STORYTELLER'S TALE

MAYHEM MAKERS

WRETCHED SOULZ MC

MANDA MELLETT

COPYRIGHT

DISCLAIMER

This book, and others in the Mayhem Makers series, are firmly set in the fictional world. Although the very real Motorcycles, Mobsters and Mayhem signing is mentioned, none of the events actually take place or exist outside of the author's imagination.

PRODUCTION
ACKNOWLEDGMENTS

Cover Design by CT Cover Creations

Edited and formatted by Maggie Kern @ Ms.K Edits

Proof reading by Darlene Tallman

DEDICATION

Authors don't work in a vacuum and rely on a number of people to keep them on the right track.

Many books ago, I was lucky enough to find Sheri Secord, an amazing person with an incredible mind and memory who's one of my beta readers. Her encyclopaedic knowledge of my characters and stories is far better than my own, and she often corrects me, and points out inconsistencies which I've missed.

To thank her, I've purloined her name and used it in StoryTeller's Tale.

Anyway, this one's for you, Sheri, and hopefully shows my appreciation of the beta reading you do for me.

PROLOGUE

"Hey, Prospect!" Rat roars out and beckons me over. "You tell it," he instructs. He gives Beard such a nudge it almost pushes him off the couch while simultaneously saying, "You'd fuck it up, Brother."

Unconcerned, Beard shrugs, repositions himself, then leans back and raises his beer bottle as a signal for me to go ahead.

Trying to suppress my grin and keep my expression serious, I widen my stance, clasp my hands behind my back, and begin, "It was a beautiful day, not a cloud in the sky, sun glinting off the chrome of our Harleys. The air was tinged by the scent of a wildfire. In the distance, a plume of smoke could be seen, but the news was that it was under containment."

Rat interrupts, "Beard wanted some new aftershave or such shit—"

I wait for the roars of laughter to fade and for the man with the waist-length beard to survive another of Rat's violent nudges. Then, allowing my lips only the faintest twitch, get back to my retelling.

"We parked up the bikes, me, obviously, being told to stand

guard while Beard went inside and restocked with extra small condoms—"

"Thought Rat said it was aftershave?" Pothead pulls up a chair and plants his ass. Glancing around, I see he's not the only one who's drawn closer.

"Poetic licence." I wink. "Anyway—"

"So what was it?" Bull approaches. "Condoms or...?"

Beard sits up straight. "Does it fuckin' matter? What happened was—"

"Nah, let him tell it," Prez, approaching, drawls, and sits on the arm of the couch. "Carry on, Prospect."

I suppress another twitch of my lips. "As I said, the sun was beating down, warming the day, and presumably heating some tempers. As I stood with one eye on our bikes, I watched Beard exit the store with a package, and he was followed by two elderly men."

Beard snorts and shakes his head as he remembers. "They were cursing up a storm—"

"Shush!" He's admonished from all sides, glared at, then the attention returns to me.

Schooling my features, I recommence. "One man was leaning on a Zimmer frame, one using a walking stick. As they walked out, their words carried clearly. 'Motherfucker', one shouted. 'You goddamn son of a goat,' yelled the other."

"They were quite inventive," Beard interrupts again.

I nod. "Yeah, I was particularly impressed by 'your mother sucked donkey's balls and took it up the ass.'"

Chuckles of laughter come from my audience, which again seems to have expanded.

"It went from verbal to physical in the blink of an eye. The dude with the stick brandished it like a sword. He was blocked by the frame being used as a shield. The moves started to get quite impressive, as though they were ninety-year-old ninjas, both trying to get hits in, and both staggering from the effort. It wasn't clear which one of them was winning, when this old broad comes tearing out of the store and starts beating both men with her purse."

I use a falsetto. "'You worthless motherfuckers. You ain't even got dicks long enough to fuckin' measure anymore.'" Guffaws sound as I return to my normal voice. "Mothers covered their kids' ears, but no one intervened to separate them. We were all watching the free entertainment." I grin, thinking back, seeing the fighting trio in my mind. "Employees came out of the store and tried to separate them, but punches, sticks and purses were flying. A man in a suit got caught in the nose or something, and blood was flowing. He tried to restrain the old bitch, but that got the men joining sides, and both started attacking him." I pause, seeing my audience is rapt.

"It was a beautiful day," I repeat. "Sun blazing down, peace interrupted by the sound of sirens."

"They got arrested?" Rat asks.

"Wait for the punchline," Beard warns him.

Chuckling, I shake my head. "Nah, the store manager, the guy in the suit, decided not to press charges. It turns out the elderly trio were a ménage à trois, and the fucker with the Zimmer frame had been arguing it was his turn tonight."

There were snorts all around. Then Prez points his finger at me. "You're making that bit up."

"Makes for a better story," I respond, unrepentant.

Beard sighs and rolls his eyes. "Should have listened to me. All I would have said was 'we were late as there were these three old fuckers fighting outside the store.'"

Rat punches his arm. "Yeah, but we like how he tells them."

Prez stands, grimaces as though he's wasted moments of his valuable time, then tilts his head as he looks at me. "You ever get patched in, Prospect. Your handle's going to be StoryTeller."

If I ever get patched in. I acknowledge his comment with a raise of my chin. I've no problem with that handle. I just want to prove my worth and earn it. I've been prospecting eleven months, and as each day passes, I get the jitters that, however hard I try, I might not make the grade. If I don't, I've no idea what my life will look like. Since starting life as a veteran, I've become completely invested in joining one of the biggest one-percenter MCs in the country with chapters all over the world. Drawn by the lifestyle, the camaraderie and the way they hold their middle finger up at authority, I can't think of anywhere else where I'd fit in so well.

But they've got to want me. So, I do everything asked, with a smile on my face, however disgusting or grim the task may be, giving no one the opportunity to criticise or question my loyalty. Sometimes, like today, I'm rewarded. I've worked my ass off and finish everything early. When Bull, my sponsor, tells me to get my ass home, sensibly, I don't argue.

I'm in a luckier position than most prospects who aren't allowed to go with the club whores during the prospecting period, as I have a girlfriend who's been with me prior to coming on board. At least I don't have to suffer from blue balls, and I've a few ideas how to use the additional free time that's been offered. As well as his permission to leave, Bull had also issued admonishments to get my ass back here early in the morning to compensate, but that's fine.

Eagerly, I head for my bike and point it in the direction of my small, one-room apartment that I share with the love of my life, who I'd met shortly after I'd finished my final tour. Not a day goes by when I don't thank fuck, I was in the right place at the right time to find her. She's pretty, petite, intelligent and witty, and I hadn't wasted time locking her down. We'd clicked immediately, hooked up, and have been together since. She's got my ring on her finger, and, if I get my patch, I'll do it properly and claim her as my old lady. Yeah, I'm pussy whipped. I'll admit to it and take all the flack that my hopefully soon-to-be brothers throw at me.

She's the one good fucking thing that's happened to me in my life. She makes me want to be a better man, and I'm never going to let her down.

As I pull into the parking lot, knowing she won't be expecting me this early, my lips curve at the thought of how pleased she'll be—she often complains she doesn't get to see me. More times than I can count, I don't stagger in until the early hours, then need to be back at the crack of dawn. But good naturedly, she puts up with me putting in the long hours, as she knows how important joining the Wretched Soulz is to me.

I park my bike, then remember the florist just up the street. Fi deserves recognition for how much support she gives. So, I detour and pick up a bouquet of her favourite blooms, approaching the apartment on foot, carrying a bunch of the aromatic flowers.

I use my key, the initial words of my greeting coming out, "Honey, I'm..." But then the words stop.

It's only a one-room apartment. Bedroom, living space and kitchen combined, so there's nothing to hide the sight of my loving fiancée getting railed on the bed directly in my line of sight.

She's clearly very much a willing participant, as witnessed by their loud grunts and groans, and frenzied athletic movements, which had it been another couple, might have impressed me. So intent on themselves, they've not noticed my voice or my entry.

With a roar, I throw the flowers down to the ground and

launch forward, grabbing the naked man by his shoulder and pulling him off her. With an equally loud shout, he spins and faces me, his erect and wet dick swinging in the breeze.

"Stand the fuck down, Prospect," he thunders. When I make another move toward him, he holds up his hands and repeats, "Stand the fuck down."

Blinded by rage, I don't listen. My fist rises and I hit him straight in the jaw, making him lurch backward.

The fucker shakes his head and grins, holding up his hands defensively. "I'll give you that one, but not one more. You want that patch, don't you?"

I want my patch.

"Jake," Fi wails. "I didn't, I couldn't..." She swallows rapidly, as though trying to gain some time. But whatever fucking excuse she's trying to come up with won't settle with me. I could see she'd been into it as much as him. She tries, though. "I thought I was helping you get your patch."

Like fuck, she did.

My brain works a million miles a minute. I'm a prospect. If I want my patch, I can't hit a fucking member, or not again, seeing as he seems to have allowed that one shot to pass. Custer has had his patch for years, and is now standing, gloating, in front of me.

"Just making sure you can share, Prospect. Look at it as part of your initiation." Then he fucking laughs.

Indecision sweeps through me. I've chased that patch for eleven months, but now I'm not sure I want to join the club anymore. The man inside wants his slice of revenge and wants to slap Custer's smirk off his face. *But I've worked so hard.* And I'm a man who thrives on self-control.

"Get the fuck out of my apartment," I roar. I may be able to buy myself time, but I won't be able to hold back unless he gets out of my face.

He holds up his hands. "I'm going, I'm going." He's still laughing as he yanks on his jeans, steps into his boots, picks up his shirt and cut, and walks out of the door.

While I may be experiencing second thoughts about wanting to join the club, I've no doubts about the woman at the heart of this. Even naked, she's trying to persuade me that I'd been mistaken in what I thought I saw, but I know my fucking eyes didn't lie.

Ignoring her protests, I go to the closet and start pulling out her clothes. "Pack your shit."

"Jake—"

"I said, pack your fuckin' shit." I growl. "Or I'll just throw it out."

Fi's weeping, begging, telling me it's all a mistake, but I know it isn't. When I ask how long she's been fucking him behind my back, she can't lie for shit. Oh, she tries, but I can see straight through her.

I just about hold it together until she finally leaves, tears streaking her face, but leaving me cold.

Then, when the door closes behind her, I wait only for the sound of her car engine to start before I fall to my knees, my hands clasping my head, as I lose my battle to hold everything together.

I thought she was it for me. My ride or die.

I was wrong.

How can I go back to the fucking club? Do I want to be patched in? Have to sit around the table with Custer? Treat him like my fucking brother?

Rocking on my haunches, I stay on the ground. Time passes and my distress keeps me down. I've lost the woman I thought I'd be with for life. *We'd been planning our marriage, for fuck's sake.* And without my club, what the hell would I do? Since leaving the Navy, I've never considered anything else.

The sun drops behind the horizon, darkness descends on the room, but still, I don't move, frozen to the spot, thoughts assailing my mind, coming so fast one after the other, but presenting no solutions on how I move forward from here.

Fuck knows how long it is before my door bursts open.

The shock does nothing more than make me lift my face. If death's coming for me, I'd be pleased if he'd take me now.

But it's not a man dressed in black, carrying a scythe. It's the prez, Chaz, along with his VP, Dane, and there's Bull, my sponsor, alongside them.

After the glance of recognition, I stare down at the floor once more, just wanting to be left alone.

Chaz doesn't give me that choice. "On your fucking feet, Prospect."

A growl enters my throat. "I don't answer to you anymore. I quit."

"The fuck you say?" Bull takes action, his meaty arm grabbing mine and pulling me up.

Shrugging him off, I shake myself, then stand my ground. "Kick me out or let me leave, but I don't want to be part of the Wretched Soulz." Them coming here, busting in, probably to give me shit about hitting one of their precious patched members, has ensured that.

Prez looks around, his face tightening slightly as they fall on the unmade bed, the site of the crime. His eyes meet mine.

"Don't give a damn what happens in other chapters, but in mine, old ladies are off limits. Custer was out of fuckin' line."

Huffing, I remind him, "She's not an old lady. I wasn't patched, so I never claimed her."

He waves his hand. "Fuckin' semantics. As for your patch, we've already taken a vote on that. Only the formalities are left, and circumstances have expedited those." He holds his hand out behind him, and as if by prior agreement, Bull puts something in it. When Prez again brings it around to the front, patches are resting on his palm—the full three patch insignias of the Wretched Soulz. There's also a name patch bearing the word, *StoryTeller*.

I reach automatically to take them, then pull my hand back. Straightening my spine, I tell them honestly, "I can't sit around the table with Custer."

Bull grimaces, Dane shakes his head, but Chaz still regards me firmly. "Guessed that." He sweeps his hair back over his shoulder. "You've been wronged... Brother." The slight hesitation suggests he's trying the new mode of address on for size. "Can understand how you're feeling. Betrayal ain't going to be a good start." He raises his foot, places it on the coffee table, and leans forward over his knee. "Here's the deal. You sew those patches on, come to the club and I'll give you the chance to take your pound of flesh, but in the fuckin' ring. You hear me?"

I raise my chin, but I still don't see how letting Custer off with a beating, even if I'm the one to deliver it, will assuage my hurt. *I fucking loved Fi. I trusted her.*

Chaz's eyes draw me in. "Just so there's no misunderstanding, there will only be one man walking away from said fight. You got me? You win? You keep your patch, Brother, and won't need to see Custer's face around the table. You lose? You won't need to worry about anything anymore as you won't be breathing. Or, you suck it up, shake hands and forget it." He pauses. "Final option, you take a beatdown and leave the club." He places his foot back on the floor. "We'll leave you to consider. See you at the club in an hour with your decision."

Having delivered that bombshell, he swings on his heels, and beckons Bull and Dane to follow him. The trio walks out of the door, leaving me with my mouth open.

A fight to the death? Shake hands with Custer? Or take a

beating and leave the club? Those appear to be my only options, and to my mind, there's no fucking choice. I won't be sent away with my tail between my legs as if it's something I've done wrong, nor will I ever be able to call Custer "brother."

It wouldn't be the first time I've killed a man with my bare hands. But before it'd been for my country, and then I'd been driven by nothing more personal than the desire to survive.

CHAPTER ONE
STORYTELLER

It's been five years since I was patched in, and in that time, the clubhouse hasn't changed. The air is still tinged with stale beer, cigarette smoke and sex. The couch I'm sitting on has been here since I prospected. Member wise, there are a few differences. After Dane met his demise, losing his battle to a man with a knife, Bull stepped into his VP shoes. Rat and Captain were arrested and sent down, and the ranks had been swelled by Legit and Skunk. But it's essentially the same place that holds the bad memories, the ones that keep me out on the road.

Leaving my bike engine still ticking and cooling, I'd wasted no time getting inside the air-conditioned clubroom where I could be confident there'd be a beer with my name on it. I wasn't wrong. Said beer was put into my hand the moment I arrived, by a prospect I didn't recognise.

This is my home chapter, but since I prospected, it's never been my home, spending, as I do, so little time here. As I relax on the couch, stretching out my legs to rid them of the kinks caused by the long ride, eyeing the stranger and wondering whether he'll measure up and become a Soul, I recall the time when I, too, was an eager prospect. Though it's long back in my rearview and tainted by history. It's hard to remember there were ever carefree days when all I wanted was my patch, and the time I was living with who I'd thought was the love of my life.

My mood sours as my thoughts turn to how it all ended. Closing my eyes, I can still see and smell the blood, both Custer's and mine. Even now I tense, as if still feeling my body reeling from his punches. I recall him smirking, thinking I had no chance and that this affair would soon be over. He'd toyed with me at first, showing off to his brothers.

With my desire for revenge, I, on the other hand, was all business. Being a SEAL, fighting was about survival not giving a show, and Custer's expression quickly changed from sneering to worried. Weight wise, we'd been even, skills wise and stamina, I'd had the edge. I'd like to say it was over in minutes, but it took quite a while, pain inflicted on both sides, movements becoming frantic as we both fought for our lives.

When I'd had him on the ground, I didn't waste time. One moment we were fighting, the next I'd broken his neck, feeling no remorse. Suddenly, instead of the cheering, the jeers, the smacking of fists into hands in encouragement, a sudden silence had fallen, almost deafening in the absence of noise.

It was then I realised my predicament, and that there was a good chance this wasn't the outcome they'd counted on. Me, a new patch, insignia hastily sewn on, had killed a man they'd ridden beside and called brother for years.

Could they switch their allegiance?

They'd patched me in. They'd sworn to have my back, to ride or die with me.

But the murmurings around warned in the eyes of some, at

least, what Custer had done hadn't deserved the death penalty.

On my part, what happened hadn't brought satisfaction. It hadn't made up for the loss of the woman I thought was going to be my life. Fi was as culpable as me for the death of the man who'd died at my hands.

It was then I'd realised I hadn't really known Fi at all. Or, perhaps, I tended to misread women in general, only seeing what I wanted to be there. While I'd gained what I'd been striving for, my patch seemed to come at too high a price for both me and my new brothers.

Chaz, a good president, wasn't blind to the implications, and he was fair. I'd prospected, earned his trust, and proved I could handle myself. So, while I stayed a member of the Arizona chapter, I was offered a chance to go nomad, at least for a short time until the dust had settled.

That had suited me fine. Without Fi, I had no home and no desire to start a new relationship. It was the best of both worlds—I had my patch and a promise of brothers at my back should I need them, but also the lonesome freedom of the road. If my prez didn't issue me precise instructions, I could just go where the wind blew. A chance to get my head together.

It should have been months.

Five years later, I'm still travelling alone.

I oomph, feeling the weight of a body sinking onto my lap, the perfume and size letting me know it's female. Opening my eyes, I raise my bottle to my lips, and glance around, seeing the room has filled while I've been lost in the past. Bull's standing by the bar, raising his glass to me, Beard by his side. They both look pleased to see me.

Custer's death is water long under the bridge now, and absent or not, I've re-earned their trust, and we share mutual loyalty.

Feeling the exhaustion of the ride slip away, I take more notice of my surroundings. Then something, or rather, someone, catches my eye.

I try to sit forward, my progress impeded. "Get off me, sweetheart," I growl.

"But I'm comfortable." The girl on my lap moans and wiggles, causing the predictable reaction from my cock, and I stifle a groan.

Lightly smacking her butt, I instruct her again, "Let me up." When I use my hands to encourage her, she reluctantly stands.

My eyes are set on my target as she breathily asks, "Can I catch up with you later?"

"Sure, Candy." Casually, I wave her off as I go to greet the man who's summoned me.

"I'm Brandy," she corrects indignantly, but she's talking to my back.

Carrying the refill of beer the prospect had brought me only moments ago, I cross the dingy, but large clubroom, my long legs covering the distance in just a few strides.

"Brother." At his greeting, I take his offered hand, clasping it firmly, and then allow myself to be pulled in for a hug, my back soon smarting from the hefty slaps landing on it.

Retaliating, I return the greeting. "Prez."

His eyes sparkle as he glances back at the couch I so recently vacated. "I only heard your bike come in a few moments ago. You didn't waste time." His raised eyebrow and smirk give me the clue to what he's talking about.

"What can I say?" I give a nonchalant shrug. "Girls like fresh meat."

His hand punches my arm. "Don't want to hear anything about your meat. Straight from the slaughterhouse or not."

Barking a laugh, I shake my head while examining the expression on his face. "Wanna talk, Prez?"

"Sure fuckin' do. Ain't called you back for nothing." He gestures toward the room at the back of the clubhouse he uses as an office.

I sincerely doubt he has. When Chaz, the prez for the Arizona chapter of the Wretched Soulz, calls, you don't wait for a second invitation.

As I follow him back, out of the corner of my eye, I catch sight of Candy, *Brandy,* already with her hand on Legend's crotch. Some things never change, no matter what clubhouse you're in. Club girls like cock and don't much care which man it's attached to.

Chaz goes around the back of his desk and takes his chair. He nods at the door through which I've just entered. Taking the hint, I kick it shut. Then, accepting his offer of a seat, I sit. Leaning back, kicking out my legs, I take a pack of cigarettes out of my pocket. Holding the lighter to the tip, I draw in air until there's a red glow.

With a shake of his head, Chaz simultaneously finds an ashtray and slides it across, while his other hand reaches back and opens a window.

"You mind?"

He snorts at my belated request for permission. Chaz doesn't smoke, never has, but doesn't usually object to second-handedly sharing the bad habits of others. While his stern eyes focus on me, I take another drag, not intimidated in the slightest. Chaz and I go back years, and I've lost count of the jobs, some dirty, many clandestine, that I've done for him. I fucking love my life, mostly alone, answering to no one, wearing the patch that's feared and respected in equal measures wherever I go.

"You've come via New Mexico?"

I simply raise my chin. He knows that I have.

He lifts an eyebrow. "Any problems I should know about?"

Filling my lungs again, I exhale smoke out, then with my free hand, reach for my beer. "Slaughter's got everything under control. Well, he has now." I take a swig from the bottle.

"After a visit from you?" He chuckles. "I bet he has. Anything else I should be worried about?"

"There's word about the Alpha."

Now he snorts. "He fuckin' hates you calling him that."

Unrepentant, I grin. "Well, he who doesn't like to be named can put the fuck up with it." At his gesture, I continue, "The Dominators think they've got a bead on him, so he's staying underground for a while."

As I name the MC that's our biggest rival and enemy, his mouth twists. "Fuckin' Dominators are always trying to catch up with him. Why don't they give it a fuckin' rest?"

The Wretched Soulz MC is made up, for all intents and purposes, of charters acting independently, bound only by name and each organisation's loose interpretation of the shared regs and rules. While there's not a mother chapter as such, we do have a national prez, though his identity and location is a very well-kept secret, one only known to patched brothers. The Alpha, as I call him, is a wanted man, and has a price on his head set by our rival MCs. And it's not just them. The feds would like his identity and whereabouts confirmed as well.

Chaz wipes his hand over his beard. "He coming our way?"

Moving my hand in a seesaw gesture, I give him what I can. "Maybe? Probably? It's hard to tell. Not sure what risk exactly attaches to him at present."

He doesn't say a word, but he's quiet for a moment. A visit from the national prez isn't necessarily something the clubs vie for. For a start, security has to be tight as a drum, and it's natural that individual prezes like to impress. Members have to be on their best behaviour, and, as far as it extends in the biker world, mind their p's and q's.

Added to that, the national prez has a habit of making suggestions, which the hosting club is expected to follow.

"Moving on," Prez states, still carefully schooling his features. "Been a long fuckin' time since you graced us with your presence. Thought you'd forgotten where the clubhouse was."

My shoulders rise and lower. "Got any complaints?" The quirk of my eyebrow challenges him. As a nomad, I'm his roving enforcer, and thus, beholden to him as much as if I were a resident in the club. Even absent, I'm at his beck and call.

His lips thin, his brow wrinkles, then he admits, with a broad grin, "Can't say that I have."

"Fuckin' asshole." I roll my eyes to the ceiling.

Immediately, he leans forward with both hands on the desk. "You and I go way back, ST, but don't take liberties."

Cockily I grin, sit back, fold my arms, and show I'm not scared of him. It's one of the traits he admires about me, and why he lets me have the freedom he does. Not many men survive on their own out on the road, but there aren't many fuckers who can take me.

Exasperated, he shakes his head, sits back down, and at last gets down to business. "Fuckin' cartel is up my ass. They want us to shift a shitload of guns for them."

My head leans to one side. "I thought we already did that shit?"

He raises his chin slightly. "We do. But this isn't a discreet small load, Brother. This will involve two eighteen wheelers."

Whistling out air through my teeth, I unfold my arms. "I take it you mean over the border?" When he again makes a positive motion with his head, I continue, "Shifting that amount could risk losing a few brothers." Even the small amounts carry risk. Case in point, it's that very reason Captain and Rat are currently serving time in the penitentiary.

"That's why I needed you back, Bro. Want your brains on it."

"Are we in that deep with the cartel that we can't refuse?"

He grimaces. "We could back out, but we get enough trade from them, our coffers would be damaged. I have made it known that we expect their marker if we do this, and it will be a fuckin' big one."

The cartel owing us favours could work out well. If, that is, we can minimise the risk, and not end up with half the brothers joining Cap and Rat. I acknowledge his comment with a dip of my chin.

"You want me to help sort that shit out?"

Chaz smirks. "Well, if you're offering, Brother."

As if I've got any choice. I snort and shake my head. "I'm yours to command, Prez."

He grunts, and his mouth twitches. We both know I answer to him and will do whatever is needed. I just hope it's not going to take long, and I'll be back out on the road before my feet start itching.

That sorted, it's quiet until Chaz slaps the desk. "I know you must be beat after your long ride today. You think you could do with some entertainment before taking a rest?"

Cautiously, I let my lips curve. "Depends on what it is."

"Couple of wannabes have been riding around, wearing colours of a pretend club. Think they're a couple of hotshots. You wanna come with and show them they're wrong?"

You don't wear colours of a different club in our territory without our permission. And as the Wretched Soulz have the southern states sewn up, there aren't many places where there's an exception. Neither do you decide to set up your own club without getting approval from us.

If someone's stupid enough to don colours without our consent, then they need to be taught a strict lesson. Despite my sore ass, I'm down to be the one to teach them.

Flexing my hands, I let my body do the talking.

"Knew you'd be down for it, Bro." Prez grins broadly. "And some of the bros here might like to see a demonstration of how the mighty StoryTeller works."

My mouth stretches and curves to match his expression.

While a member of the club, it's not often I visit, and when I do, it's more of the flying type, where I dip in, show my face, then dip out again. I learned long ago after what happened with Fi, I have an aversion to setting down roots. So, while I know the brothers, I've not often had occasion to step up beside them. And I'm completely okay with the opportunity to display my talents.

My cigarette has long been smoked down to the stub, and my beer bottle is empty. "Let's go do this." I'll go bust some heads, then perhaps come back and this time take what Candy, *Brandy,* was blatantly offering, or one of the other sweet butts. My cock isn't particularly fussy.

Only half an hour later, I'm pulling up outside a local bar, noting the couple of flashy Harleys outside. As well as Prez, Claw, Pothead, and Skunk have come with us. After we dismount, Chaz gathers us into a group.

"He," he dips his head toward me, "will take the lead." When Claw, thumping one fist into his palm, looks disgruntled, Chaz chuckles. "Watch, listen and learn, Brother." He slaps my back.

At that moment, the door opens, and a man walks out, checking behind him, then approaches our group. He respectfully inclines his head toward Prez.

As soon as he's close enough, he leans in and quietly informs us, "They're at the bar, trying to act tough, regaling the bartender with their supposed prowess."

Chaz wraps his arm around my neck and indicates the man who's spoken. "This, 'eres, our latest prospect. We just call him Shitface." The other men around me chuckle, but the man in question pulls back his shoulders and doesn't look upset. Name calling is all part of the initiation.

"Well, Shit," I address him directly, unable to hide my smirk, and get down to business. "There's two of them?"

"Three," he corrects. "Looks like they may have been recruiting."

Prez cocks a brow, but I answer with only a rise of my chin. *I got this.* Taking off my cut, I hand it to him for safe keeping, then warn the others, "Come in, but stay back."

Pothead rolls his eyes. "We've got your six, Brother."

Yeah, like I'll need it. But again, my chin rises, this time in polite appreciation.

I head for the door, knowing my brothers will give me a minute before following me in. It's a bar, nothing remarkable about it—chairs, tables, slot machines, and rock music playing courtesy of a jukebox. It takes but a moment to see the three men grouped by the bar, and the sight of their illegitimate colours makes my blood boil.

Wannabe bikers either don't know, or don't give a damn, that it takes more than owning a two-wheeler to make them a biker. Or that putting on a rag and planting patches on the back is a million miles away from being an official MC. Whether it's ignorance or blatant disrespect, these three will soon learn the error of their ways. And it just so happens, it's a lesson I love to teach.

People always underestimate me. I'm built but wouldn't

win any body-building competitions. My long hair makes me look like I'd be more comfortable strumming a guitar.

The bartender, proving he's not stupid and that he can read the glint in my eyes, quickly moves the glasses he's polishing to safety. "Don't want any trouble here," he warns me.

Proving they're not so observant, the three guys turn, give me a quick glance, then, just as fast, dismiss me as a person of any interest to them, and return to their conversation.

"Beer," I demand. When the bottle's placed in front of me, I don't touch it. Instead, I lay my hand on the cut of the man who's standing next to me, a big disrespect in my world. For good measure, I tap it lightly a couple of times. When he turns sharply, I say, casually, "Haven't heard of your MC before."

He puffs out his chest. Sure, he's bigger than me, not taller, but wider than many men are. Him making more of himself doesn't intimidate me.

"And what do you know about MCs?" he asks sneeringly.

"A lot more than you, apparently," I calmly reply. When he snorts, I add, "Enough to know that you haven't cleared the setting up of your club with the dominant."

"Bikers don't need no damn permission from anyone." He scoffs. "You have no idea what you're talking about."

"This fucker giving you problems, Jack?" One of the other men leans forward.

"Nah, I can handle it." Again, he puffs his chest out. "Just going to teach this asshole not to mess with us."

That's my opening. As I see his fist clench, his eyes viewing up his angle, my punch, already sighted and lined up, is flying. I don't want to drag this out, so I put all my strength behind it. The single punch to his jaw lays him out.

I sense one of the others behind me, so I donkey kick back. From the scream, I've scored a direct groin hit. The third man comes flying at me, but I allow his punch, lessening the impact by turning my face slightly, while my fist takes him straight in his throat. He collapses, gagging and heaving.

"You fuckin' cunt," the man I got in the balls shouts and launches at me, but I'm ready. I use his own momentum, side-step, throw my arms around him and guide his head into the bar. He drops to the floor, dazed, his pupils pinpricks, his face bemused as if wondering how he got there.

As wannabe one starts to come around, holding his head, and wannabe two stops gagging, Chaz and the others step up. Chaz hands me my cut. Sliding it on, I shrug my shoulders to get it to settle right. The three punks' eyes go wide when faced with real versions of the men they thought they could emulate.

"Wow." Pothead is staring at me, his eyes gleaming. "I can fuckin' see how you survive by yourself. You're a fuckin' one-man army."

That's the SEAL training, I think to myself, but acknowledge his admiration with a rise and dip of my chin.

"Take their... cuts." Prez says the word as though the leather the wannabes are wearing is barely worth the description.

The three men start to protest but come to their senses when my brothers take up a threatening stance. When Shithead has their leathers, Prez issues one further instruction. "Take those back to the clubhouse and fuckin' burn them." Then he turns his attention to the bikers on the ground. "Outside." He jerks his head.

When they're slow to comply, Pothead and Claw give them some encouragement. With Skunk's help as well, they make their way through the patrons who seem to be making a point that none of what happened is any of their business.

Chaz opens his wallet, takes out a few notes, and passes them over to the bartender. No words are spoken, but an understanding passes between them.

I step to his side as we leave the bar.

Outside, the entertainment is just beginning. I might have warmed them up, but my brothers are just as eager to show them just what they think of men who think all they need is a Harley and a leather vest to call themselves a biker. I've already had my fun, so standing with Chaz, we leave them to it.

When all that remains is a groaning heap, some of which, at least, might need emergency room attention, Chaz beckons Skunk, Claw and Pothead to stand down.

He kicks at the prone men until he gets all their attention and warns in a menacing tone, "If I see any of you fuckers again, wearing your pretend colours, you won't get off so lightly, you hear me? If that's your thinking, then my advice is to get measured for your coffin, as that's what you'll be needing."

He spits on the ground and turns away from them. Putting his hand to the back of my cut and Pothead's, he urges us and the others back to our bikes.

Skunk shakes his head as he swings his leg over his Harley. "You were poetry in motion back there, Brother," he tosses at me. "Turned me right on. I could actually fuck you right now." He blows me a kiss.

"Me too, Bro. Me too," Claw echoes.

Snorting loudly, I mount my own steel horse, and as Chaz's finger circles, start my engine. We pile out of the parking lot in practised formation.

CHAPTER TWO
STORYTELLER

With no permanent room in the clubhouse, I crash in one of the spare rooms that are used for visitors or fucking, or both. While I'm used to sleeping anywhere—out under the starry skies isn't unknown—the mattress has got lumps in it. Deciding to complain to Prez and insist he purchases a new one if he intends on me sticking around for any length of time, I give up on sleep soon after day breaks.

Last night, after having our fun, we'd returned to the clubhouse where I proceeded to have a few drinks, catch up with my long unseen brothers, and let Brandy have her wicked way with me. As CeCe didn't want to miss out, I also gave her a taste of my cock. When Brea looked a bit lonely, I took the blow job she offered as an easy way out. I'd ridden a few hundred miles before taking out those three punks, so if I wasn't up to my A game, who could fucking blame me?

Today's a new day though, and while tired from the lack of meaningful sleep, I'm looking forward to getting on with it.

Brothers from other chapters I visit are normally

welcoming enough, offer their sweet butts—some even their old ladies if there is a mutual interest there—but it's nothing like being in your own clubhouse and not having to worry whose toes, or dick, you might be stepping on.

The room I've been given is bare other than the bed and my worn-looking rucksack. As the facilities are down the hall, I dress before leaving. Then, taking a book from my pack and suppressing a yawn, I enter the clubroom.

The only person around is Shitface who's making an effort to clear up bottles and empty ashtrays. When he starts polishing the tables with a rag he pulls from his pocket, I hold back the comment he might as well try to polish a turd.

Interrupting his work, I snap out, "Get me a coffee, Prospect."

Another good benefit of being home, prospects are even more accommodating, knowing your vote will be counted when it comes to patching in.

"Creamer? Sugar?"

"Black," I growl. "As nature intended." Or what I've become used to when it was just me and my camping stove.

Turning sideways on the worn sofa, I place a pillow behind me, and put my feet on the seat. Now comfortable, I open my book, and start reading.

I've no idea how long Shitface has been chasing his patch, but he's close to wooing my yay as he keeps my coffee topped up, wordlessly removing the empty cup and replacing it with a full one without me having to ask. Having gotten lost in the words on the pages in front of me, I've no desire to be interrupted.

The book is a satisfying length, and I'm only a third of the way in before the clubhouse starts to fill up around me. Men enter, burp, fart, scratch their balls, and, yawning, embrace the morning in a variety of masculine ways. I'm only disturbed when Iron pushes my legs off the couch, allowing him room to sit.

"See nothing's changed." He chuckles.

The sergeant-at-arms and I go way back, and yeah, I've always been a reader, finding books a great place to escape and take your mind off more unpleasant matters.

He reaches over, pulls the book out of my hands, and checks the cover. His eyes widen. "Not your usual style, Brother." He snorts, giving it back.

So what if the cover shows a half-naked man? He's wearing a cut and is obviously a biker. The story inside is good, not something I would have picked that's for sure, but the writing is pulling me into the plot. I'd given it a cursory glance at first until I realised that the author knows what they're talking about. For a start, they have to be a motorcyclist, the descriptions of riding are so apt that wasn't pulled from the imagination, and though I was dubious about their knowledge of clubs, they've got it right in so many aspects. In fact, I've pretty much decided that the author must be a dude masquerading under a pen name, surely no woman could write like this.

"It's good." Raising my shoulders, I don't need his opinion or approval.

"Tangled Threats on the Nomad Highway." He leans forward to read the title again, then snorts. "Must be because the word nomad is in it."

I half-turn away, opening it back to the page I was on, and try to ignore him. I'm only successful for a few moments before another voice brings me out of the pages.

"Ooh. That's a MariaLisa DeMora book. I love that series."

I glare up at the newcomer.

Camilla is Bull's sister, a stunner, though no one in their right mind would touch that. Not unless they wanted to go toe to toe with the VP, who didn't earn his road name for being small and timid. One punch from his fist and it's probably the last thing you'd ever feel. She pops into the club from time to time, to visit her brother, and it usually coincides with a breakup in her love life. We tolerate her, fix her up, then send her out to make her next mistake. Unfortunately, she doesn't have good taste in men. Bull would kill any man who actually hurt her, but it's usually her who walks away, having found the "love of her life" to be a disappointment.

Her status though, gives her some amount of leeway, so when she reaches forward and snatches the book out of my hand, I have to restrict my response to a growl instead of instinctively ripping it out of her grasp.

My glare hardens as she flicks through the pages, losing my place. "Camilla." I grit my teeth and ask politely, "Can I have it back, please?"

She waves her hand dismissively, and shoeing Iron away, settles down next to me on the couch. "I've read this. It's a good one. Have you read the rest of the series?" I'm just about to answer in the negative, when she flicks again through the pages, ending on the title page. "Oh. Who's Sheri?"

I lean toward her, and check what she's pointing out. "No fuckin' idea."

"It's been personally signed by the author and dedicated to her. Look." She traces the words as she reads them out. "To Sheri, thanks for being a great fan. MariaLisa DeMora, MMM 23." She glances my way and her eyes narrow. "How the hell did you get this? Are you certain you don't know this Sheri?"

"Fuckin' certain," I growl, reaching to take the book from her. "I found it, okay?"

"Found it?" Her eyes widen. "You know what MMM is, right?"

I couldn't give a damn. I just want to keep reading, but

she's intent on enlightening me. "It's a big signing for authors of Motorcycle, Mafia and Mayhem romance."

"Romance!" Iron snorts. "Why you reading that shit, Brother?"

I shoot him my finger. "Give it to me," I demand, as Camilla seems to have taken possession of the book that I was enjoying reading.

Instead, she continues in a dreamy voice, "I wanted to go to the signing, but I couldn't make it to Houston. But this?" She taps the signature page again. "This is a personal dedication by the author. It's not something a woman would treat casually." She squints at me. "She'll be devastated to have lost it. A book like this is a prized possession, especially as the signing was only a couple of days ago. How the hell did you get your paws on it?" Her eyes narrow. "You steal it?"

I shift awkwardly, not comfortable with her accusation. "For fuck's sake woman, I don't need to steal a fuckin' book. I found it, alright? At a rest stop in New Mexico." I'm probably sounding more aggressive than I should, but I'm on the defensive, for some reason feeling guilty. "It was lying abandoned on the ground. Must have fallen out of her purse or something." I think back and add, "There was no one around."

She harrumphs. "I bet she went looking for it as soon as she realised she lost it." Her reproving stare makes me react.

I did nothing wrong. I just saw a perfectly good book that looked interesting, lying around and took possession of it. "Finders, keepers," I tell her, snatching the book out of her hands. Standing, I give up any thought of reading peacefully in the clubhouse.

Going back to the room where I'd left my bag, I start to slide the book into it, when guilt makes me pull it back out. *Prized possession.* Guiltily, I straighten the corner which I'd bent over to mark my place.

I snort at my action. Well, Sheri, whoever the fuck she is, had clearly been careless about keeping it safe. Her loss, my gain.

With the object that had spurred such fascination safely stored, I stretch my arms over my head. As I do so, my stomach grumbles.

Book forgotten, seeking out some breakfast becomes the first item on my agenda. Then, after checking that Prez has no other plans for me, I spend the day tinkering with my bike. It's in need of some loving attention after the miles I've put on it recently.

Hours later, while my hands are covered in grease and dirt, my bike is gleaming. Oil has been changed, filters renewed, belt adjusted, and the timing is spot on. I stand, lovingly staring at it for a moment, wishing I could pack my saddlebags and ride. I've gotten used to not staying in one place for long, and, despite only having been back for one day, the open road is already calling.

"Looks fuckin' good, Bro." Skunk pauses in the middle of making adjustments to his own bike and spares mine an admiring glance.

I raise my chin, acknowledging the compliment paid to the possession that I treasure most in the world. As I turn away, then glance back at my bike, that thought reminds me how devastated I'd be if anything happened to it. Though it's not in the same league, my guilt returns about taking an unattended book when it might have meant so much to the person who lost it.

Sheri.

One name. That's not much to go on, and I'm unable to conjure an image to go with it. She could be nineteen or ninety, or anything in between. Despite not knowing, my mind races with questions.

Does she know it's missing, or is she oblivious to its loss? Did she go to that signing just for the one book? Or did she go home with bags overbrimming and losing one won't be much of a thing.

I snort, laughing at myself. Why am I, a one-percenter biker, even worrying about it? She lost it. I found it. End of story.

Except...

Scrubbing my hands free of oil and grit, I wheel my bike out of the workshop and park it alongside those of my brothers. Then I take my cigarettes out of my pocket, and lighting up, go lean on the fence and stare out into the desert, wondering why I can't seem to get this strange Sheri out of my mind. Perhaps I feel some kinship down to the pleasure I'm gaining reading the book that she'd chosen. Why do I feel so pained at the thought of her disappointment when she discovers it's missing?

A clearing of a throat behind me warns someone's approaching. *Wise man.* You don't walk up on an unsuspecting SEAL and expect to survive the encounter.

I turn, and on recognising him, greet him briefly. "Legend."

"Good to see you back, Brother." When I offer him a cigarette, he takes one, as well as the lighter I hand out. Drawing smoke into his lungs, his mouth quirks. "Longing for the open road already?"

I chuckle. "Always longing, Brother. Always. But Prez wants me here for a reason."

He sucks in smoke then breathes it out. "Yeah." He sighs. "The fuckin' cartel." He spits out the words with derision. "Got to do this right, Bro, else we're going to lose brothers."

"You know the timescale?" I'd forgotten to ask Chaz.

He frowns, thinks, then informs, "Couple of months?"

Shit. Longer than I want to stay rooted to one spot, but I can see the logic in it. If a job's worth doing right, it's worth doing well, and for something like this, we'll need to do a lot of planning.

Legend inhales nicotine and lets out the cloud of smoke. "Think Chaz is getting antsy with you being gone so long, ST." He cocks his eyebrow toward me. "Thinks you might go loco." He circles his finger around his brow.

"He's got nothing to worry about." Or, at least, I don't think so. Or maybe it's too late and I've already gone crazy. "My heart's out on the road."

Riding alone doesn't come without its risks. I'm probably lucky to have survived as long as I have. Some people may think I have a lack of self-preservation, but after Fi's betrayal, I find the lifestyle suits me. Always moving means I never put down roots, nor stay in the same place long enough to form bonds. I lost my heart once and swore I never would again.

In my view, what I do isn't any more dangerous than staying grounded in the club. Over the five years, brothers have come and gone, some in jail, some underground. But me? I seem to have the luck of the devil and just keep going on.

I don't mind the occasional visit, but this clubhouse is itself a reminder of betrayal. Even after all this time, there are too many memories here for me. I've more of a chance of going loco, as Legend so kindly put it, if I'm forced to stay here for a long while.

To get my mind off my uncertain future, I light another cigarette out of habit, then bring up the other thing on my mind. Legend's the one to ask. He's our go-to computer guy and all-around security expert. "How would you go about finding someone when you've only got a first name?"

Legend's head slowly turns to face me. He barks a laugh. "Unless it's completely unique—and with nearly eight billion people in the world the chances of that are limited—then I think you'd have a better chance of winning the lottery."

I wince. The answer was what I expected.

"What's on your mind, ST?" His eyes alight as if I've caught his interest. "Who do you want to find?"

I started the conversation, now I'm of two minds whether to finish it. Turning around, I lean my back on the fence, bend my leg and place my foot against it. "So," I start.

"Ah." Legend grins. "A story. I best get myself comfortable." He shuffles his feet and rearranges himself so he's leaning next to me. He waves his hand in an indication I should go on.

Knowing what he expects, I make sure I don't disappoint. "It was a long, hard ride. I was answering a summons from our prez, travelling through New Mexico. My bike was running low on gas, and the dust had gotten into my throat, so I decided to stop, top off my tank, take a piss and have a drink. There was a rest stop coming up, so I pulled into it." I pause, take a drag of my cigarette, then continue, "I was coming out of the bathroom when I saw a book lying on the ground. Fucker in front of me kicked at it, kind of bringing it to my attention. When I looked down, the title caught my eye. It mentioned the word nomad, so obviously I picked it up. There was no one around, no one who could have dropped it. I carried it out, but no one hollered it was theirs. So, when I got outside, I put it in my saddlebag and brought it along."

Legend tilts his head and looks confused as well he might.

"Started reading it this morning. Good fuckin' story as it happens. But as I was reading, Camilla appeared and took it out of my hand. She found there was a dedication in the front and told me it had been personally signed at an event only a few days ago." As Legend cocks his eyebrow, still at a loss where I'm going with this, I shrug. "Seems like it would have been important to the girl it was signed to, and she must have dropped it by accident."

He chuckles. "A bitch. Might have guessed there'd be a woman at the bottom of this."

I shift awkwardly. "It's the principle," I try to explain. "Would have been the same if it had been owned by a man." But would it? Somehow, I doubt my reasoning.

And I haven't fooled him. "*Principle*?" He snorts. "Since when have you had principles, ST?"

Throwing up my hands, I start to walk away.

He comes running after me. "You saying you want to find her to give the book back?" His mirth has gone and for that reason, I reply truthfully.

"I don't know what the fuck I want, or whether I should even bother." My shoulders rise then lower. "But yeah, I suppose I do. If Camilla is right, she might want it back."

CHAPTER THREE
STORYTELLER

My own words sounded ridiculous to me, so I'm prepared for Legend to resume laughing, slap my back and walk off. The crazy task I've suggested to him is pointless, as is my non-reason behind it. But a sideways glance suggests I've caught his interest.

"The book was dedicated to a woman called Sheri," I say hesitantly.

His palm meets my leather, but not as a farewell. Instead, his face lights up. "Well now you've given me something, Brother. Her name, and presumably you've got info for the signing if you knew when it took place and the name of the author who scribbled her moniker?"

"The author's name is on the book. Camilla gave me some other details." To me, that all adds up to a whole heap of nothing, but seeing the flare in the eyes of our computer guru, it's obviously a start. I tap ash from the cigarette. "So, what do you suggest?"

Legend's brow develops crease lines. After a moment, he

suggests, "You could try and contact the author. They've probably got a Facebook page."

My mouth drops open. For a start, Facebook is like an alien complex to me. I avoid social media like the plague. "Aren't authors like rock stars or something? Why would they respond? And the only name I've got is Sheri. Though that's not as common as some, with thousands of books they've probably signed, why would they remember this one?"

He snorts. "Rock stars? Authors are ten-a-penny nowadays. Anyone can write and publish a book. Remember Cowherd from LA? He got something published a year or so back. Only sold a handful of copies, but it's as easy as shit." He looks at me then barks a laugh. "What, you starstruck, Brother?"

Indignant, I shake my head. I'll go toe to toe with anyone be they pauper or prince. I don't give a damn. "Even if they know who I'm talking about, why would they share info with me? And even if I get her full name, how's that going to move this along?"

"Okay, okay." Legend bites his lip, and his face creases again. "What was the signing?"

"MMM apparently." I think back to what Camille had said. "Motorcycles, Mobsters and Mayhem. It was in Houston last weekend."

He squints into the sun. "There's bound to be a Facebook group or something. Maybe you could join that, look at the members list, and then check out all women called Sheri."

"You're speaking a foreign fuckin' language," I warn him.

Swinging around, his eyes are wide. "You're not on Facebook?"

"Not fuckin' likely."

It's as if I've made a big joke. I don't understand why. Why would I want to share with the world what I'm doing? I've enough dirty laundry to keep to myself. I don't want anyone up in my business. And as far as what we do, going public is dangerous. "You got a profile?"

He shrugs. "If you can't beat 'em, join 'em. You'd be surprised what people brag about. So yeah, being in the business I am, I have." He glances at me and grins. "A fake profile, of course. Nothing that can be tracked back to me. On there, I'm a twenty-something nerd."

In practice, he's a thirty-something person of the same description, but far be it from me to tell him that.

A hefty slap to my back then, "Leave it with me. I'll see what I can dig up. I've got it right, haven't I? The mighty Story-Teller wants to find this mystery woman and give her her book back."

Raising my chin, I confirm that's it. But I smirk. "But not too fast. I haven't quite finished it yet, and I want to know the ending."

That seems to amuse him. As Legend walks off chuckling, I re-enter the clubhouse.

I might not spend much time here, but it's enough so no one's a stranger to me, nor me to them. I exchange a few tales and share a blunt with Pothead, then take up a brother on his offer of beating my ass at pool. Yeah. Right.

Fuck. It seems Weasel's far better at potting balls than I remember. I've given up trying to regain the contents of my wallet that I've lost when Legend reappears. Glad of the excuse not to embarrass myself further, I replace my cue in the stand and step forward when it's obvious he's heading for me. It's then I notice his customary smile is gone, and instead, he approaches me with brows drawn down.

"A word?" he speaks while still a few feet away.

"Sure. What's up, Bro?"

He waves toward the bar. "I think we need a drink for this."

A little unnerved by the expression on his face, I follow him over. Shitface, having spied us approaching, is ready to hand us two beers. When Legend asks for whisky chasers, he's quick to get them.

Picking up his two glasses, Legend leads the way to a table, and again I'm right on his heels. I straddle my chair and place my drinks on the table.

This time it's him who gets out his smokes. When we've lit up, he stares at the glowing tip held between his fingers, then sighs deeply. "Kind of wish you hadn't asked me about that woman."

My brows knit. "What have you found out?"

"A shitstorm, Bro."

Without the faintest idea what he could be talking about, I make a gimme gesture with my hand as I instruct, "Tell me."

After a raise and dip of his chin, he starts, "I was right. There is a Facebook group for the signing. And shit's going down on that group right now."

Confused, I look at him with narrowed eyes. "What kind of fuckin' shit?"

"Your woman... this Sheri," he corrects when he interprets my growl. "Well, she visited the signing alone, apparently. She drove down from Austin, but never returned. Her housemate reported her missing when she didn't get back."

"What?" That wasn't what I expected him to say.

Legend nods. "The cops gave it their obligatory twenty-four hours before they even started to look. When they did, they found her car abandoned in a rest stop just outside Houston."

My eyes crease as I stupidly repeat, "Houston?"

He shrugs. "That's where her trail disappears."

"Fuck." I let his findings sink in for a moment, then observe, "I found the book in New Mexico."

He gives a slow nod. "Yeah, not exactly on her route from Houston back to her hometown."

I talk half to myself. "She went off with someone, or she was taken."

"Latter seems more likely. There are loads of theories circulating, but the long and short of it is, no one has a clue what happened."

"Apart from the abandoned car, have the pigs made any progress?"

Legend shakes his head. "Nah. Presumably, CCTV didn't show anything. And no one's been able to contact her so far. She seems to have disappeared off the face of the earth." He eyes me carefully. "You know, you may be the only person to have found a piece of the puzzle. A possession of hers found in another state."

I shoot him a quick look. Damn it. He's right. I have. The police will be chasing their heels, trying to find her in Texas, while I've got evidence she might be far away.

"Do you think I ought to say something?" But even as the words come out of my mouth, I know me fessing up is unlikely. For a start, what help would that information be? I found her book, no proof she'd been anywhere near at the time. And, being who I am, a member of the Wretched Soulz, it's likely suspicion will fall on me. The feds are only too eager to want to get a warrant out for the club, and even an innocent, "I found a book belonging to a missing person" is likely to start a sequence of events we might not be able to stop.

Legend seems to be aware of the thoughts going through my head. "Don't see how you can. Oh, if it would help, maybe. But if she was there, I suspect it was only a brief stop. Fuck knows where she went, or was taken, after."

"And the book's not proof of anything." I find justification for keeping my mouth shut. "Anyone could have picked it up and left it there. You only want to read a book once."

"And it was dog-eared and looked used?"

Bashfully I turn away, unable to meet his eye. It was pristine, never been opened except to be signed. Fuck. It looks like Sheri's on her own. The pigs will be chasing their tails, trying to find her in Houston where she was last seen. I try to console myself with the sensible thought that just because she was in New Mexico a day or so ago is no proof she's there now. As Legend had mentioned, it was probably a pit stop. If she'd even been there at all.

Finders, keepers. That book is now mine. But for some goddamn reason, I get no joy from the thought I'm enjoying the book that's rightfully hers, and while I'm getting lost in its pages, she could be going through hell.

"This housemate, she had no explanation? Sheri might have met up with a friend, a man, family member?"

"All those suggestions are on the responses to the post the housemate, Agatha, made. All discounted. Sheri, it appears, was a bit of a loner. Even going to the signing was out of character. If she had a boyfriend, she'd never mentioned it to Agatha, and she thinks it's unlikely."

Women disappear all the time, and often for the worst of reasons. It seems like an innocent reason is going to be hard to find. Would coming clean help in some way? If it might, I shouldn't discount it. I rack my brains for some way I can help. "What about an anonymous tip-off?"

Legend shrugs. "Maybe, if there's no way they can track you down." As I turn back, I notice there's a thoughtful look on his face, as if the wheels are turning in his mind. His lips press together, and he rubs at his forehead. "Only thing the cops would be able to do is get a hold of the CCTV footage at the rest stop and start trawling through it." When I start to nod in agreement, the corners of his mouth turn up. "And it just so happens, I'm also able to do that."

I don't know how Legend works his magic, but he does. He's the one who checks all the backgrounds of people who want to join up. Of his own, however, we've all a suspicion there are things in the past he doesn't want us to know. But he's proved himself over and over, and how he got the skills and knowledge that come in so handy can remain shrouded in mystery.

"Legend, that would be—"

"Nah, don't fuckin' thank me too early. I've got too much on my plate to trawl over security videos for hours. You want to find her, you fuckin' look for her."

Doing something has got to be better than sitting on my hands. "Just show me what to do, Brother." Unless Prez has a need for me, I've got time. I bounce on my heels, suddenly eager. "When can we start?"

Slapping my back, he chuckles. "You have no fuckin' idea how tedious this is going to be." Then he considers, and suggests, "How about now?"

Feeling the need to be caffeinated, our other prospect, Ryder, is issued with instructions to bring coffees to Legend's lair, and I follow him into his sanctum hidden deep in the club-house, waiting while he unlocks the door. He's not paranoid about security with regard to our brothers stealing anything, but more worried about a drunken fucker wandering in and causing mayhem to his carefully set up equipment.

As always, I'm in awe of the array of monitors that hang from the walls, the PCs under and on the desk and at least two laptops which are there. Carefully, I step over the trip trap cables which no Occupational Safety and Health officer would approve, and take the seat opposite his expensive computer chair.

He grills me for a moment on exactly where the rest stop was, the time that I was there, and where exactly I found the discarded book. Then his fingers fly over the keyboard. It takes more than a moment as he inputs instructions, then finally, after both cups of coffee have cooled and been drunk, a look of triumph appears on his face.

"I'm in," he says, with satisfaction. "Now, there are several cameras. I suggest you start from the one showing where you found the book." He points to one of the monitors, and flicks through some views. Excitedly, I point out the one which shows the location, and chuckle softly when he rolls the footage back and I appear.

"Looking shady there, Bro." He laughs, then pushes the keyboard over, and gives me some brief pointers about what to do.

Suddenly, the problem hits me. "How will I know that it's her?"

Rolling his eyes, he snorts. "Give me a mo." He pulls a laptop toward him, and only seconds later is turning it back around. "This is her Facebook page, and these are her photos. Now you'll know if it's her who drops the book, or someone else."

Interested, I pull the laptop closer.

Until now, the Sheri to whom the book was dedicated was just an anonymous name. Now she comes alive in front of me. For some reason, I'd expected an immediate connection, in that there was one already, as the book she'd chosen had appealed to me. But the lithe beauty my imagination had summoned is not what I see.

It's hard to tell, but unless she's surrounded by dwarfs, she's a little taller than I thought she'd be. About five foot nine I'd estimate. She's curvy, pear shaped, and not immediately a person who'd attract me. But it's her smile that gets me right in the gut. There's a twinkle to her eyes that's captured in most of the pictures, a curve to her lips that suggests she's in love with life. A carefree way in which her red wavy hair is allowed to blow free with no attempts made to contain it, and clothes that don't try to hide the body she was gifted with. Some people might complain her attire would look better on someone slimmer, but not me. For some reason, the character I can see makes me smile.

Until I remember there's good reason to suppose this happy-go-lucky creature, I'm seeing in the two-dimensional images in front of me, is missing, and possibly dead, dying, or in a place of misery.

I wish I hadn't bothered to look at her profile. It was easier to ignore when she was a faceless name. Lowering my head into my hands, I rub at my temples, suddenly knowing I can't finish the book that doesn't belong to me. Why should I have closure learning the ending in the fictional world, when the conclusion of Sheri's story is yet to be written?

CHAPTER FOUR
STORYTELLER

Legend settles down, working on something or another while I stare at the monitor that shows the rest stop in New Mexico. I've gone back in time from the image of me looking, I must admit, fairly furtive, as I pick up the book, checking to see whether anyone's around.

In reality, I did so in case I could spot someone who's bag it may have fallen out of, but without that context, a different connotation could certainly be put on my actions. Viewing it again, I look guilty as fuck. I snort, momentarily catching Legend's attention, but at the shake of my head, he gets back to his own work again.

I start working back through the footage. I thought it would only be minutes because who'd leave a book lying there for long? But it seems most people aren't readers, and they pass it without giving it as much as a glance. A couple seem to actually notice it, though don't slow their pace, let alone stop. I suppose most are too focused on what they're doing to allow themselves to be distracted by a book.

In my case, it was only the word Nomad in the title that

had made me stop. If that hadn't caught my eye, maybe I wouldn't have picked it up. It could have lain there until an industrious cleaner swept it into a garbage sack, and Sheri would have been lost forever.

I realise I've been staring without really watching, and the next frame shows the book isn't there. Guiltily, I look at Legend, but he's too engrossed and hasn't noticed my lapse. I let the footage advance frame by frame, sitting forward, eager to get sight of the woman. On the screen, a crowd walks past, and when they've moved on, the book has suddenly appeared.

Damn it. I go back over the same footage again. There's a group who don't seem to be related, and my view is blocked of the actual event. Worse, they are all men except for one elderly woman who's limping along with a cane. None of them could be Sheri.

"Ledge?" When I get his attention, I voice my problem. "I need to follow some fuckers, see where they go."

He stands, comes around, and flips something on my screen. "Anyone in particular?"

I shake my head. "It could be any one of this lot. Except the old bitch. I doubt that it's her."

He's quicker than me, obviously used to assessing visual information. A couple peel off to go to the heads, and two more into the restaurant. One, though, he's more interesting, as once we have a clear view of him, he's loosely carrying a rucksack. When I see it's unbuckled with flaps hanging open, my interest is caught. *A book could easily have slipped out of that.*

We both watch as he glances around, as though making sure he's not being watched, before approaching a garbage container and pushing the rucksack inside. Then, he straightens, and confidently walks off.

The hairs on the back of my neck stand up. "Follow him," I demand.

Legend freezes the screen, but the face of the fucker is unclear. So, he does what I suggest and switches from camera to camera as we follow his progress out into the parking lot, Legend taking the occasional screenshot.

The sun's light makes the film a little hazy, but I suck in air sharply as I see our target walking out toward a group of bikes. As he approaches, a man steps forward and hands a cut to him.

"Fuck this shit!" Legend suddenly roars. "He's a fuckin' Dominator."

"Can you see the chapter?"

Legend's already zooming in. "Ari-fuckin'-zona." But I don't need him to tell me, enlarged, I can see it myself.

We continue to watch, me feeling helpless as the half dozen bikes surround a white van which pulls out of the parking lot. I'd bet good money that the Sheri I'm after is held captive inside, and they've just rid themselves of anything that would lead someone to her.

"Jesus Christ!" Legend exclaims, pushing himself to a standing position. "Fuck." His eyes find mine. "Doesn't look good for your Sheri."

She's not mine. She has nothing to do with me. Our only connection is that I've got something of hers, something that was important to her. The only thing we have in common is her taste in books.

She's nothing to me. I owe her nothing. In fact, I feel less of a thief now I know she hadn't meant to come back and reclaim that book. Nor had she left it as a clue for someone to follow her.

If someone else had found it, they could have thrown it away, or disregarded the inscription inside. Not many people would have a Legend who could track the owner down and find out she was in trouble.

Why hadn't I let sleeping dogs lie and not looked the gift

horse in the mouth? I could have gone on with my life, completely oblivious, have finished the book or not, and never again thought about the woman I've never met.

But having involved Legend and found out what I have, I can't leave it alone now. Knowing our arch enemies are involved, and particularly what we know they're involved in.

The Wretched Soulz aren't angels, far from it, and most of our lives are spent on the wrong side of the line. But what our chapter, at least, never gets involved in is treating human beings as commodities to be traded. On that front, the Dominators haven't just crossed the line, they've moved so far away, it would be impossible for them to see where it had ever been drawn. They trade in flesh, trafficking people over the border, and bringing migrants in with a promise of a good life, only for them to end up kept as slaves—the women for sex, the men to work until they drop.

If Sheri's fallen into their clutches, and on current evidence I've no doubt she has, she'll be headed to Mexico and from there onto a life she could only have dreamed up in the worst nightmare she could ever have.

Two days. Two days and she's been in their clutches.

Legend must be thinking along the same lines. "There's probably only a very short window in which to save her."

"You think we should?" While I don't like the thought of what the Dominators could be doing to a woman in their hands, I hadn't thought as far as actually doing anything about it.

Cupping his chin in one hand, Legend gives a long sigh. "It would bring us into a war."

"We're already at war." I scoff.

"We have the odd skirmish," he refutes. "But interfering in the Dominators' business would be seen as outright hostility."

He's right. I stand, use what unoccupied space there is in

his office to pace, though two steps and back is about all there's room for. Apart from me and Legend, no one else has a clue about what has happened to Sheri. They don't even know where to start to look.

I could ditch the book and go about my life as if nothing happened. Doing anything else could involve my club in something too dangerous to contemplate. Yeah, that's what I should do. But... The image of those sparkling eyes comes into my mind, and I know I hate the thought of them dimming.

But what to do? Go to the cops? I don't trust any pig to be able to find their asshole even with a map, let alone a missing girl. And the Dominators' connection means local cops will probably want to involve the feds, especially being as she's been taken over state lines. They'll probably take time getting a team together, and if I'm right, Sheri hasn't got that long. They might not even listen to me. Me being who I am, they might even view my info with distrust. The feud between the Soulz and Dominators is well known.

Even so, the thought of leaving Sheri to her fate without doing anything makes my gut roll. I rake my hands through my hair.

"Fuck it." I suddenly round on Legend. "I've got to do something, Brother."

His eyebrow rises. "You listening to yourself? You proposing to single-handedly take the Dominators on?"

I shrug. I haven't gotten so far as putting together a plan.

He sighs. "You can't go alone. You'll have to bring it to the table." At my dismissive gesture, his eyes narrow. "Or have you been nomad so long, you've forgotten how this shit works?"

"I fuckin' remember," I snarl, again brushing my long hair back with my hands. Church isn't until Friday, and it's only Monday now. Four days and fuck knows where Sheri might be taken, or what might be happening to her. Already it might be too late to prevent the worst. Sheri hasn't got four days. Fuck, she might not even have four hours. I make my decision. "Gonna go see Chaz."

"Good luck with that," Legend remarks.

It's not just luck that I need. I need a fucking miracle. The Dominators are a club similar in size to the Wretched Soulz, and while we're sworn enemies, we tend to avoid direct confrontation. In the past, when tempers have run high, a clash between the two clubs has attracted law enforcement's attention, with the result that those members who didn't die were rounded up and sent to the penitentiary.

If a Dominator comes into our territory, or we enter theirs, that biker is fair game. When I ride through, I'm careful not to display my colours.

Like any huge club, it's made up of separate members, not all of whom are assholes. I had a drink once with one in a neutral territory bar. He was much like any of my brothers, our conversation revolving around bikes. But had his chapter and mine met each other en masse, it would have been a bloodbath.

Going head-to-head with them is a decision Chaz won't make lightly, if he agrees at all. He could well decide finding Sheri is none of our business, certainly not enough to risk the club. As I walk through the clubhouse, trying to locate him, I'm having difficulty explaining my desire to rescue her to myself, let alone to him or anyone else. I've never met the fucking woman, so why do I feel this need to save her?

Shitface is wiping down the bar. I pause to ask him, "Seen Prez?"

He jerks his head to the left. "Think he's doing some work on his car."

The garage was my next destination, a fair bet if he wasn't

in his office, which I've already established he is not. I head that way, still undecided how best to approach him.

Delaying the conversation, I go stand under the raised ramp, looking up to the underside of Prez's first love after his bike, a beautifully restored Ford Mustang convertible from the 1960s. Even from this view, it's a work of art.

"Problems?" I ask, knowing the way to Prez's heart.

Wiping his hands on an already dirty rag, he confides, "Was. Isn't now."

Well, that tells me heaps. "Got a moment, Prez? I need to run something by you."

His eyes narrow as he turns his head to face me. "Yeah? Am I going to want to hear it?"

I grimace. "Probably not."

He throws down the rag, lowers his car, then parks it in its place out in the parking lot. When he's happy it's situated, he comes back to where I've been waiting.

Gesturing back to the clubhouse, he suggests, "Let's take this to my office."

On the way, we grab a couple of beers from Shitface, then only moments later, I'm sitting opposite him sat behind his desk. He takes a long swallow from his bottle, then wipes his mouth as he places it down.

Sitting back, he folds his arms over his chest. "Speak. But only if it's not going to be anything about the Dominators."

I clamp my mouth shut.

He stares at me for a moment. "Fuck, ST. I've just heard the Alpha's heading our way. I can't afford to have trouble or draw their attention. Can it wait until after his visit? He's only, hopefully, going to be here a few days."

Wiping my hand over my face, I disillusion him of his hope. "Chaz, I'm fuckin' sorry, Bro. But no, it can't wait."

His cheeks puff as he sucks in air, then hollow as he blows it out. "Hit me with it."

Sitting up straighter, I clasp my hands between my legs. "I was travelling through New Mexico. Hungry, thirsty, both me and my bike needed a top off—"

"Fuck, I've no time to hear one of your stories. Just give me the punchline, Brother."

Frowning, my oratory brought to a halt, I try to focus on the important bits. "I found a book in a rest stop. It was autographed by the author. I didn't realise the significance at first."

"Significance?" He cocks an eyebrow.

"Long story short, it wasn't dropped by accident. Evidence points to the owner, a woman named Sheri Secord, having been taken by the Dominators. It happened two days back— saw them clearly on the CCTV footage Legend dug up. I want to get her back."

Chaz raises his hand. "Hold on. You've lost me. Who's this Sheri to you?"

"See, she's the owner of the book I picked up—"

He waves his hand. "Got that bit. But how long have you known her? What's she to you? Some chick you fucked?"

My brows drawn down. "I've never met her."

His eyes widen and he snorts. His head moves sharply side to side, then he repeats the action. Finally, he wiggles a finger into his ear. "Sorry, for a moment there I thought you said you didn't know the bitch at all."

I know her choice in books, but nothing more than that. I feel my cheeks redden as I admit, "You heard right."

He drums his fingers on the desk. "Let me get this clear. A woman's gone missing, and you've got evidence she's been taken by the Dominators, so we can suspect what her future looks like. But you don't know her and haven't a clue whether she's worth saving. Yet, you're proposing we go to war to get her back?"

Put so starkly like that, it does seem ridiculous.

"I don't ask you for much, Chaz."

He gives another snort. "And this isn't much?" He sits forward, placing his elbows on the desk and clasping his hands. His blazing blue eyes stare into mine. "This isn't like you, ST. Any other brother, and I'd dismiss it out of hand. But what's the bitch done that's got you so invested in her?"

What can I do but respond lamely. "I took her book."

"You took her book." His eyes widen incredulously. In disbelief, he asks, "Is it any good?"

I shrug. "So far it is. I haven't finished it yet."

He harrumphs. "Well, I suggest you go finish it. Maybe take a bit of time to think through what an ask this is. It's not as if we can walk up to the Dominators and ask them for the woman back."

It isn't. Such a request is just as likely to get her killed as a way of making a point to us.

He waves to the door and growls, "Get out of here, ST."

CHAPTER FIVE
SHERI

BEFORE...

Agatha snorts. "I can't believe you're really going to do this."

To be honest, neither can I. My shoulders rise to ear level as I try to explain it to my housemate. "It's so close. It's an opportunity I can't miss. It's only two hours away!" To me, it's a sign that the gods have meant it to be.

"A rock concert, sure, I could understand that. But authors?" She rolls her eyes dramatically. Then frowns. "It's so unlike you, Sheri."

She's right. It is. But it's time I started pushing myself, grabbing life and doing something with it instead of letting it simply sweep me along.

I'd grown up not knowing things weren't quite right between my parents until I was old enough to realise how different our family was. Other people's parents talked to each other, maybe kissed or showed signs of affection. My mom? Well, no one could please her, least of all me or my dad. They probably should have gotten divorced years earlier, but I was sixteen before my dad had enough and moved out.

Whether it was the shock or coincidence, Mom was diagnosed with an aggressive form of cancer. Dad never returned, despite how ill she was, or that eventually I had to leave school and become her full-time nurse. In those final months, she'd softened, and we'd settled into a relationship that meant, despite some of the hard truths she'd left me with, I was devastated when she was gone. A girl misses her mom whether she was the best in the world or not.

It was then I found out she hadn't changed her will, and because they'd never gotten around to making their separation legal, everything had gone to my dad. A man who, at last, returned home.

Having lost a parent, regaining one and staying in the house where I was brought up seemed comforting, until he quickly remarried and brought a stepmother, and stepsister home.

I'd run the house when my mom was ill, but now I was pushed to one side. Furnishings changed and soon the place no longer resembled where I'd grown up. My new sister, one year older, had a privileged place in the house. She was the favourite and could do no wrong, while I, who hadn't finished school because I'd been home playing nurse, was stupid, had no future, and was just a weight to be carried, or that was the view of my stepmom.

My dad wasn't blind, he could see what was going on. He'd even apologised to me. In his words, I was young and had my whole life ahead while he deserved to grab some happiness while he still could. And happy, yeah, that's what my stepmother made him. She was completely different from my mom. Ultra-nice to him, while being as cruel as she could get away with to me.

I thought it would be nice having a sister, but hey, lucky me, I ended up with one who was everything I was not—slim, pretty, full of confidence oh, and a total bitch to go along with it.

Obviously, I didn't last long. I stayed for a few months before discovering my stepsister in bed with my boyfriend. That was the last straw.

Desperate to get away from the home where I was no longer wanted, I answered an ad for someone to share the rent in a rundown apartment. By then, I'd had a waitressing job and could just about afford what was asked.

Until I was sixteen, I thought my life was in a neat little box, but one blow after another had had an impact. Rather than outgoing, I became introverted. I went from a child who thought they were wanted, to someone without parents or roots. A psychiatrist would probably say I not only feel unloved, but unlovable. But my life isn't how I originally planned it, nor what I want. My housemate is okay, but the total opposite to the person I am myself. But we gel together, agreeing on the major elements, such as the importance of keeping our hovel clean, tidy, and as nice as we can make it. Perhaps how we're not up in each other's business has helped us get along, and the three years have passed fairly smoothly since I moved in.

As real life had knocked me back, I escaped to a fictional world, reading voraciously, picking through the genres until I settled on one I liked. Now, I devour books about motorcycle club romance as though they were going out of fashion. In every spare moment I've got, I'm to be found with my head in a book, dreaming of being part of the world that exists in the minds of the authors who fascinate me. What draws me to the trope are the ideas of brotherhood, that MCs are a mismatched family, where people who might not otherwise find a place are welcomed and accepted. And above all, the loyalty that binds them, and the raising of their fingers to the blind following of citizens' rules. Justice is delivered swiftly, no need to take wrongdoers through the courts. No chance for a fork-tongued lawyer to sweet talk a jury and get a perpetrator off. Or sisters that steal your men.

The books I've read aren't sweet, and they are so often about the underdog. They are full of violence, swearing and sex. They're not sweet romances. They're ugly and raw. The men though, are protective, and one hundred percent into the woman when they find the right one. Oh, how I dream of finding a man like that, who only sees me.

Dreams. Just dreams. In real life, no such man would be attracted to me, not when there were people like my stepsister around—intelligent, witty and pretty.

I also doubt any such men really exist. The words that I read paint a rosy picture of life in an MC, while the reality is very different. There's little chance of me ever coming across anyone like the bikers who populate the pages of my books, however much I wish I could.

However unrealistic, something about that created world has caught my imagination, and I read little else. A little Mafia, perhaps, which is like swapping leather for suits. Sometimes in a complete turnaround, I'll read about heroes in uniform. But it's the MC books I always return to.

Agatha, who I share the small apartment with, can't understand how I read so much. She's an extrovert and my complete opposite, going out and having fun, while I stay home with my books.

She's shaking her head at me now. "You do realise this signing will be full of women? There won't be unattached men for you to find."

I can see why it wouldn't appeal to her, but I don't give a

damn. The kind of men that attract me are far safer to remain within the pages of the books that I read. If I met a leather-clad hero in real life, I wouldn't know what the hell to do with him. And, as I've found, flesh-and-blood men are likely to end up in bed with someone else.

"I'm going to meet the authors," I tell her primly. "And I'll have fun."

Though she rolls her eyes, I know that I will. When I heard that a big signing was coming to my home state again, this time to Houston, I did something spontaneous, being one of the first readers to splurge my meagre savings to buy a ticket. Then I watched the announcements, growing more excited each time one of my favourite authors was announced.

Knowing Agatha would laugh at me, I'd prepared in secret, stitching patches onto a denim jacket so I could fit in, putting away what pennies I could to buy a couple of signed books as a souvenir. While I don't expect to actually buy many books, the main reason for attending the signing is to fangirl over, and meet with, my favourite authors, and of course, meet new ones who might capture my interest and lead to more reading material in the future. Of course, I know, when I meet the authors of the books that I love, I'll be tongue tied and awkward.

As an introvert, my life is lived vicariously through stories in the books that I read. I'm no beauty, I've not got a model's figure, and I'm clumsy as fuck. The heroes are sufficient boyfriends for me. They'd never cheat. And the women are the people I'd love to be surrounded with in real life.

As the day of the signing approaches, I realise perhaps there was more pleasure in the anticipation, as my nerves start to make themselves felt. The only thing keeping me going is the camaraderie in the online readers' group. I'm far from the only one having nerves about attending their first signing or worrying about being starstruck.

The day has arrived. I wake up early, dress carefully, and apply makeup sparingly. Knowing I'm no raving beauty, I don't bother too much with my looks. After giving myself a pep talk, I go to my car that I'd already refuelled and give it a quick status check. Yup, I've got my phone and wallet in my purse, and that goes into a backpack with spare room for any books.

My hands shake as I turn the key and get the engine running, and I steady myself with a few deep breaths. I set out to start my two-hour journey, a little bit proud of myself. Today is taking me out of my comfort zone, and if I do this, I'll feel I can conquer the world.

The drive goes smoothly, and soon I'm navigating through Houston. My GPS guides me unerringly, and, swapping lanes when told, I find it relatively easy to navigate the big city. Eventually, I'm turning into the driveway of the hosting resort, and easily find the parking lot.

Mentally giving myself a pat on the back for arriving safely, I again steady myself with deep breaths. After giving myself a short uplifting lecture, *you've got this,* I exit the car, taking more time than necessary to make sure the locks are engaged, pausing and looking back twice to check the position of the telltale mirrors. Satisfied, I progress slowly toward where the signing is being held.

I show my ticket then pause at the door. *There are people. Wall-to-wall people.* I start to hyperventilate, then berate myself, *what did I expect?* Knowing there are people wanting to enter behind me, I force myself into the room.

Suddenly, instead of a jigsaw puzzle just opened and in a thousand bits, pieces start to assemble themselves, and what I'm seeing begins to make sense. There are people queuing around the most popular authors, some of whom I'd hoped to talk to myself. A few authors sit behind more meagre displays, looking just as unnerved as myself.

Pulling up my big girl panties, I approach a table that others seem to have forgotten. The author gives me a welcoming smile, and when I ask, starts a spiel about her books. She's a fairly new writer, and only has recently started publishing, but her work attracts my interest. When offered, I take a bookmark and a pen, and promise to check her out in one of the online stores. Walking away after a few moments, I feel a new confidence inside. If I'm not mistaken, that author was as nervous meeting me, as I was her. I'd done a small service by showing interest in her books.

Still anxious about meeting the big names, I avoid the lines and continue to spend time on authors I haven't read before. As I wander around, although guilty I'm taking the offered swag without making a purchase, I start to realise it's par for the course, and that I'm going to fulfil my promise, and definitely read the e-versions of their books. My pack becomes laden with bookmarks, pens, leaflets, keyrings and magnets, and, to my amused delight, a chocolate dick.

Something to eat when I'm on the long journey home. I have to suppress a snort, as I picture getting caught at a red traffic light, sucking on that particular chocolate delight.

As the day goes on, I become more relaxed, and am thoroughly enjoying myself. I do end up speaking to some of the authors whose books I've read and loved. I've still not yet made a purchase. Feeling guilty as the day draws on, I approach one of my all-time favourites.

I'm nervous as hell as I walk up to MariaLisa DeMora's table, waiting while she finishes animated conversations with readers ahead of me. By this time, her table, like many others, is depleted, with only a small selection of books. I'm pleased for her that she's obviously had a good day, well worth her making the trip, but disappointed for me. I really wanted to get the first in the *Neither This nor That* series. Twisted's book is my absolute favourite. But she's down to only a few copies of the later books, so I plump for *Tangled Threats on the Nomad Highway,* a book I've not read yet.

Although I must be the hundredth person she's talked to today, she's so lovely and treats me as though I'm her first, even recognising my name from some of the comments I've made in her reader group. She's so down to earth and friendly, she makes an impression on me, just like some of the other authors I've met.

I suppose that's a bonus for them for attending a signing. If you connect with an author, you're more likely to read all their books. But whatever, she signs the book I've purchased, making sure she spells my name right. Then she hopes I enjoy the rest of my day and, reluctantly, I move on.

That ends up being the only purchase I make, but I leave with a huge mental list of books to read, and swag to remind me of all the authors' names in case I forget. I make them a silent promise to read at least one from each of the authors I've met.

The venue is starting to empty, and authors begin packing away their books. Not wanting to hold up any of them from getting their well-deserved break, I leave, albeit with a smile on my face after having had such an amazing day.

I might have only ended up with one book, but it's one I know I'll always treasure.

I'm tired, hungry and thirsty, but I've got a long journey home, and stopping off to eat at one of the chain restaurants is probably going to be cheaper than eating here at the venue. I decide to get on my way.

The traffic's a little heavier from when I first arrived, but it doesn't really take me long to get out of Houston and on the freeway. My phone is playing a selection of my favourite songs through the car's audio system, and I'm still buzzing from having a great day. For an introvert, I feel what I've done is quite an accomplishment.

A sign's coming up, advising me this is where I can get a cheap meal. I pull off the freeway and stop. I grab my backpack and take it rather than digging down to extract my wallet.

Going to the counter, I order my food and beverage, wait for my number to come up, then take my meal to a table in an empty area near the back. Making sure I don't have grease on my fingers, I take my prized book out of my backpack and examine it. Almost scared to open the pages in case I muck it up, I read the blurb, gaze at the cover, and peek carefully at the inscription inside. It's the first signed book I've ever had, and I still can't believe the author signed it for me. But she did. After a moment's perusal, I put it back in my pack.

I flick through the bookmarks and leaflets I picked up, to occupy my time while eating my burger, mentally cataloguing those which I first want to look up. When I've finished eating, I slip them into my bag, my eyes falling on the chocolate dick which makes me smile.

"Hey, a pretty lady like you shouldn't be eating alone."

I startle, having been so lost in the book world, I hadn't seen the man walk up. Quickly, I turn toward him, my eyes opening wide as I see he's tattooed and wearing a cut which, along with a hefty chain securing his wallet to his belt, and his boots, the left scuffed by operating the gears, screams that he's a real-life biker. Stunned with this feature of my dreams coming to life, I'm lost for words for a moment.

He's not alone. Two companions similarly dressed are with him. I quickly realise that rather than my fantasy being answered, these bikers are nothing like those I read about in books. Their features are hardened, their skin battle scarred. While big, at least one carries a full paunch. One's teeth are yellowed with gaps showing he's lost some, and the one who addressed me has an unpleasant leer. I get an unpleasant whiff of stale sweat.

My excuse isn't made up as I grab my pack and start to stand. "You can have the table, I've finished."

The first biker puts his hand over his heart. "Darlin', you wound me. Just wanted to have some pretty company for a while."

I may have a fixation for fictional bikers, but the real thing has my heart beating fast from fear and is a million miles from arousal. Danger exudes from the trio, and I'd rather be anywhere but here right now. My innate recourse is to be polite and give in to their demands, but something tells me that wouldn't be good for my health.

I continue to get to my feet, my hand gripping my pack as I swing it over my shoulder.

"I'm sorry, I have places to be."

While not particularly crowded, I take comfort in that there are sufficient people around to make me feel safe, a fact the biker's glance around shows he's equally aware of. With a smirk and a mock bow, he steps to one side, allowing me to leave.

I scuttle away, only belatedly realising I haven't put my garbage in the trash, but I'm certainly not going to go back to rectify my omission. Instead, I head straight for the ladies' bathroom, quickly sliding in, hoping I've evaded any of them if they had any thought of coming after me.

A pit stop was what I was going to make anyway. I've still got a distance to drive. After doing my business, I wash my hands, stare into the mirror and laugh at myself. The bikers hadn't wanted anything more than to unsettle me and have a joke at my expense. Unless, the likes of them, so far removed from the handsome specimens who populate the pages I read, think they'd have a chance with an ugly duckling like me.

Now I've been faced with the real thing, I'm more certain than ever, I'll be sticking to bikers of the fictional variety.

I hurry myself up, the altercation having unnerved me. The bikers had presumably come into the restaurant to eat, as well as taunt the curvy girl. If I tarry too long, I run the risk that they'll have finished and will be leaving the same time as me. I decide if I see them in the parking lot, I'll fake a medical situation and run back to the bathroom again.

But what if they're already waiting for me?

Oh, for goodness' sake, why should they be? Maybe I'm worthy of a few minutes' entertainment, but not of a lot more of their time. Haven't they got club bunnies or sweet butts to satisfy their needs?

They won't be waiting for me. And if they are, I'll just have to bring on my inner badass just like the women I read about in books. A few lashes of my sharp tongue will soon have them under control. *Who am I kidding?* I snort to myself.

My internal arguments are getting me nowhere, unlike the glances of a few women who've entered and left, giving me strange looks at me taking so long washing my hands. The recommended twenty seconds turning more like twenty minutes.

It must be the signing getting to me. Having spent a few hours immersed in a fictional world, I'm now unable to separate fact from stories in the novels I've read. Nothing is going to happen, and those bikers certainly won't be waiting for me.

Shaking my head at my silliness, I pull my back straight, again settle my pack on my shoulder, and open the door.

I needn't have worried about anything. As I pass the restaurant, the bikers are long gone. While I peer gingerly into the parking lot, my way is unimpeded between me and my car. With a final huff directed at myself, I step outside into the evening sun, and walk boldly toward my vehicle, with my eyes fixed straight ahead.

There are four yards between me and my car, now three. When I'm reaching into my pocket to bleep my key, a van suddenly screams up the lane between the parked rows of cars. Before I can blink, men jump out and grab hold of me.

I have time to give a startled scream before I'm thrown in the back and the doors are slammed closed. Then two other doors slam and the van speeds away.

I tumble and fall with the speed they set off, and try to jam myself in.

I'd only gotten a brief look at my kidnappers, but enough to confirm I was right to be wary of real-life bikers. One, at least, was one of those who'd accosted me in the restaurant.

CHAPTER SIX
STORYTELLER

Chaz had pointed out how ridiculous it was for me to want to send my club into war, to rescue a woman I'd never met or knew anything about, other than that she had good taste in books.

That should have been the end of it. His pep talk should have brought me to my senses. I've far more important things to worry about, like going through the logistics of moving the guns the cartel will soon have coming our way. But, as I leave his office, instead of having my head straight, Sheri's predicament plays on my mind.

I try to tell myself I know nothing about her, her likes and dislikes, whether she's got family she's close to, or even if she's a good person. Maybe if I knew more about her, I'd know whether she deserves to be rescued. Of course, being trafficked and sold isn't a fate anyone should be subjected to, but if Sheri's a cruel, horrible person, then maybe it's karma come knocking at the door.

My problem is, although I know nothing about her, my

imagination is conjuring up the very opposite of a person deserving of punishment.

I stop in the corridor, gently knocking my head against the wall. *Why the fuck can't I just give this up?*

What choice have I got, though? I might be a nomad and used to fighting battles for myself, but if I were to try to get Sheri out of the hands of the Dominators singlehanded, I might as well be committing suicide. I like my life too much to throw it away on a mission that has no chance of success.

But damn it. Why do I feel so much like a failure? And why, when I think about the book lying on the table beside my bed, do I feel guilty about picking it up to finish reading it.

"Hey." Skunk holds up his hands in a submissive gesture as I approach. "Whatever you think, I ain't done it."

What? As I watch him nervously take a step back, I realise my features are composed into a scowl. I shake my head, as much to dislodge it, as to refute his assumption.

"Nothing to do with you, Bro. Just got a lot on my mind."

Claw kicks out a chair at the table he's sitting at. The noise gets my attention, and at the jerk of his head, I accept the invitation he's offered to me.

"So, what's on your mind, ST?"

He's barely waited for me to get my ass on the seat before asking. I consider carefully before answering. This is my home chapter, but I'm away more often than I'm here. I've not really got rights to criticise my brothers. Instead of telling the enforcer that Prez has got shit wrong, I sigh, lean back in my chair, and link my hands behind my head.

"Prez handed my ass to me." I shrug. "He's probably right." Deep down, I know he is. What's inexplainable is my wish that I could say he was wrong.

Claw starts shuffling a pack of cards he brings out of his

cut. It's not like he wants to start a game, but it's an ingrained habit to keep his hands busy. "Wanna tell me what it's about?"

For the second time today, I find myself sticking to just giving the highlights of the sorry story. When I finish, I take my cigarettes out, offer him one, then light both. Shitface appears with an ashtray.

Claw shakes his head. "I'd love to beat some fuckin' Dominators' heads together. I hate the fuckin' skin trade they're all up in. But, Bro, Prez is right. That's one of their biggest businesses. We go for that, then it's all-out war."

Despite that my words indicate I've accepted Chaz's reasonable position, I tense as Claw backs him up. If I was looking for someone to be on my side, then the enforcer is showing he's not going to be it. For a moment, I wonder if it would help my frustration were I to challenge him to a bout in the gym. Rearranging someone's face might soothe my soul a bit, though it would probably be sensible to go up against someone other than him. I might have been a SEAL, but Claw served as a Marine. Unless he's using the knuckleduster he's named for—the custom made one with knives that shoot out when he clenches his fist—the odds are probably no better than even on which of us would win.

Curving my nails into my palms, I force myself to stay calm, and admit through gritted teeth, "You're probably right."

He taps ash off the end of his cigarette and sits forward. While his mouth opens, before he can get any words out, there's a roar of bikes approaching the clubhouse, and more worryingly, the sound of shots.

Ryder bursts through the clubhouse door. "Soulz, coming in hot."

Even before the words are out of his mouth, I and my brothers are already on our feet and rushing toward the door.

Gun in hand, I crouch. Taking advantage of any cover I can

find, I sum up the situation. *Fuck.* I identify the leading bike and rider, raise my gun and take aim, ready to open fire at the riders closing on him fast.

Iron and Ryder have the gates open wide, then drop to their stomachs and start to provide cover.

"Hold fire!" Iron suddenly screams leaping to his feet. "Hold your fuckin' fire."

My gun's already back in my holster as I've, too, noticed the riders "chasing" our dear leader are actually part of his entourage, and they're not firing at us. All their weapons are pointed upward. Our guns might have been stood down, but our heart rates? Well, they're quite a different matter. More than one of my brothers has their hand to their chest as the adrenaline that had risen so fast needs a moment to go back down.

"Fuckin' cunt!" Chaz, not cowed in the slightest in the presence of greatness, approaches Slugger. "Asshole," he spits out for good measure as he draws closer.

The man I call the Alpha is uncontrite. He's still on his bike, leaning on his tank, staring around with a shit-eating grin on his face. He watches Prez approach, and only when he draws close, throws his leg over the saddle and dismounts.

I follow behind Chaz as he goes to greet the newcomer, raising my head at Slugger's companions as I pass. I've met both before. Like me, Oak and Fart are nomads, and often end up as the Alpha's unofficial escorts, as I've done myself.

Having received chin lifts in return, I wait while the prez and Slugger perform their greeting ritual. Then, as Chaz steps back, I move forward and am enveloped in Slugger's meaty arms, forcing myself to endure the pounding that's being given to my back.

"Way to make an entrance, Bro." I roll my eyes.

Slugger snorts, but Chaz glares at him. "You could have

been fuckin' killed. You couldn't have come in like normal fuckers, eh? Or used the fuckin' phone and given us a heads-up?"

"What's the fun in that, Brother?" The titular head of the Wretched Soulz snorts as he responds. "Now, where's this Arizonan hospitality I've heard so much about?"

Chaz indicates Slugger should precede him into the clubhouse, and behind his back he gives me a scowl. I shrug, raising my hands, silently indicating I haven't been extolling the virtues of our chapter. I certainly didn't recommend that he come here, but I don't know whether Chaz believes me or not. And, after that entrance, I doubt Slugger will be making any of our lives easy.

When I've been in his company before, I've often thought the Alpha's got a schizophrenic personality. He can be the craziest asshole you've ever met, then, in the blink of an eye, be the most serious and deadly. Woe betide anyone who tries to predict which side of him you'll get. But then, anyone who leads the vast organisation of the Wretched Soulz has to have balls made of fucking steel.

Chaz places his hand on my back and uses it to steer me to the side. "You know why he's here?" His eyes bore into me.

"Not a fuckin' clue." I push back my hair. "It was on the cards as I already told you."

"He's not fuckin' coming in like a man trying to stay under the radar," he observes.

"He's fuckin' crazy. You know this."

As I state the obvious, Chaz just stares at me, before shaking his head and rolling his eyes once again. "Well, I guess we're not going to find anything out without talking to him."

By the time Chaz and I reach the bar, Slugger's already got a beer in his hand and a sweet butt, Ce Ce, hanging off his arm. He's got an easy grin on his face, and he'd look like any other brother out to have a good time. That's if you weren't aware of who he is. Instead of being approached, men are standing back, only cautiously acknowledging him. Going by the various looks being given to him by those all around, some brothers are wary, some full of admiration, and some down-right ready to do some sucking up.

Shitface shoots beers over to myself and Prez, and I take mine to go join Fart and Oak, and stand with them, juggling my bottle while trying to light a cigarette.

"Quite an entrance, Brothers."

Oak grins at my dry tone. "Thought you'd like some more material for your stories, ST. The one about how the Alpha gets killed, approaching one of his own charters."

Fart chuckles. "What you even doing back here, Bro? Thought you were still out on the road?"

"Chaz called me back. Seems even a nomad has to do work sometime." I grin back at him. We all know how it goes. The freedom of nomads is an illusion as we can all be summoned at any time. It's the price of the patch that we wear. I take a drag of my cigarette, then ask, "You got a new ride, Fart?"

He has, as I've already noticed. We spend a few moments discussing his latest sled, and the abrupt demise of its prede-cessor, an unplanned dismount involving oil on the road and a disgusting amount of road rash indelicately described. I commiserate, as expected.

The music turns up, the other club girls appear, and in Soulz fashion, we begin to party. Word has obviously gotten out and women turn up from the nearby town. My usual self would be leaning back against the bar, checking them out, choosing one, then taking her to my room where we'd fuck. Then, kick her out, and depending on how I felt, maybe target another.

I don't do ties. I don't want relationships, but like every red-blooded man, I need to get my rocks off.

Tonight though, I try to take part. It's not that the scantily clad, heavily made-up women are any different, there's something wrong with me. My dick doesn't so much as twitch. For some reason, my brain's tied up imagining a girl I've never met, being forced to endure what women should enjoy. The thought of her being raped has my blood running cold.

Fuck it. I grow angry at myself. What the hell do I know about her? That she went to a signing entitled Motorcycles, Mobsters and Mayhem suggests her reading matter is hard core. Maybe she jumped at the chance to move on from fiction and experience bikers in real life. She might have gone with them voluntarily. She might even be a sweet butt right now, happily spreading her legs for any Dominator who requests it.

There's nothing to stop me from grabbing one of the girls and using my cock for what nature intended. But try as I might, not one of them makes it stir, even when a pretty, buxom, twenty-something comes over and all but pushes her cleavage into my face.

I can't find fucking pleasure while I don't know what's happening to Sheri. Which is so fucked up, I don't even have a name for it.

It's not just the women. My brothers seem intent on pulling me out of my funk, but I can't be bothered to join in with a game of poker, nor try my hand at the pool table. Fed up with my dismissive snarls, my brothers gravitate to those wanting to have a good time. It leaves me sitting alone, nursing my fifth beer of the evening.

Slugger breaks free from the entourage surrounding him and makes a beeline for me. With a chin lift, he joins me at my table. "So, what's going on with you, ST?"

My shoulders rise to my ears, then drop slowly. "Same old, same old," I tell him.

"Nah." His sharp eyes stare into me. "You're not your normal self, Bro. Been here a few hours and you've not been regaling me with any stories."

"Maybe I just haven't got any worth telling."

His eyes narrow. "You're sitting here on your own. Not like you, ST. You're normally the heart and soul of the party."

Suddenly, I growl. "You want to hear a fucking story? Try this one on for size."

Without meaning to, I start spilling, in my normal expressive fashion, how I came to find a book discarded by a woman's kidnappers. Said kidnappers appear to be the fucking Dominators. When I finish my sorry tale, I'm surprised when he bursts out laughing.

Disgusted, I stand with the intention of walking away, but his hand snakes out and stops me.

"No disrespect, ST, but you can't blame me. You're caught up with a bitch you've never met, let alone spoken to. Sit your ass down and let's talk this through."

Slugger could easily end me, or at least my association with the Wretched Soulz MC. He's not a man you cross lightly. Annoyed, partly with myself, because if it were anyone else, I too would be laughing, I plop down my ass. When Slugger signals for more beers, Ryder comes running.

"Come on, ST. You've gotta agree it's funny as fuck." He leans back into his seat and stretches out his legs. "You don't know this bitch from Adam but you're tied up in knots about her." Suddenly he leans forward, pointing an accusing finger at me. "I know you. I know your fuckin' history. You're not a man to go soft on a bitch."

I'm not. I can't understand it myself. After my one and only disastrous attempt at a relationship, I wasn't going to put myself into the position of getting involved again. Fuck no.

Grimacing, I try the impossible, to explain my reaction. "At first, who the book belonged to was a mystery I wanted to solve. Then, when I knew she was in the hands of the Dominators…"

"Ah," he states, his eyes blazing as if he's having a light bulb moment. "It's because it's *them*, not because it's *her*."

Feeling relieved as he must have gotten the gist of the strange emotions I'm feeling, I agree. "Kind of feels like they've got one over on us. All I wanted to do was find the bitch and return her book to her. And because of them, I can't."

"Who fucking says?"

Startling, I look at him sharply. "We can't start a war. Not for one anonymous woman."

His eyes narrow, then he looks quickly away and zooms in on a different target. Suddenly, his hand is waving in the air, beckoning someone over. I suppress a grin, seeing by the stiffness in Chaz's gait that he doesn't much appreciate the way he's been summoned.

When he reaches us, my prez stands by the table, arms folded, an eyebrow raised, waiting for an explanation.

"ST's got a problem. Says you're cockblocking him."

The beer splutters out of my mouth, and I slam my bottle down, using both hands to raise in supplication. "Chaz, I didn't—"

"You've been running your mouth?" Prez's arms unfold as he rises on tiptoe before placing his heels back down. I can read the signs. He's angling for a fight. And probably one where he'll be backed up by the enforcer and sergeant-at-arms if I don't find a way to defuse this.

But when my lips part for my defence to come out, Slugger stirs the shit again. He leans back on his chair, and there's a gleam in his eyes. "Heard you're too chicken to take on the Dominators."

The beginnings of a growl coming from Chaz gets me leaping to my feet. "He's shitting you," I tell Chaz, my words coming fast. "I didn't say anything of the fuckin' sort."

"Both of you, sit your asses down." Slugger's voice is loud.

"I don't like being told what to do in my own fuckin' clubhouse." Chaz swings around, his eyes leaving me for the first time since he'd answered the summons.

Slugger chuckles. "You're both too fuckin' easy to wind up." The mirth leaves his face. "Sit, please. I'm in mind of sharing an idea that I've had."

Chaz doesn't look happy, but he does take a chair, while I resume a seated position in mine.

Slugger lights a cigarette, blows smoke out, then stares at the glowing tip. "Fuckin' Dominators are getting too big for their britches. Time to take them down a peg or two."

"You're in my state, in my clubhouse," Chaz reminds him. "Not certain I like the idea of you stirring shit up then moving on, leaving me with a mess to clean up."

Slugger looks at him sharply. "Have faith in me, Bro. Remember, I've got the good of the Wretched Soulz at heart. And I'm not talking about starting a war, just putting a dent in them a little." He takes a drag then taps off ash. "What's your relationship like with them in Arizona?"

"As much as possible, we avoid each other. Toss insults around if we happen to come across them, maybe bloody a few faces, but there's a kind of truce with a common hatred of the cops."

Slugger nods as if it's what he expected and states, "When we come to war, the pigs always seem to get involved. And neither of us want them poking their noses into our business."

He's right. If the Soulz and the Dominators go head-to-head, pigs turn up en masse to try to arrest as many of us as they can. When we can, we try to avoid direct confrontation. But hell, we're bikers, it comes with the territory, and it's hard to resist when you meet head-on with your enemy.

Chaz seems to relax a little, enough so that he kicks out his legs and leans back. He gestures toward me. "ST doesn't know the bitch. By his own admission, he's got nothing invested in her. If she was his ol' lady or something, and they weren't the Dominators, maybe I'd have been willing to help. But she's not, and they are." He shrugs.

Shitface is watching us from a distance. I wave him over, and being a good prospect, he brings fresh drinks. We wait until he's removed the empties and replaced the ashtray with a clean one.

"You might say she's not his ol' lady, but ST's acting like a man in love," Slugger jokes as I snort, my features composing themselves into an expression of utter disgust.

Chaz chortles loudly. "ST, in love?"

"Not fuckin' likely." Been there, done that. Not going back.

"Watcha thinking?" Chaz has a glint in his eye which I'm not sure I like.

Slugger smirks at him. "I'm thinking ST here should man up and go ask for his ol' lady back."

Again, I splutter. "What the fuck?"

"You think they'll just pony her up to him?"

The head of the Wretched Soulz snorts. "Not fuckin' likely, but there is a chance. Honour among thieves and that. Might do to keep the truce between you."

"Or I might get a bullet between my eyes for just having the balls to ask." I point out the obvious.

With his mouth turned down and his eyes hooded, Slugger shakes his head sadly. "Never took you for a pussy, Brother."

They can't be fuckin' serious. I look from one to the other. "Yeah, yeah. Good joke."

The way Chaz is looking at me makes me worry I can't trust him one bit and remember I had annoyed him earlier when I'd asked for help that he wasn't prepared to give. Add to that the way Slugger's treating him like a second-rate member, not someone in charge of his club, well, if I was facing down a train at the moment, I wouldn't trust my prez to pull me away from the tracks.

"You wanted to save her." Chaz lazily rolls his shoulders. "I'm thinking that Slugger has an idea that could work. This is your chance. What's the worst that could happen?"

"Um, a bullet as I said?"

Slugger chuckles. "Or they might not be against adding a white boy to their collection." He eyes me up. "Some rich sheikha might fancy some pale meat to serve her."

My eyes go wide. "I'm the fucking StoryTeller, not the fuckin' story. And this bitch isn't worth dying over or ending up as a rich woman's sex slave. As you said I don't know her—"

"As I said, pussy."

Chaz nods. "Seems like our brother's got a white streak."

"Now wait a fuckin' moment." I stand, my chair flying back.

Both men start laughing, and for the second time, I'm instructed to sit my ass down.

Slugger leans forward. "You'll be wearing your colours, ST. Worse that will happen is they give you a beatdown. They won't kill you or take you as that would start a war." He pre-empts my question about why the Dominators should do anything for me by saying, "If they let you have her, they'll have your marker. If they don't, they'll be in deep shit with the Wretched Soulz. I'm betting they'll take the easy route and won't cause problems."

Could he be right? Could it be that easy? I just walk in and take her? I have to admit to being intrigued. A direct approach hadn't occurred to me. "And if they do kill me?" My mouth twists as I suspect it wouldn't be a quick or clean death. If we caught a Dominator, they wouldn't die easy.

"It's a risk," Slugger agrees. "But if they take you out, the Wretched Soulz will avenge you." He catches Chaz's eye. "*All* charters." He laughs softly. "If they want a war, so be it. I'm sick of pussying around them."

Chaz picks at the label on his bottle for a moment, then sighs. "Up to you, ST. You want to ride in like a knight in fuckin' armour, then we'll have your back. Though it might just be your bones we're rescuing."

It's up to me.

Now how do I feel about that?

CHAPTER SEVEN

SHERI

BEFORE...

I t's stupid how inane things occur to you in the worst of situations, including thinking how lucky it was I was snatched after, rather than before I'd managed to have a pit stop. If not, my bladder would be screaming as we've been driving for literally hours. I've no way of knowing exactly how long, but the light's grown darker in the back of the van, and light that was coming in through the cracks has totally disappeared now.

I've gone through all manner of emotions and reactions. I've cried until my eyes are sore, screamed enough to make my throat hoarse, but nothing stopped or even slowed the truck's movement, and beneath mc, thc road just rumbles on. I've gone from being terrified about what these men might have in store to me to furious that they've the audacity to snatch me away from my not vcry rcmarkable life.

Through it all, there's a sense of incredulity. This can't be happening to me. I read stories, I'm not a part of them.

Like any victim, I end up questioning, *what did I do wrong?* But I can't think of anything I did to contribute to the situation I'm in. I gave no one come-hither glances, nor encouraged the bikers at all.

There could have been a hundred ways to avoid this predicament. I could have eaten at the resort and then driven straight home. But who would think I was risking my life by pulling off at a rest stop?

How soon will people come looking for me? Agatha surely will raise the alarm when I don't arrive home, unless she thinks there was maybe a man at the signing after all and I got lucky. While she should think it unlikely, it's what she would do if she was me.

But even if she got people looking for me, what are my chances of being found? People disappear every day. The thought I've become just another statistic makes me want to vomit.

Real-life bikers have stolen me away. It's nothing like I ever imagined it would be. It's not a dream. It's a freaking nightmare.

I may be an introvert, but I'm not a coward. That I enjoy my own company best and hate being in a crowd, doesn't mean that I'm helpless and won't fight back if I'm given a chance. I don't like to think about the fate that might be in store for me, but I won't accept it meekly like the proverbial lamb.

While I've got no actual experience to call on, surprisingly, I've never been kidnapped before, I've got a whole armoury within the pages of books that I read. Although all is based in a fictional world, I'll take my strength from the heroines who've managed to escape, or at least, stay alive, until rescue comes.

I toss out of my mind the thought that while Agatha might raise a cursory alarm, there's no one who'd put themselves out to find me, and definitely no one who would put themselves in danger. I can't allow myself negative thoughts. Being here is deleterious by itself.

Wedging myself into a corner, exhausted from the emotion and adrenaline flooding through me, I let my eyes close, drifting off to the drone of the engine. Again, with no way to measure time, I could have been asleep for minutes or hours when the truck comes to a stop.

I wake fast, my head spinning, my ears ringing, even though the noise has cut off. Pushing myself away from the corner, I prepare to run as soon as the doors are opened. I'm wearing sneakers as I knew it would be a long day on my feet, but that's the only thing athletic about me. I don't exercise or work out. But I'll give any chance of escape a damn good try. Anything has to be better than staying in the arms of the enemy, even if I give myself a heart attack in the process.

But the doors stay shut though the engine is switched off. After a few minutes, there are sounds of doors slamming and the engine again roars to life.

I doze once again, then the process is repeated. This time, my preparations pay off. As the doors are flung open, immediately, I throw myself out... straight into the arms of one of the bikers who oomphs as he catches me then laughs aloud.

"And where do you think you're off to?" he asks, using my own momentum to spin me around.

"There's nowhere for you to fuckin' go," the second says as he takes a hold of my arm firmly, pulling me along.

I stagger and try to drag my heels, but he's far too strong. He has no problem ignoring my attempts to escape and pulls me along with him. I eye the building ahead with utter dread. It's an old farmhouse, out in the middle of nowhere, and it's obvious nothing good will come of me going inside.

But that's where I'm heading, and there's nothing I can do about it. I struggle, stumble, but end up being half dragged along the overgrown pathway and in through the doorway. I'm pulled upright and to a halt in the middle of a room.

I stand, my chest heaving as I hyperventilate. My mouth is completely dry. Shivers rack my body as I'm subjected to an unpleasant scrutiny by a number of bikers who are lounging around. Movement catches my attention, and my eyes focus there as one stands. Idly, I notice the letters on his cut denote he's called *Tats*.

He walks over as the biker behind me draws my hands firmly behind my back and holds them tightly. When Tats is directly in front, he stares at me, his eyes tracing down, lingering on my breasts, my stomach, and then to my legs.

"She fits the description." Half turning, he nods at one of the men behind me approvingly. "Tall for a girl, long legs. Got meat on her bones, and the red hair requested. The face isn't much, but maybe the rest of her assets will make up for that."

"I'm happy to try her out," one of those seated calls out, his offer being received by a round of laughter.

"Sure you will, Fang. That's mighty big of you." Tats rolls his eyes.

The man making the offer rubs at his crotch. "Glad you noticed."

Someone else snorts.

Though my mind is fogged with terror, I try to think through it. Physically, I'm unable to beat them. I've only my brains to depend on now. These men seem to have taken me because I match some kind of warped shopping list, though I'm not sure any of the assets they've mentioned are worth very much. It's clear I'm not going to be able to stop them from having their wicked and probably very unpleasant ways with me, unless there's some way I can increase my value for being untouched. The merit of a certain predicament had come up a time or two in the stories I've read. Now, I've just got to be believable.

I let my lip tremble, not having to feign the shakes that are racking my body. In a quivering voice, I blurt out, "I'm a virgin."

"Sure you are," the one named Fang retorts. "Nice try." Lazily, he gets to his feet, his hands starting to unbuckle his belt. "But all the better if you are. Breaking them in is the best part." He starts walking toward me. I try to shrink back but I'm still being firmly held. Jeers and chuckles start sounding and just when Fang's within touching distance, he's interrupted.

"Hold up." Tats raises his hand in the air. His rheumy eyes meet mine. "You wouldn't be lying to us, would you, sweetheart?"

"N-n-no." Keeping myself from being raped immediately relies on how well I can spin this truth. "I'm a good Christian girl. I've got a fiancé. He's waiting—"

"Bollocks she has," a man with a distinct British accent states, his words punctuated with an exaggerated roll of his eyes. "She's just trying to keep us hands off, Tats."

Tats swings around to face him. "And if she's telling the truth? We fuck her, get our rocks off, bloody her up and then find we could have asked double, triple for her?" He scrubs a hand across his bald head. "You want to explain to Knuckles about that?"

"And if we sell her under false pretences, who's going to cop it then?" the British man insists.

"We could check her out." Fang enters the conversation again.

Tats eyes go wide. "Yeah? And you're a fuckin' doctor who can tell?"

Fang shrugs. "Well, it should be obvious. She'd be tight as fuck."

And I want dirty fingers touching me about as much as I want one of their cocks. My stomach rolls and I feel like I'm going to vomit.

Tats walks close and stands right in front of me. It's as though he's trying to read my mind. I don't have to pretend for real fear to show on my face, I might be trying to be brave, but I'm terrified. Experienced or not, no woman wants to be raped.

As he stares into me, my mind works, but try as I might, I can't think of a way out. These aren't the bikers I've always read about. They don't give a damn for anyone but themselves. Idly, I find myself wondering if I do get out, whether I should sue the authors of the books who so misled me. Maybe if I'd been more scared of them at the start, I wouldn't have let down my guard.

There was nothing more I could have done.

It's not the authors' fault, nor mine. I knew these were bad boys in the worst possible way as soon as I'd seen them, and I'd always known the bikers I read about lived only in a fantasy world. I just doubt I'll be reading those books with the same enthusiasm ever again. And that's if I even get the chance.

Instead of holding Tats' stare, I drop my eyes in a show of submissiveness. *That's what a virgin would do, isn't it?*

"Please, please don't hurt me." My voice sounds as weak and helpless as I'm feeling, but perhaps that bit of begging might help. Reading the room, any defiance isn't going to go down well. I've been used to bullies trying to take advantage of the quiet weak girl. There are times when standing up for yourself earns you respect, but sometime staying quiet and demure better serves your purpose.

"Tats—?"

"Oh, fuck it. Just throw her in with the others," Tats snarls as if he, too, was anticipating playing with a new toy, only to have it taken away. "I'll need to talk to Knuckles to see how he wants to play this."

"Knowing Knuckles," another unnamed biker states in a voice that sounds whiney, "he'll want to break her in himself."

Another sneers, "She'd wish it was one of us."

I don't even bother to look at who's talking, but I'm even more terrified. If their leader, or whoever Knuckles is, is indeed worse than any of these men in front of me, what kind of hell could I expect?

But, as I'm taken away and led into a basement, and, to my horror, pushed into a cage, I try to congratulate myself on getting a reprieve, even if that might not last forever.

The door is slammed, and a padlock snapped into place, after which the bikers leave. It's only then I take a moment to inspect my surroundings, only able to see by the light from a single, dim, overhead bulb.

There are six cages, women in various stages of undress in each. A couple are looking my way inquisitively, while the others are curled up in balls or rocking, lost in their own distress. Swallowing rapidly, I realise the latter could have been me if I hadn't come up with a way to distract the men who'd been prepared to rape me. It could be me with my clothes torn, or, as I see, completely naked in a couple of cases.

The woman in the cage closest to mine rattles the bars. "They didn't touch you," she tosses out, almost accusingly.

Quickly, I study her. She's pulling the remains of a blouse around her, and there's a large bruise on her face. But though she's clearly been molested, there's a challenge in her eyes, a sign of a spirit that hasn't been broken.

I need information, and I need it fast. While I doubt there's a way out of here, I can't give up without making a try. Though I'm tempted wallow in my own misery, I force myself to respond.

"I'm a virgin." I make it sound positive, leaving no room for doubt. I wouldn't put it past the bikers to have planted some kind of listening device.

"Really?" She cocks an eyebrow.

"Really," I confirm, as firmly as I can, knowing my only course is to make anyone who can hear believe it.

I examine the padlock holding my cage shut. It's unfortunate I have no handy bobby pin on me, or the knowledge how to open such a lock if I had. I take hold of the bars and shake them, but they're not flimsy enough to pull apart. Reluctantly, I accept I'm a prisoner until someone releases me.

I decide to get information from the person who's spoken to me. But first, I personalise myself. "I'm Sheri." I turn to her, then pause.

She doesn't disappoint. "Carole," she responds, still viewing me with curiosity.

I let go of the bars and turn to face in her direction. "Do you know what's going to happen to us?"

"Can't you guess?" Her brow wrinkles in disdain. "We'll be sold."

That's obvious. But I want detail, like, how, and, "When?" I want to know how much time I've got. Though why, I'm not sure. There's going to be no one rushing to my rescue, no one to know where I've gone. I swallow down the wave of nausea that threatens to overwhelm me. *This can't be happening.*

She snorts. "How the hell should I know? They don't exactly let us in on their plans."

While my legs shake and threaten to fail me, I make a determined effort to stay standing, and to keep talking to the only person here who seems capable of holding a conversation. Otherwise, I'll end up curled into a ball just like the others around me.

"How long have you been here?" I ask.

Carole purses her lips. "Two days? Three? It's hard to know." She jerks her head toward the other cages. "Some of them have been here longer."

While not feeling optimistic, I have to know. "Do you think there's any chance we'll be rescued?" Carole doesn't seem as bothered as the others by her situation, so is she hanging onto some hope?

But she disavows me of that immediately. "Honey," her eyes roll, "there's no chance in hell. This isn't the first rodeo these boys have been to. You can see by the setup. They're running a smooth operation here."

I clasp my hands together to stop them from trembling. Half of me is convinced this is a nightmare from which I'll soon awake, while the sane part of my brain realises however unlikely, the situation is real. I watch as Carole turns away, sinks down to the floor, pulls up her knees and rests her chin with a sigh. I wonder how she seems to be resigned to her fate, unlike the others who are openly crying or frozen with fear.

As my heart rate speeds up, knowing however strong I think I should be, everything is against me being able to influence the outcome by positive thinking. Once I finally accept my predicament and it sinks in, I'm more likely to be ranting and railing against my fate. Right now, even with the evidence in front of my face, I can't bring myself to believe it. Other women get kidnapped and sold, not me.

"What makes you so calm?" I suddenly throw at her. "Why are you different?"

She raises her chin and gives me a sad smile. "Oh, honey, I didn't have much to begin with. I was taken off the street." She grimaces, adding "Where I was working," in case I was in any doubt as to what she meant. "There's probably not a lot they can do that I haven't experienced before. And if the end comes fast, so be it. I probably wouldn't have lasted long anyway."

I swallow hard. Maybe the trick is accepting you haven't got much to lose. I haven't got much either.

Copying her action, I sink down to my knees, clasping my hands around my head. I might not have reached rock bottom like the woman in the next cage, but if I was gone, who'd miss me? Agatha, maybe, but she'd soon find a new housemate. My dad? No, he doesn't go out of his way to contact me, and as for my stepmom, she'd be pleased to be finally rid of me. I exist day to day. I have no big dreams I'd have to give up.

But I'm me. I've got a life, and no one should be able to take it away. I'm not a possession to be owned, used and discarded. I can't stifle the sob that comes unbidden from my throat. I might not want to give in, but I can't see any way to escape.

And, unlike all the stories I get engrossed in, there's no group of good bikers, SEALs, Marines or other alphas, all currently plotting how to rescue me from my fate.

CHAPTER EIGHT
STORYTELLER

How the fuck did I let myself be goaded into this?

Slugger and Chaz had issued a challenge and I know they half-expected me to respond with a middle finger. Unfortunately, if a gauntlet is thrown down in front of me, I'm the type of man who picks it up instead of walking away.

Leaving them, returning to the crash room I'm using as mine for the time being, I bang my forehead against the wall, wondering why returning the book to its rightful owner had become so important to me. How the fuck have I gotten into the position that I'm proposing to put my life on the line for a woman I only know by name.

I barely know what she looks like. She's got a mass of red hair, that's to be admired, but while the camera is known to add on weight, even allowing for the couple of extra pounds, Sheri isn't slim by any stretch of the imagination, and certainly isn't my normal type.

And while I don't much like the human trafficking trade, I'm not normally driven to stop it. I know it goes on, but it's easier to turn a blind eye. Much like the guns that we shift, I rarely think about the outcome—sure a gun is a weapon, but it only becomes dangerous in the hands of the wrong man. Call me shallow, but it's a dog-eat-dog world, all of us just doing what we have to do to survive. Normally, I don't lose sleep thinking about the victims. Life's cruel, and fate can end it in too many ways.

But then, normally, I don't have any connection to someone who's been stolen away.

Even now, I could throw that damn book in the trash, and act like I never found out a fucking thing about its owner. Yeah. I could do that.

Resting my forehead against the drywall, I scoff at myself. Like fuck I could. For better or worse, I do know what's happened to Sheri, or can take a good fucking guess. And for some reason, I don't like it.

Knowing my head won't take much more punishment, I throw myself down on the lumpy bed. *What are my chances? Will the Dominators really honour the ol' lady code? If I convince them she's my woman, is there a chance in hell that I could get her back?*

I doubt it. Okay, I could bargain as suggested with a Wretched Soulz marker, a kind of *get out of jail free card* or, in other words, escape unscathed if we happen to catch you. Would one bitch be worth that?

I'm not convinced it will be that easy. They might prefer me to offer to buy her. While I've money in my bank account, why should I spend it on rescuing a bitch who means fuck all to me?

A loud knock at my door has me raising my eyebrow, wondering who'd be disturbing me. I go and wrench it open, not in the mood for company. There, holding a bottle of whisky in one raised hand and two shot glasses in the other, stands Chaz.

"You going to invite me in?"

My eyes narrow. "I wouldn't have, but you had the foresight to bring that." I nod toward the amber nectar he's holding, and then step aside.

It's a crash room, one used for fucking and not a lot else. There's nowhere to sit except on the bed.

I don't miss Chaz's grimace as he sits down, shifting position as a broken spring clearly touches his ass, or his rueful glance. "Fuck, Bro, didn't realise I was sentencing you to sleep on that."

Overlooking that I was going to complain about it, I minimise my discomfort. "It's only temporary, and I've slept in worse places." As a SEAL, I certainly have. The luxury of even a lumpy worn-out mattress would have been very welcome at times. Even as a nomad, I don't get offered the best pads. And there's many a time I've slept out under the stars without griping.

Chaz shrugs. "As I'm hoping you'll stick around for a few months, we'll get you something better."

I'm not sure I want to stick around, as he puts it, at all, in the current climate. I feel like a chew toy both Chaz and Slugger are throwing to the dogs, without much concern whether it's going to get ripped to shreds and spat back out.

He pours a generous portion of whisky into each glass and passes one across. Taking it, I feel like a condemned man being offered his last meal.

Hoisting my leg onto the bed, bending it at the knee and leaning back on the pillow, I tiredly ask, "What do you want, Chaz?"

His lips purse as he studies the contents of the glass in his hand. "I wouldn't have come up with Slugger's plan. Knew not doing fuck was eating at you, but I couldn't see how we could get this bitch of yours out, not without bloodshed."

"But you're quite happy if it's mine?"

He looks at me sharply. "Not at fuckin' all, ST. That's why I wanted to keep you out. You don't even know the bitch, let alone owe anything to her."

I open my mouth but I'm not sure whether it's to protest the safest route is the one he'd planned—for me to keep well out of it—or to say Sheri doesn't deserve the fate she's facing at the hands of the Dominators. When pushed, I wouldn't be able to explain what drives me, and I'm undecided how much risk to myself I'm prepared to take in her rescue. In the end, I use the parting of my lips to take a swallow of the liqueur, relishing the burn as it goes down.

Chaz gives up on waiting for me to say something. "Slugger didn't get where he is by being a stupid man," he comments, his eyes unfocused, suggesting he's speaking his thoughts aloud. "He also didn't get to be the Alpha, as you call him, by keeping his head buried in the sand. Slugger likes taking risks."

"Seems like it's me taking all the risk in this instance." I hate that my voice sounds like a whine. "I'm going in on my own. Wretched Soulz won't pick up any flack, but the Dominators will love a Soul just delivered into their hands."

As if I hadn't said anything, Chaz carries on. "As I said, Slugger's a risk taker, but he likes to take calculated ones." He wipes his hand over his head. "You know this club, Brother. We're all Wretched Soulz, bound by the patch on our backs, but apart from loyalty to that, the charters run as they see fit. We know some aren't so strict about the treatment of women as we are in Arizona, but wide-scale trafficking isn't part of our brand. The Dominators are different. They don't give a damn who they hurt and don't seem to have any morals."

I suppress my snort. Morals, in my view, are relative. Most

of the citizen population would question ours. "Why are you telling me what I already know?"

Chaz gives a quick grin. "I couldn't commit the Soulz to taking the Dominators on, but Slugger? Well, if he decides he wants to bloody their noses, that puts me in a different place. He's got a plan, ST, and it doesn't involve losing one of his best enforcers."

After taking another sip of my whisky, I tap a cigarette out of my pack. Lighting it gives me a second to try to work out what he's saying. It is comforting to know he believes Slugger doesn't want to lose me. "Got a plan to stop me putting my head in the lion's den?"

He chuckles. "Not what I'm saying. You're definitely going to be doing that. But Slugger's got the yearning to kick this business of theirs to the kerb. At least in Arizona."

"We even sure that's where they're holding her?" That doubt has been growing in my mind.

"Oh, ST, you of little faith. Slugger's got his best IT guys already tracking them down. The Dominators that took her have been identified, and their holding den is indeed local." He takes out his phone, taps at it, then passes it across. "Plans of the building where they hold the women before transporting them to auction. Looks like we've long known about it but haven't had a reason to go after them until now."

Using two fingers, I enlarge the image as best as I can. "The basement?"

"Seems the most likely place."

I suck in smoke, hold it for a moment, then blow it out. "So, what's the plan?"

Chaz tops up our whisky, then starts to explain. As he speaks, my lips curve upward as my interest is piqued. *This sounds more like it.* The gist being, while I'll be going in on my own, risking them shooting first rather than talking, I will have something to offer them as long as I'm given enough time. And while out of sight, my brothers will be there with me, ready to come in and attempt a rescue should I end up imprisoned along with her.

Standing, I ponder the situation. As a SEAL, I was given no guarantee that I would survive. From the time I first put on a biker cut, I accepted that my days were likely to be limited as a result. The benefit being, during the time you're wearing it, you can really live and feel alive, unlike the morons who work nine to five, with no other object in mind beyond surviving to get their pension. I've long been prepared not to make old bones.

I live for danger and excitement.

Is the cause worthy? That's the question. Is Sheri worth the ultimate payment? Probably not, but sticking one to the Dominators? Yeah, that's something I can get behind.

"So, what do you think?" He salutes me with his glass as he raises an eyebrow.

I grin and don't hesitate. "I'm not backing out."

CHAPTER NINE
STORYTELLER

The whisky and beer combine to provide the sleep medication that I need, and I wake early the next morning actually feeling refreshed. Sure, I have to stretch my back to iron out all the kinks from that fucking mattress, but my mind is definitely in a better place than where it had been yesterday.

With the plan Chaz and Slugger have come up with, I may actually have a chance of getting out of this alive, and, finally, reconcile Sheri with her precious book. I snort to myself, thinking, if this works, maybe she'll need to send a thank you note to the author. If it hadn't been for me finding the novel lying around, I'd never have known she was in trouble. The cops would still be chasing their tails, and I know, left to them, no trace of her would ever be found. She'd end up as a missing person statistic, her memory gradually fading like the weather-worn posters left on lampposts.

I know I can't save everyone, but perhaps I'll be able to save her. Maybe it would earn me some points in my favour with the universe. Fuck knows I could do with some.

Down in the clubroom, Brandy and Brea have got some breakfast cooking. I wait my turn then fill my plate with hash browns, eggs and bacon. I'm chewing on a mouthful when Iron steps up.

He eyes me carefully before he sits down, folding his meaty hands on the table. "You happy with this?"

The sergeant-at-arms will be able to see the same flaws that I can, and possibly some more that I can't, or haven't yet thought about. Whatever, I notice he doesn't look particularly happy. "Ride or die, Brother. Go big or go home, isn't that the saying?"

"We'll give you a good send-off if you don't make it back."

I turn and give Beard the finger that comment's worthy of, noticing the kitchen's slowly filling up, and all eyes seem to be in my direction.

"Who you going to leave your sled to?" Pothead asks.

"Not you for a fuckin' start," I growl.

"Children, children." Bull appears, slapping his fist into his palm. "Whose heads do I need to knock together?"

"His probably." Legit points my way. "He's the one committing suicide."

I shrug. That's not my intention, though there's a chance I might never come back, and it's not too hard for me to accept that. Not much different to being alone on the road without a club backing me up. I take my life in my hands every day as a nomad. Living life on the edge is what it's all about.

When Slugger appears with Ce Ce—the reason that she missed breakfast duties abundantly clear—I know my time is running out. As my brothers start busying themselves, I down another cup of coffee and visit the heads. Then, before leaving the clubhouse, I have to suffer my back being slapped multiple times as I say my goodbyes. By the time I reach the exit, my skin is stinging.

"We'll be right behind you, Brother," Iron, standing by the door, promises, touching his fist to mine.

"Got a nice burial spot picked out for yah," Skunk confides with a twinkle in his eyes.

Fire nudges him. "And the epitaph will simply read, 'Here lies the man whose story came to an end.'"

Again, my middle finger gets some use.

Legend's farewell is far more practical. He pulls me aside and takes a moment to talk me through how the almost invisible earpiece that will go into my ear will work. Although by itself it's already well camouflaged, my long hair will also work to disguise it.

Finally, knowing I'm as prepared as I can be, and that I'm looking at a couple of hours ride before reaching my destination, I leave with a cursory wave toward Prez and the Alpha who are waiting by their bikes, ready to ride.

As I paddle walk my bike out of its parking spot and switch on the engine, I try to clear my mind of anything but the mission in hand.

Find the Dominators' lair and rescue the damsel in distress.

Yeah, perhaps I do think of myself as a modern-day knight in armour, be it that my protection is only made of leather, and my steed is of steel.

No stranger to riding alone, it doesn't feel unusual as solo I head through the gates and the road leading to Phoenix, dutifully following the instructions of the GPS that Legend had programmed for me.

For a while, I focus on the asphalt disappearing under my wheels and the growling thump of my engine underneath me. I could spend the journey planning exactly what to do or say but know improvisation will be better than any practiced routine. I have no idea how the Dominators will take either my sudden appearance or my request, whether words will be adequate or whether I'll need to use fists.

Hopefully, it's my wits that will be sufficient, and that I'll be given time to say my piece before they resort to bullets.

I ride on, enjoying the feeling of the sun on my face, the wind blowing through my hair that while tamed by a tie, isn't constricted by a helmet, that not being necessary in my home state.

Finally, I reach the vicinity where I will find my prize, my princess to be rescued in this particular story. I pull to a halt and take out a cigarette, relishing it as I draw the smoke in deeply, hell-bent on enjoying what could be my last ever nicotine hit.

Not wanting to be taken at any disadvantage, I piss against the nearest tree, then, back at my bike, bend over the tank and rub at my temples. Finally, I tap the button that triggers the earpiece's connection, and quietly state, "I'm going in."

"*You can still back out,*" Chaz suggests, his voice sounding tinny and thin.

"What, and spoil Slugger's fun?" I shake my head.

Slugger's snort comes loud and clear down the line.

Without waiting for another reply, I turn the key and start the engine once again, and this time don't deviate and head straight for the building where we're pretty certain Sheri is being held.

I don't get very close. A loud gunshot makes my bike veer as I try to make less of a target of myself. I pull to a halt, kick down the stand, and swinging my leg over the seat, get off.

With my hands held up high, I face the farmhouse that's seen better days. When, despite me making myself a target, there's no more gunfire, I start to approach.

"That's far enough," a voice rings out.

I try to stand as nonchalant as a man with his arms up over

his head can. This can go one of two ways. They'll either shoot me on the spot—I obviously have shown I have knowledge about where at least one of their safe houses is—or question me to find out what I want. I'm hoping it's not the former, and that they'll be intelligent enough to guess that if I've found their location, others are in the know. At the least they'll probably want information.

Within seconds, I'm surrounded and given a thorough pat down. They're no slouches, the search conducted done by experts. Even if I'd been stupid enough to try to sneak in a hidden knife, they'd have found it.

I don't feel naked without the weapons I left behind. I can do enough damage with my hands. So, I stand stoically and take it.

One steps forward, eyeing me cautiously. "What business have you here, Soul?"

Although I've not been given permission, I lower my hands. "Got a proposition for you, Dominator."

He snorts. "Yeah?" As he looks around at his companions, they dutifully laugh. He turns back to me. "You think you've got anything to offer? Seems like we're in the driver's seat here. And it could be we just fancy sending a Soul to fuckin' Hell."

Feigning a confidence I don't really feel, I sigh. "Sure, if that's what you want, but you'll never know what you're missing."

"Fuckin' wankers, the lot of them. I say we have us a bit of fun."

"Shut it, Limey," the first man growls.

"How did he find us, Tats?" another asks.

"That's what I want to know." Tats steps forward. He raises an eyebrow as if expecting me to answer.

It's no skin off my nose to enlighten them. "It's easy to follow Dominators and see what they're up to, especially when they use the same pattern time and again." I purse my lips, almost as a challenge to him.

"Fuck." His grimace shows he's not stupid. If we found them, the feds probably aren't far behind. This hideout is blown.

"What does the wanker want?" the one with the British accent asks.

"Good question." Tats uses a jerk of his head to redirect the query to me. If all I wanted was for them to be caught, I could have held back and waited for the feds to do the work. I've caught his interest. I can see by the gleam in his eyes.

Here comes nothing. "What I want is my old lady. Somehow, she got herself picked up. A mistake I take it?" I'm taking a chance that the relationship between a biker and his woman are respected by this club. If not, my request is a non-starter.

"Your old—"

Before Tats can finish whatever he was going to say, a man emerges from the building behind them. He's shouting even before he gets to me.

"That's fuckin' StoryTeller. What the fuck does he want?"

Fuck. I recognise him. It's Knuckles. I've met him before. He's a nasty piece of work and there's no love lost between us.

"Just finding that out." Tats scratches his bald head. "He reckons we've got his ol' lady."

"Ol' fuckin' lady?" Knuckles' eyebrows go to his hairline, then his eyes narrow suspiciously. "He ain't got no ol' lady that I know of. He rides with Slugger."

There are multiple sharp intakes of breaths at that declaration, and collectively, they take a step toward me. The atmosphere, which was of amusement, turns decidedly nasty.

"Whoa." I raise my hands. "I'm a nomad. I don't ride with no man. And sure I've got an ol' lady, but I don't take her on the fuckin' road with me." I add a roll of my eyes as if to suggest the point is obvious.

Knuckles proceeds to approach, getting so close a lesser man might take a step back, but I stand my ground. "You were riding with him. I'd have fuckin' taken him out if it wasn't for you."

I rub my shoulder ruefully. Truth is, I'd seen the gun being aimed, and like any good enforcer had thrown myself in front of my overall prez. Luckily for me, Knuckles was a fucking bad shot, and he only winged me. I decide not to criticise his gun skills.

I settle for, "Still got the scars."

"I would have had him." His face has gone red, showing how angry he is.

It was one time the Dominators had gotten close enough to make a serious attempt on our Alpha's life. Luckily, I'd been there to save him, but that meant taking away Knuckles' glory. He'd have been venerated by the whole of his club if he'd been the one to take Slugger down. To say there's a price on the Alpha's head is an understatement, and why he keeps moving around.

Knuckles stares at me for a moment, then states to his men, "Whatever he says, StoryTeller ain't got no ol' lady."

"Hey." I can't let that ride. "What the fuck you saying? You calling me a liar?"

"You ride with Slugger, and we all know who he is. You ain't got time to have a ball and chain."

Briefly, I turn my back, allowing them to see the patch. "Nomad, remember," I stress again. "Sure, one time I was with Slugger, met him on the road and travelled a few miles. Parted ways, and that's all that was. And as it so happens, met my girl soon after and claimed her. And now I want her back."

Knuckles chuckles, but not pleasantly. "I want to know more about you riding with your national prez."

I snort and shake my head. "Soulz ain't got no national prez."

"Sure you haven't." He rolls his eyes. "Probably the worst kept fuckin' secret in the world."

Sighing heavily, I want to get him off this track. "Look, all I'm after is my ol' lady. I'm hoping you'll give her back, so we don't have trouble between our clubs. I can't help you find Slugger, why ever the fuck you'd want to. I have no idea where he is now." It's the truth. He could be waiting back at the clubhouse or be just down the road.

Knuckles turns away as if he's lost interest. "Just kill him now."

I hear the cocking of weapons and a shiver runs down my spine. But outwardly, I show no sign. "I wouldn't be so hasty. You don't know what I'm offering."

He swings back and again snorts. "Some halfhearted notion about preventing trouble between our clubs. And for your information, *son*, there's always been, and always will be, war between us. No getting away from that." He pauses. "I can't fuckin' believe you thought you could ride in and claim your property back. Don't you think that just makes me want to keep it even more?"

I speak fast. "Guns. Many guns. Two eighteen wheelers full of them to be exact."

He stills, then his hands make a grabby motion.

"Arizona Soulz have been asked to move them by the cartel, but to be honest, they don't have the balls."

I hear a muffled curse in my ears. Okay, so it wasn't quite what had been arranged I would say, but it comes to about the same thing.

"So, you're a fuckin' traitor to your club."

"No, no way." I grimace slightly. "They don't want to see brothers in prison or dead, so are quite happy to pass this business your way. As long as you return my ol' lady."

Knuckles' eyes crease, and it looks like I've caught his interest. "Spell it out for me. As if I'm stupid. You want us to take the pittance from the cartel for delivering guns over the border?"

I allow a grin to come to my face. "No. We tell you where and when, and you step in, take the eighteen wheelers and the cargo. Bloody a few faces, but don't cause serious damage. You end up with two truckloads of guns to do with what you want, and Soulz don't have the hassle of getting them to their destination."

His eyes go so wide they dominate his face. "And you reckon the cartel are just going to accept you lost their guns?"

"Won't have much choice." I chuckle softly. "But you can be damn sure they won't be asking us to move their cargo again."

"Why should we care what the cartel does to get revenge? It won't be on us, Knuckles." Tats certainly looks like he wants to take the bait.

Knuckles doesn't look convinced, but there's a spark in his eyes. "So, you're offering us guns, all for the release of one bitch."

Well, now seeing I'm here, I'd rather not leave before freeing all the women they're holding. But I'll lie if that's what it will take to get me inside. I nod my head.

"Which of the broads are you after?" Tats asks, clearly as intrigued with my offer as the man he defers to.

"Sheri," I tell them, mentally crossing my fingers that despite all the odds, this is going to work.

But Tats is shaking his head. "We don't bother with names. What does she look like?"

Hastily I think back to what I saw on her profile on her social media page. "Red hair, long and curly. She's curvy." I use my hands to shape an hourglass. "Tall for a girl." I hold my fingers at shoulder level. Surely, they can't have many like that?

Suddenly one of the bikers bursts out laughing, and I can't tell what I've said that's so funny. Sure, she may not win a beauty contest, but she wasn't that bad. I look around for someone to enlighten me, but most are grinning and chuckling as well, and not eager to let me in on the joke.

Knuckles isn't so reticent. "Well, one of you's fuckin' lying. Never took you for a *gentleman*, StoryTeller."

"You don't know me," I reflexively answer, while wondering what the hell he's talking about.

"Maybe he can't get it up?" Limey suggests. "Did you shoot his dick off when you had him in your sights?"

What the hell?

"Think, Brother. What the fuck are they talking about?" The voice in my ear isn't comforting when they've got no answers to give me.

I don't know how to act. The truth is, I know fuck all about my 'ol' lady. They've got the advantage of meeting her when I have not. What the hell are they alluding to?

I think of something to say that won't betray my ignorance. "My ol' lady's an acquired taste," I settle for at last, wishing like fuck I knew what they know that I don't.

"She's something." Tats laughs. "Which makes us have doubts about you, Brother. Are you a fuckin' man or a mouse?"

"I think she was lying. Thought that all along."

"Think you might have been right, Fang." Tats throws him a glance.

Lying about what? The safest thing for me to do is to stay dumb. All I know of her is her taste in books, and that brief information on her profile. It gives me fuck all to go on. For a moment, I wonder whether my ol' lady might be transgender and have a cock like myself. Hell, if that's the case, no wonder they're laughing. But in that instance, I'll have to go along. I've got nothing against dicks, but the only one I want to play with is my own.

"You gay?" Limey's question catches me off guard. It's so aligned with my thoughts, for a moment, I fear he can read my mind.

"Perhaps he's a virgin too?"

Knuckles gives the speaker a long look. He narrows his eyes, then examines me carefully. "Well, are you?"

"She's told them she's a virgin," the helpful voice in my ear says, just about the time as I also add up two and two. Hmm. That might make her a clever girl if she's saved herself from being raped. But if these fuckers believe it, then it would raise her value in any buyer's eyes. *More than the guns are worth?* Fuck knows. For a moment, I wonder if I should call her out in the very obvious lie, but then I remember I know nothing about her.

She could be telling the truth.

My thoughts have zoomed through my brain in a split second. Without missing a beat, I respond, "Nah, but my ol' lady is a good Christian girl. She wants to wait until I've put a ring on her finger."

"Christ." Tats stares so hard I wonder if I've got bird shit in my hair or something. "You're kidding us, aren't you?"

Nonchalantly, I shake my head. "Got dozens of other pussies in the clubhouses I go to. Ain't no bother giving her the time she needs." I leer and wink. "I reckon she's going to be worth waiting for."

Several heads nod. Knuckles looks like he's received the explanation that at least makes some sense.

"Nice one, Bro," I hear in my ear.

But nothing's quite so easy, is it? Knuckles jerks his head toward Tats, and the two of them take a few paces away. They bend their heads and confer quietly. Only a moment or two passes before Knuckles returns.

"Ain't quite decided what I'm going to do. But I will be magnanimous and let you see your ol' lady. Foghorn? Trots? Take him to her."

Two large men that I could easily take, but at the moment see no reason to, come alongside me and grab both my arms. They half guide, half drag me forward and into the door that's gaping open like it's the mouth to hell. I could get out of the grip they've got me in, in two seconds flat, but don't bother as they're taking me to my objective.

My problem? Sheri doesn't know me from Adam, and I'm hoping I'd be able to pick her out of a line up. She'll be traumatised, upset, terrified of what's happening to her. I'll have no chance to warn her, and with just one word or expression, she could give me away.

Glancing back, I take a last look at my bike, sitting forlorn as though waiting for its owner. Taking in the daylight I might be seeing for the final time, I step inside, wondering whether there's even a chance I might make it out.

Fuck. Why does one book matter? Why hadn't I walked on and never picked it up.

CHAPTER TEN
SHERI

PRESENT...

Carole thinks we're being held in Arizona, but it's hard to tell. My flesh is covered in goosebumps, and I continuously shiver. I'm not sure whether it's from fear, or whether the sun doesn't permeate here.

Where I'm being kept is hell, belying tales from the Bible that tell me that would be warmer.

The air is stale, permeated with the most unpleasant smells. There's no toilet or proper facilities, and each cage has a bucket which may or may not be emptied, depending on the day's particular jailor. Being a private person, I'd held off using it until my stomach had cramped. In the end, I, like my companions, had been reduced to relieving myself in view of everyone else.

I'm tired, I can't sleep, nor can I relax. Even if I did close my eyes, the almost continuous desolate crying and weeping would keep me awake. I've shed my own useless tears, but all they did was make my throat and eyes raw and did nothing to improve my situation.

As well as Carole, I've spoken to a couple of the other women, but it's not really worth trying to make conversation. All we can do is commiserate with each other and swap stories of how we were taken. MaryAnne was simply walking home from work one day and was pulled into an alley, Kelly's car broke down, and a Dominator posed as a mechanic. Angie's and Leah's stories were a version of about the same thing. We can only guess at what the future holds, and that, we don't want to contemplate at all.

I try to stay strong, but I'm hungry, the meagre food and few water bottles our captors supply are only the minimum necessary. My body aches. There's no bed or mattress, just the rough floor and a thin blanket to lie on. Even a dog would be treated better. I wonder whether it's to break our spirit, or just to keep costs low, as our time being kept here is probably limited.

When footsteps sound on the steps leading down to the basement, like the others, I retreat to the back of my cage, not wanting to draw attention to myself. I've suffered enough comments from them, describing ways they could check my declaration of being untouched, and their suggestions of how is enough to make anyone's stomach turn.

Has it been that long since our last meal? What do I know? There's no way of telling time, how much has passed, or whether it's going fast or slow. But while an unexpected visit might interrupt the boredom, there's always the chance it signals our time here is done. I might hate this basement and long to be free, but I suspect what comes after will be even worse.

The door bangs open.

"Sheri? Sheri Secord?"

It's not just the words, it's the authoritative deep voice barking them. A voice I've never heard before, but one so loud it echoes around the walls.

"Sheri? Where are you?" There's a hint of anxiety in the tone.

Is it a rescue or someone come to buy me? I don't know which, and while I'd like to say it's the futility of refusing to identify myself, rather than the effect that booming, commanding voice has on me, it's the latter that has me stepping forward.

"I... I'm here." I move to the front of my cage, wrap my hands around the bar, and stare as my fate approaches.

My God—he's beautiful. If this is someone who wants to own me, maybe I won't bother to protest. I ignore the voice inside that asks why such a vision should need to buy a kidnapped woman, when surely a crook of his finger would get him anyone he wants. It has to be something like he's got such a devious nature, only the forced would comply.

Mesmerised by his insane good looks, I jump a little at his voice.

"Sheri, babe. Looks like MariaLisa DeMora has brought us back together again."

His words might no longer be shouted, but the low tone vibrates, creating the sensation that I can feel as well as hear them.

Has the thickness of the air down here affected my brain? Maybe it's the lack of daylight and stimulation, but it takes a moment for what he's said, rather than the manner, to sink in.

He called me babe. And, he mentioned my favourite author.

Could she have sent him to rescue me? A kernel of excitement starts to grow inside, as I realise no one else would think to mention that name to me. Even Agatha hasn't taken notice of the actual books I read. But my hopes are dashed fast. How would she know I was missing? I shake my head in a vain attempt to clear the fog enough to solve the mystery. It doesn't work.

"Haven't you anything to say to your ol' man?" the delicious stranger asks, his deep voice sending tremors shooting through me. His brown eyes captivate me, speckled as they are with flecks of gold that seem to glimmer in the weak overhead light. His long, unrestrained hair is such a gorgeous brown, that I find myself swallowing. He wears a cut with a name patch which reads, *StoryTeller*, and even that fuels fantasies which at this moment I really shouldn't have.

Entranced with the vision in front of me, I take longer than I should to interpret the words. *Ol' man.* In my bikers' books, that's a serious claim. How could this man I've never seen before in my life, because, believe you me, I'd have remembered if I had, claim such a relationship with me?

Glancing at him quickly, I see a pleading in his eyes, a slight loss of confidence in the way he's looking at me, as if I'm not responding in the way that he wants.

I have no idea what he wants me to say, so I just plead. "Get me out of here, please."

Sotto voce, so low I half imagine I hear it, are the words, "Go with it."

"You going to let my ol' lady out of here?" He half turns as he says the words, letting me see the back of his cut.

I swallow my gasp. He's a member of the Wretched Soulz. They have the worse reputation of any outlaw club. I start to think I'm going to be leaping out of the pan and into the fire if I'm depending on this man to get me out.

I could disavow him. Make it clear we've never met before. But to what end? It won't change a damn thing. I'll still be a prisoner of the Dominators.

Swallowing again, wondering if I'm being led by my pussy

and not by my brain, I take a leap into the unknown. "Story-Teller, please make them let me go."

A dry, unpleasant voice sounds, as Knuckles approaches the door. "Well, well, what a touching reunion." He grabs the back of StoryTeller's neck, holding it so hard I can see it must hurt, yet my *ol' man*, barely flinches. "Open the cage, Foghorn."

Is this it? Is this the moment I'm freed?

The door starts to open, and things happen simultaneously. Instead of me being allowed out, Knuckles rips the cut off StoryTeller's back and then throws him in the cage with me. I'd have fallen had it not been for his quick reflexes, and the way he grabs for me, and holds me up.

"Go with it," he hisses, repeating the words he said before.

I don't have time to process anything, as without any warning, his mouth crashes down onto mine.

Instantly, I know this is something special and far out of my league. I've been kissed before, or, at least, I thought I had, but never like this. His lips cover mine with enough pressure to bruise, and his tongue demands entry into my mouth. My breath must smell, my teeth are furry, but he kisses me as if I'd been sampling the finest wine. My toes literally curl, and without conscious thought, I rise on tiptoe, realising to my surprise that my hands have tangled in his hair and I'm kissing him back as tingles travel the length of my spine and sparks alight something in the very core of me. My senses of where I am, who he is and who's watching, completely flee. I've no room for thoughts other than allowing myself to enjoy the sensations flooding my body. As he angles my head for better access, my nipples peak and become sensitive as they brush against my shirt.

I'm under no illusion that he's got all the control. Where he leads, I can only follow. When I think he's pulling away, I whimper, but he's only repositioning himself, and allowing us a chance to take in much-needed air.

For the first time in days, I smell something other than the foul odour surrounding me. Leather, cigarette smoke and the shampoo or soap that he uses fill my nostrils, the scents combining to form a perfume I'd make a fortune from if I could bottle it, though I wouldn't. I'm selfish. I want that to be just for me.

His lips are firm. His tongue, strong as it fights for dominance with mine, makes me wonder what other use he could put it to. And that's not the only part of his body I'm aware of. Being as close as we are, there's no doubting that he's also turned on, as a very hard cock is pressing into my stomach. *Is that me? Or does danger get him off?* I decide it has to be the latter. I don't think I've ever had that effect on a man before.

Nor has just a kiss ever turned me on, or got me to the point where the slightest touch to the right part of me might make me explode in a blinding white light like fire set to magnesium.

A slow hand clapping suddenly breaks through the fog that seems to be surrounding us, breaking into our bubble and reminding me where I am.

As StoryTeller pulls back, slowly in his own time, he grins at my murmured complaint and quietly whispers, "To be resumed."

After one last, soft touch of his lips to the corner of my mouth, he turns, his arm pulling me tight to him. I never want him to let me go. If this is my future, my punishment, I'll go willingly.

"Touching," the leader of the Dominators says, his mouth turned up in a sardonic grin. "Think we'll leave you lovebirds to reconnect for a while."

As Fang and one other I know is called Trots start to push

the door of the cage closed, instead of protesting or trying to force his way out, StoryTeller just stands still and raises his chin.

"I thought we had a bargain." I feel his voice rumbling against my chest. "You reneging on that now?"

"Not at all," Knuckles replies. "But you'll forgive me if I want to check things out. Make sure what you're offering is compensation enough."

"I want my cut," StoryTeller says brusquely.

"I'm sure you do." Knuckles laughs. "But I think I'll keep it hostage for now."

StoryTeller flicks at his ear as though a fly's bothering him, a gesture I don't understand. Then again, I don't comprehend a word of what they're saying, of whatever compensation he's talking about, or even why StoryTeller is here in the first place. Let alone why he's pretending I'm someone he knows intimately. I am certain, though, being locked inside this cage with me isn't the way he expected the situation to play out.

But the Wretched Soul, who I should be terrified of, just shrugs, seemingly unbothered, replying confidently, "Everything will check out."

"Well, you can just stay here, making out with your ol' lady, while I go make sure of it." He turns, gestures to the others, then marches toward the stairs.

StoryTeller waits for the Dominators to leave, then, seeing me open my mouth to let all my questions come spilling out, he places a finger to my lips and his eyes signal an unspoken instruction to keep quiet. He leads me to the back of the cage, sits on the rough ground, and pulls me down beside him.

Now, reality has brought me back to my senses. I realise kissing me had all been an act just to impress our audience. Of course, such a magnificent specimen of a man wouldn't really want to kiss a girl like myself. Now there's no longer anyone watching or a reason to act a part, I try to evade his arms, but he doesn't let me go, instead tightening his hold on me.

"Who are you?" I hiss.

"Shush." He puts a finger to his lips this time, then jerks his head, his eyes looking to the roof of the basement.

I follow his eyes, don't see anything, but gather his meaning fast. "They're listening?" I ask quietly.

"Probably got cameras as well," he murmurs directly into my ear, as though he's whispering sweet nothings. Nipping my earlobe, probably for effect, he continues in a low, but oh-so commanding voice, "Just go with it, huh? Don't contradict me, and we'll both have a chance of getting out of here."

"Why are you here?" Copying his example, I nuzzle into him, conscious that for some reason, he wants any possible camera to see that we're close. While I tell myself it's all a ploy and worth going with if there's at least a chance of getting free, it's actually no hardship. I've never been so close to such a perfect example of manhood before, and even under the circumstances, it seems churlish not to take advantage.

"I'm here to get you out." His rich voice oozes confidence, as if he has no doubt in his plans.

Strangely, he cups his hand to his ear and frowns. He grimaces before his attention comes back to me.

"Give me info. How many Dominators have you seen?"

I rise to the challenge. "Well, there's Knuckles, he's the leader, and Tats acts like his second-in-command. Then there's Fang, Limey—"

"Foghorn," Carole supplies from the next cage.

I toss her a nod to thank her, then finish, "A guy called Trots, and there's one who I think is a prospect. He's called Handle."

"Six members, one prospect." StoryTeller repeats, then

again touches his ear. I wonder whether he's got an infection or something.

"Hey, you," Carole calls out, rattling the bars of her cage. "You going to get all of us out of here?"

StoryTeller stands, leaving me feeling bereft on the floor. He stares at Carole for a moment, then glances around at the occupants of the other cages. A couple of women are looking at him, eager for his response. The other two are so lost in their own misery, it looks like they couldn't care less.

Finally, his eyes turn to Carole again. "No."

Carole rattles the cage again. "Why the fuck not?"

He shrugs. "Only have enough payment to get one person out of here, and that's got to be my ol' lady."

Standing, I suddenly feel disgusted and unclean. My release shouldn't come at the expense of others. For some inexplicable reason, he's here for me, and though I long for freedom, I'd at least want to try to free the women also kept captive.

Reading the signs that my temper is in danger of flaring, he closes the distance between us and holds me tight. I try to pull away, but he's too strong for me, so I content myself by lowering my voice to a growl and disputing, "I'm not your ol' lady. We've never fuckin' met." Then I remember one of the first things he said. "And what was that about MariaLisa DeMora? How do you know her?"

"I don't," he says simply, then pulls me to him again. Keeping his arms wrapped around me so I can't move away, to any onlooker it would look like a lover's cinch. "Your fuckin' life depends on doing what I say." He snorts softly. "Mine too, for that matter. Sure, I had to claim a relationship that I've no right to, but the ploy is simply to get you free."

But he's locked in this cage. He's now a prisoner as much as me. Rolling my eyes, I can't help observing, "And that seems to be working like a charm."

He glances sharply at me, then his face breaks into a grin. "Yeah, all is going as planned." When he winks, he seems to be indicating he hadn't factored in being imprisoned himself, but even so, he isn't particularly worried.

He might not be, but I am. I might have company, but other than that, nothing has changed. I'm still a prisoner and unless he can persuade them to release me, I'm faced with a fate I don't want to imagine.

CHAPTER ELEVEN
STORYTELLER

Okay, so my initial plan had been that they'd accept the exchange—the guns for Sheri's release. Though it had been on the cards they'd find a way to have their cake and eat it too, I hadn't really expected to be locked into her cell, nor lose my cut for which I've already had a deafening earful of abuse and derision.

Though that was welcome confirmation I've Slugger and my brothers on the outside looking out for me. No need for me to be concerned as for now I'm still breathing. And while the location hasn't got much going for it, my companion, well, she's something else.

I hadn't known what to expect. All the information I had was a few brief details from her social media profile, and her profile pic, which in truth does her no favours. While I haven't seen her at her best, with eyes red raw from crying, her skin is covered in the most attractive freckles, her face rounded, her lips... well, they're perfect. The kiss that had started off as a way to impress our audience turned into something else. If Knuckles hadn't interrupted us, I was probably only a few seconds away from throwing her on the ground, tearing off her clothes and having my wicked way with her. Fucking her would have been no hardship. My cock was already fully engaged. She's soft with curves in all the right places and that hair, well, I just want to fist my hand around it and…

Fuck. I should slap my own face for allowing myself to get distracted.

After the kiss, her pupils had been dilated. I know she'd been turned on as much as I was. And even if it's true that she'd never been close to a throbbing dick before, she didn't act as if as if she'd have any objection if I'd been the first man to take her.

I suspect, like me, she'd forgotten where we were and exactly who was watching us, which on my part was unfathomable seeing as I'd had Iron speaking into my ear, telling me to try to get information.

Now she's leaning away from me, as though trying to put distance between us, probably embarrassed about her reaction to me, just as I'm examining mine to her. I know I made her upset when I refused to confirm I was going to try to get the other women free. But suspecting ears at least were listening to us, and suspicious that there were probably cameras as well, I couldn't say anything that would cast doubt on my already flimsy cover story.

I hold tight to her to put on a show, but I can't deny enjoying having her close. She's curvy and soft and fits in my arms as if she's made to be there.

Wary of listeners other than my brothers, I can't say much else to her. Then again, I wouldn't be spilling our plans, that apart from rescuing her, our aim is to put a dent in the Dominators' operation. Slugger couldn't hide his joy at finding this location, and them knowing by me turning up, that this safe house is now a bust and can't be used by them again.

I'd told her it was all going as planned, but I hadn't factored in being made prisoner. At least I'm in contact with my brothers, and I know they won't desert me. Well, I'm pretty damn sure. Or I think so, anyway.

"Iron?" I say softly when I haven't heard his voice for a few moments.

"Hold on, ST. We're thinking."

I hear a tinkling sound and realise it's one of the other women, forced to use the bucket which is their only facility. They're being kept like fucking animals and that doesn't settle well with me. Already I know it will need a ton of therapy to get those taken away from friends and family back to the equilibrium they enjoyed before.

Something confirmed when the door opens again. The British Dominator saunters down the stairs and unlocks a cell opposite. Without a word, he drags the reluctant woman out by her hair. I don't need any explanation of what he's going to do to her, nor for anyone to tell me it's not the first time. Her clothes are already torn and more of her is uncovered than hidden. She goes, not willingly, but as if there's no fight left in her.

There's a collective sigh of relief from the others remaining, and I close my eyes briefly, thanking the universe that Sheri's quick thinking had saved her from a similar fate.

"Think faster," I say softly, my mouth turned away from her ears, knowing Iron will pick my words up, and hear my urgency.

I can feel the woman in my arms shaking as she watches the scared woman being led away.

I turn my attention back to her and tell her quietly, "I'm not going to let that happen to you. And good thinking, by the way, to say you're untouched and keep yourself safe."

Her cheeks glow as red as her hair. She turns her head away

as though embarrassed. Mumbling, she admits, "They use them all. They come down, take one, or two, and…" She sobs.

"Hey, no need to feel guilty. You did what you needed to to protect yourself." Gently, I move her to face me. "It's on those motherfuckers, not you." Now, when I pull her into my chest, she relaxes against me.

I feel a surge of protectiveness rise inside. She's kept herself relatively unharmed. From now on, it's down to me. While I hate what's happening to the other women, I'm only one man, and I can only take care of one. I silently vow that whatever happens, she will get out of here and be able to go back to her life.

Once again, I sit on the hard ground, pulling Sheri down with me and folding her back into my arms. We stay like that as if neither of us want to break the spell, nor lose the comfort afforded by human touch. Eventually the door opens again, and Limey brings the girl back down and throws her into her cage. She collapses in a heap, folding into herself and weeping. If I had my gun on me, I'd have shot him dead. I will him to try opening this cage door. If he does, I'll happily rip him limb from limb with my hands.

Time drags. I'm already bored. I don't know how these ladies can stand it. Still held in the safety of my arms, Sheri is dozing. Something loosens inside at the trust she's giving me, and for some reason, I nuzzle my lips to her hair.

"They're bringing in transport. Looks like they're getting ready to move the women."

The voice in my ear brings me back to myself. I turn away from Sheri and mumble, "Going to plan or are they escalating the timetable because I'm here?"

"Hard to tell. But the result will be the same." The connection clicks and then another voice comes on.

"ST. You been asked about the pickup for the guns?"

"Not yet," I respond to my prez.

"Not sure I like that."

Me neither, come to that. Unless Knuckles has another way of checking my story out, which I can't believe he has.

"He could be playing with you. We're thinking of ways of getting you out."

Alive would be my hope. I didn't survive this long to be killed like a pig in a slaughterhouse. Sure, my death might always have come at the hands of a rival club, but I'd rather go out with a gun in my hand.

Being caged doesn't suit me.

"Is something wrong?" Turning, I see Sheri rubbing her bleary eyes. She looks slightly startled as if surprised she's been asleep.

I tighten my hold on her briefly. "My brothers have everything in hand." I'm not sure whether I'm reassuring her or myself.

She looks understandably dubious. "How do you know?"

Just in case the lack of that information is the thing that's going to keep her safe, I shrug, and don't confide that they can hear everything we do, and that the contact works both ways.

Bikers don't like riding in cages or being confined in any way. The lack of anything happening is getting on my nerves, and it's easy to see it's also getting on hers. I'm trying not to let my frustration show.

"I asked you before, but you didn't answer." Sheri turns so she can look into my face. "I don't know you, yet you know my name, and mentioned one of my favourite authors."

Stretching out my long legs to ease the stiffness, I begin, in my normal way, to tell her the tale about the lone biker who stopped off for a piss and ended up with a book that was inscribed with her name. She looks rapt as I explain.

"You liked the book?"

"I haven't finished it yet. But from what I've read, yes."

"And you're a nomad? Like Einstein?"

I chuckle softly. As far as fiction can resemble real life, "Yes."

"So how did you know I was missing?"

I continue the story, noticing her eyes light up at the thought that her disappearance had been a topic of interest. I start to wonder about the life my ol' lady had been leading.

To fill in the gaps, I ask, "You go to the signing on your own, or with a friend?"

She shifts a little awkwardly. "Alone. I've not really any friends who'd want to come with me."

"What about a boyfriend?" Belatedly, I realise I know nothing about the woman I've claimed. If there is a man in the wings, I'll just have to get rid of him.

What? I shake my head to clear it. Stating she's my ol' lady was just a ploy to get my club on my side. I'm not seriously going to continue the fiction once we're outside. Am I?

She kisses so well and fits in my arms. She's curvaceous and has the type of body that I discovered I like. I love her hair, the colour of her eyes, and her taste in books.

Again, I shake my head, more vigorously this time. I know nothing important about her. If I was looking for a partner in life, I'd want more than eye candy to hang on my arm, and thousands, if not millions of women could have my cock interested. It's probably easier to list the types that turn me off.

Sheri's looking at me oddly, and I realise she probably answered my question while I've been setting things straight in my head. "I'm sorry?" I sheepishly admit I hadn't been paying attention.

Her brow furrows. "I just said I've never had a relationship that really worked out."

I glance around, peering up at the ceiling as though it holds the answers. When I hear and see nothing to suggest we're running out of time, I decide continuing the conversation is better than us just sitting, ruminating about our fate, outcomes I'm unable to influence right at this moment.

I cross my legs at the ankles and get as comfortable as I can. "What do you expect from your relationships?" I wait to hear her tell me about her requirements for the white picket fence, the man with the good job, fancy car, and ability to support her and the two-point-four kids I'm sure she'll think they should have.

Her brows have drawn down, and she bites at her lip. Her mouth quirks as she starts. "Well, for one thing, I don't want someone who thinks they should control what I think or what I do. I'm a person in my own right, not a possession."

"Is that a dig at the ol' lady label?" I know there's a twinkle in my eyes as I ask.

She's straight off the mark. "I don't want to be anyone's property. I have my own thoughts and ideas. I don't want to be someone's little woman. I want a partner, someone to be by my side, not walking in front or behind me. I don't want to be tied to the kitchen, nor have kids hanging on my apron strings. I want to have fun."

"And what's your idea of fun?" I raise a brow toward her.

She sighs deep and gives a charming self-deprecating smile. "I read a lot."

"You go out with friends? Party?"

Not wanting to meet my eyes, she looks down at her hands. "I kind of keep to myself."

"By choice?" I press, interested.

"Of course." But the way she refuses to meet my eye suggests circumstances have forced the way she lives upon her.

Something clenches inside as I realise I'd love to see her

truly happy, hear her laughing, and watch her smile. "You ever want to get some excitement in your life?"

Her attention comes back to me. "Of what type?"

I chuckle softly. "Babe, you just went to a massive signing of motorcycle club books. I'll take a leap and suggest you like what you're reading. Ever think of being in the starring role yourself?" She catches my eye, flushes red, then quickly looks away. *Oh yeah, she does.* "You dream of riding on a back of a bike? Heading off into the sunset? You dream of a biker sweeping you away?"

Her deepening blush shows I'm right on the money. I start to grin, but a closed look comes into her eyes.

She pulls her shoulders straight and her voice sounds prim. "I think I'll forgo any fantasies I might ever have had about bikers. Now I've met them for real, going forward, I think I'll steer clear of any coming my way."

I don't blame her, but something inside me wants to show her that not all bikers are like the Dominators, and some might even have her best interests at heart. A strange desire to break her out of her shell and show her some real-life excitement start to fill my mind.

She seems deep in thought, so I pause my questions for now, even though she intrigues me, and I want to know more about her.

Minutes pass, the voice in my ear is silent, but the basement is full of sound, mainly women weeping. As something else comes to my mind, I open my mouth to ask her, but before I can speak, heavy footsteps sound on the stairs.

Immediately I stand, my hand going for the gun in my cut, but of course neither are there. Nor is the spare in my ankle holster, or my knife that I keep on my belt.

I'm completely helpless and I hate it.

Especially as it's Knuckles who's first through the door, with Tats and Fang following closely.

There's the soft swishing sound as all the women move to the rear of their cages. There's a collective indrawn sigh as if all are holding their breath, worrying who's now going to be taken and used, or worse, whether their time is up, and the Dominators will be moving their captives on to their buyers now.

Even I feel uneasy though my fear isn't as great as theirs. How could it be? I'm not going to be raped. I might have death coming for me, but I've long been prepared for that fate.

My shoulders draw back as Knuckles makes a determined line straight for our cage.

Keeping my worry off my face, I cockily tilt my head.

CHAPTER TWELVE
STORYTELLER

"Either she's lying, or you are." Knuckles stares thoughtfully from outside of the cage.

I stare back. As far as I'm concerned, both of us probably are, but we won't be giving anything away. The thing about lies is that once you've started, it's hard to take them back. You're caught in that web of deceit.

If I admit I've never met this woman before, there goes my bargaining chip. If she takes back that she's a virgin, then she'll be fair game. But he's right to be suspicious that a man living this lifestyle would leave such a luscious woman untouched.

The Dominators' prez fondles his short beard. "See, I've got sympathies with you, Brother. Don't like any man going short. I might be thinking of how I can do you a favour and sort that."

Raising my shoulders toward my ears, I remind him, "Ain't going short." *And I'm not your fucking brother.*

He raises a brow and turns his attention to the woman who's in my shadow. "Hey, sweet cheeks, you don't mind your ol' man getting other pussy while waiting for yours?"

While I keep a nonchalant expression on my face, I'm

holding my breath, waiting for what she'll say, knowing I haven't prepared her for this. I'm only able to let air out when I hear her response.

"Until I've a ring on my finger, he can do what he wants."

Seeing as she knows nothing of the situation and has successfully joined the dots, I'm impressed as hell with her.

"My boys ain't happy I'm considering passing up a virgin." He glances over his shoulder at Tats and Fang who stand, nodding as if to confirm. "Can get a lot of money for someone untouched and needs breaking in."

I step forward, wrapping my hands around the bars of the cage. "I thought we had a bargain with the guns."

"Guns. Yeah. Guns." He sighs and points to Sheri. "You're asking me to give up a sure thing on the basis of some mythical prize. How do I know the guns even exist?"

He's got a point as I can't even tell him where they are, only where they will be once the cartel hand them over for delivery. "They exist," I growl. "And will be worth far more than one fuckin' virgin."

He snorts. "Or not fuckin', more to the point." Tats and Fang dutifully laugh at his lame joke.

Extracting a pack of cigarettes from his pocket, he takes one out, then offers them to his companions. As they light up, I suppress my instinct to ask for one myself. This imprisonment is forcing me to go cold turkey on my nicotine addiction, but I'm not going to give him the pleasure of knowing that. I wish I'd had the foresight to put my cigarettes and lighter in my pocket rather than leaving them, as I had, in my cut.

"Tell you what." Knuckles brightens as if he's suddenly had an excellent idea. "If we get rid of that pesky hymen of hers, the brothers won't have anything to complain about. She wouldn't be worth anything more than anyone else."

Tats slaps his hand down on Knuckles' shoulder. "Excellent idea. Wish I'd fuckin' thought of that."

Sheri, not being stupid, slides even more behind me. I reach back and place a reassuring hand on her arm. *Over my dead body will these fuckers hurt her.*

Knuckles' hand disappears, slides around his back, and reappears, holding a gun. I take the threat seriously. Outside this cage, I could take them all down, but with the bars between us, I'm at a disadvantage. Even I'm not immune to bullets.

Sheri inches closer, her chest to my back, her hands gripping my belt. My gut rolls, first for the trust she's showing in me, if only by regarding me as a lesser enemy than them, and secondly, knowing there's little I can do to protect her. The Dominators hate the patch I wear on my back, and I'll give them more pleasure dead than alive. Sheri, though, well, she represents a paycheck. Regrettably, I'm coming to the conclusion there's only one way out of this for me. And that's dead.

Knuckles cradles his elbow and, with the hand holding the gun, rubs at his chin. "I'll give you a choice, Soul. You can have her, or we will."

"She's my ol' lady. No one's touching her," I rasp out, clenching my fists, not one hundred percent sure what he's trying to say.

His next words though, spell it out clearly. "As you say, she's your ol' lady. You're going to take her sooner or later, so why not now? Serves two purposes. We get a show, and she'll no longer be a virgin. My men won't have to worry about losing the premium for her being untouched. I may be able to persuade them that the guns might be enough to let the both of you go."

I hear Sheri's intake of breath, but have to ignore her, concentrating instead on trying to come up with a plan to stop her getting raped and me killed. Getting out of this basement would be a step in the right direction.

"I'm game," I tell him. "Let us out, give us a room, and I'll fuck my ol' lady."

Knuckles exchanges a look with Tats and Fang and both chuckle loudly. "Nah, you do it here. You're a fuckin' biker. You should be able to perform with an audience."

It's not something I haven't done before—shared women and fucked them in front of my brothers. But not under these circumstances and not someone like her.

"Your choice, Bro," Knuckles says lightly, as if he doesn't give a damn. "But if you're not up for providing the entertainment, then I'll go with plan A. Shoot you and sell her." He raps his gun against the metal bars, causing an echoing ring to punctuate his words.

As Sheri whimpers, I turn my back on the Dominators, calculating that a bullet to the back of my head will do the same damage as one to my front.

I pull her to me and speak quickly into her ear. "I'm not averse to fuckin' you, Sheri. You're one sexy lady. But I'm no fuckin' rapist. You've got to be willing to play your part else neither of us is getting out of here." She's shaking like a fuckin' leaf in a gale force wind. Softening my voice, I tell her, "It's me or them."

"I don't want to be raped by them." Her voice trembles, but it's her expression, her fear, that completely undoes me.

"Not sure how you're going to get out of this, ST." The voice in my ear reminds me I'm not alone. *"We can't make a move while they're in the basement with you."*

If anyone is going to take her, it's going to be me. I've no option but also, no guarantees. If I provide them with the show that they want, there's nothing to say they won't kill me and take her anyway.

Though if these are my last few minutes on earth, maybe there are worse ways to go than being cock deep in someone like Sheri. Maybe it's the danger, or the anticipation of what I've decided to do next, but my cock thickens.

Holding her tight with one arm, I smooth my other hand up and down her back. If our kiss had been anything to go by, it won't be too hard for us to make sparks. I've just got to lead and persuade her to follow where I want to take her.

I'd called her my old lady, and on looks and what little I know of her, it wouldn't be a hardship to stake my claim. Already, she appeals to me on so many levels. My problem? I've no fucking idea whether my interest in her is reciprocated.

My hand grasps her chin, holding her in place as I close my eyes briefly, take a breath, then open them and dive in. For the second time, I plunder her lips. She's hesitant, reluctant, but ignoring the comments of *get a fuckin' move on* coming from outside the cage, I take my time, pressing my mouth firmly to hers.

Her taste, her tentative response, has my cock throbbing. Despite the impatience of our audience, I don't speed up, but increase the passion as my tongue fucks her mouth.

Our chests meld together, and through the thin material of both our shirts, I feel her nipples harden. Her mind might not want this, but her body is showing signs that it's game.

Adjusting my arms, I take her weight and ease her down to the ground, covering my body with hers. She struggles, panics and tries to get free. I put my mouth to her ear. "I got this. I got you, babe. I got you." She stills slightly, as I murmur, "We've no fuckin' choice. Trust me, babe. It's either me or them."

She doesn't need to tell me she's scared, it's written all over her face. But after a second, she gives a small nod of determination, as if accepting there's only one way this can play out.

"You," she breathes, her voice hitching, showing she knows what's at stake.

Pausing only for a second, I ease down the zipper of her jeans, adjust them on her hips to give my hand space, then move my fingers down. She gasps as I find her clit and my fingertips start to strum.

"For fucks' sake, just put the damn thing in her," Knuckles demands.

"Dominators might not know how to pleasure a lady, but I do," I growl back. Then to her, I say, "Forget them. Keep looking into my eyes."

She does, and I continue to play, leaving my thumb on her clit and allowing my fingers to enter her tight slit. She might not intellectually want this, but as her gaze stays locked with mine, her hips make little motions, putting pressure on my hand, trying to get my touch where she needs it. I comply, following her unspoken instructions, reading what she desires.

This is far from the first woman I've pleasured. I know my way around a female body, and where to find the G-spot that will send her wild.

Her eyes glaze and widen. Her breathing stutters, then stops on a lungful of air. She clasps at me, her fingers digging into my shoulders as I take her over the top.

While she's still in the throes of ecstasy, I quickly free my dick then shuffle her jeans further down and spread her knees to make myself a cradle between her hips. That way I'm hiding her from anyone else's eyes.

Then, along to a chorus of *Just shove it in*," I position my dick.

She's tighter than any woman I can remember, but wonder if that's just the position I have her in. Still, I retreat, then pushing forward, get another inch of myself inside.

The pained expression that takes the place of the sated one

she wore only seconds before suddenly has me questioning whether she had been lying to save herself, and instead ask whether she'd been telling the truth. A second later, I no longer query it, as I've become sure.

I'm the first man who's ever been inside her.

Feeling such a weight of responsibility, that despite the situation, regardless that I'm probably not the man she would have chosen for herself, I'm determined I'll do everything in my power to make this memorable for her, for all the right reasons as well as the bad.

Giving her a moment to adjust, I lean my head to her ear. I growl in my most dominant voice, "You're fuckin' beautiful, Sheri. Your cunt feels so fuckin' good."

Her eyes widen at the compliment. When my fingers find her clit again, within a few seconds, she's tentatively pushing against me as if trying to get my stilled body to move.

"Might have started as nothing, but you're fuckin' mine. You hear me, babe?" I'm hoping my eyes show my sincerity. This woman is tough, brave, not easily cowed, and once she'd realised our lives depended on her giving herself to me, hadn't wasted time to protest or complain.

"Not the way I wanted our first time, babe, but this was going to happen. You're mine, aren't you?" I add just a little insecurity into my tone and am rewarded by a minute dip of her head.

Though I doubt she realises what she's just agreed to, I move so I'm able to take her mouth. As I thrust my tongue inside, my hips jerk hard, sending me deep inside her, piercing through into never before reached depths. I swallow her gasp and again still myself, letting her work through the sting of invasion.

Then I move my fingers again and begin thrusting with small pumps. I doubt either of us now are thinking of our audience as we both strive to reach a peak. That she's forgotten or chooses to ignore them becomes certain as she does nothing to muffle her scream as her body contracts and her already tight channel squeezes the hell out of my dick. I lose rhythm, and fuck, am pushed to remember my own name, as cum literally explodes, shooting ribbon after ribbon inside her.

A slow hand clapping brings me back to myself and I open my eyes to see hers wide with wonder, and her features soften as she cups a hand to my cheek.

Audience be damned, I just had my first fuck with a woman who's blown my mind. Ruefully, I do admit it might have had something to do with my first time ever going bareback, but we'll deal with any implications once we make sure we're both going to live.

I pull out, jerking up her pants and zipping her up. Then I sit up straight on my knees and look down at my dick. *Well, lookie there.* I stand, turn, and unashamedly let the onlookers get a good sight of the blood on my now flaccid cock before I lazily tuck myself in and zip myself up.

Knuckles eyes widen. "Goddamnit! You motherfucker!" he screams, raising his gun and taking aim.

Tats, showing he's got fast reflexes, lashes out and grabs his arm.

Trying to shake him off, Knuckles growls at him, "It was your fuckin' fault. You said the odds were against her being a virgin."

"Odds against," Tats says, his eyes coming to mine momentarily. He's glaring daggers. "Not outside the realm of possibility obviously, but you agreed it was unlikely. Knuckles, think. We might have lost the extra we'd get for her, but you can't shoot him. What about the guns he promised?"

"Guns be fuckin' damned. I want him dead."

Tats lets out a heavy sigh. "Up to you, Knuck. But I'd advise against it."

When Tats releases his arm, and Knuckles growls and aims again, I'm wondering if I've time to make good with a maker I don't believe in, when a body pushes itself in front of me.

Sheri snarls. There's just no other word for it. "You wanna kill my old man? You'll have to go through me."

I'm not sure who's the most stunned—me, Knuckles, Tats or Fang. But while I'm not in the habit of using a human shield, I'm betting they won't want to kiss even the diminished amount they'd get for her goodbye. So, for the first time in my life, I hide behind a woman. *My* woman at that.

I'd thought I'd had it before, but now I realise that was an illusion. If any woman is going to be it, a woman like Sheri is likely to be my ride or die.

After a moment's standoff, Knuckles puts his gun away. He spits on the ground. "You two are fuckin' welcome to each other."

He spins on his heels, and, followed by Tats and Fang, makes his way out of the basement.

All bravado leaves Sheri as she sinks to the ground, the breath she's clearly been holding, now coming and going in heaving pants.

I'm not much better myself.

"Not heard a shot. You still alive, Brother?"

I turn away and say quietly, "I'm alive." Under my breath I add, "And royally fucked."

CHAPTER THIRTEEN
SHERI

When the Dominators leave, all the strength washes out of me and I fall to the floor as though my limbs are weak, my brain having trouble processing what's happening to me. I want to pinch myself to see whether I can wake from this nightmare, but I know however outlandish it seems, this is no bad dream.

When I'd pushed myself far out of my comfort zone to attend the signing on my own, I never thought I'd end up with a starring role in one of the most outlandish stories I've ever read. Although I know it happens, I never thought getting kidnapped would happen to someone like me.

But here I am, locked in a cage. And the most unbelievable part is that I've a hero from one of my books captive with me. Well, maybe the author's plotline has gone awry, as in fiction I'd already be rescued, and I wouldn't be sitting here with the stickiness of our joint release staining my underwear.

I've had sex. I've lost my virginity. Not that that by itself matters too much to me. I hadn't preserved my virtue for a future mythical husband, nor had I taken any pledge. It was more that no one had ever showed any particular inclination in taking it from me. Or at least, not someone I had a reciprocal urge for.

I never would have had the audacity to even dream of losing my virginity to someone like StoryTeller, a man straight out of one of my fantasies. My thoughts were more likely to envisage a mutual fumbling experience with a man who was my equal, and like me, didn't know what he was doing. Then, I'd have more expected to lose it in the back seat of a car, if not in a bed, instead of a dingy, stinking basement, where I was being held captive.

I'm stunned that it happened, and even more shocked that it's not the act that I regret. I do feel cheated that I couldn't relax and enjoy it more than I had. My own machinations with a vibrator hadn't prepared me for the things StoryTeller had made me feel, and that being despite the audience and the less than desirable situation that we're in.

I'm embarrassed that I responded to him, ashamed I put him in that position. I can't quite believe he managed to get hard for a nobody like me. Yet he had, and he saved me by doing so. I'm no longer a virgin, and the despicable Dominators hadn't been the ones to take that from me.

I shudder, remembering it, not with disgust, but with remembered pleasure. When he'd spoken into my ear, his voice, so full of dominance, had left me no choice other than to obey. When he'd used his hand and body, he'd made me forget where we were, and who was watching.

Freaking hell. I lost my virginity to a biker.

It's unreal, like something out of a fantasy.

On my knees, I place my head into my hands and rock back and forth as thoughts flood through me. On the surface, nothing has changed. I'm being held captive by the Dominators with no prospect of being set free, except that I've a member of another feared outlaw club being held captive with me.

Underneath though, I know I'll never be the same.

I spend my time devouring books about fictional heroes dressed in leather and riding bikes, and living a lifestyle I could only dream about—one based on trust, hard won loyalty and love. About men who'd never let their women walk into danger and would die before they got hurt.

Of course, someone like StoryTeller was going to attract me, at least on the outside. He's the epitome of any biker I've ever read about. But he's not make believe. He's real just like the Dominators who snatched me and locked me up. There are elements to these men that I previously hadn't thought so much about, the air of danger that surrounds them, and that their loyalty is to themselves and no one else.

Bikers, like the ones I read about, only exist in the pages of the books. In real life, they capture, rape and sell women.

But StoryTeller came to rescue me.

He came with no other intention than of returning my book to me. Shaking my head, I muse how disappointed he must have been when he realised whose book he had. I mean, just look at him, and then at me. He's devastatingly handsome, built and oozing confidence from every pore. Me, on the other hand, well, I'm overweight, far from being the beauty that should be on his arm, as well as being naïve, inexperienced and boring along with it.

As I shift position, an unfamiliar soreness in my muscles reminds me I'm not a virgin anymore. Should I be ranting and raving? Should I be distressed? I know if I had a choice, I wouldn't go back and change a thing. StoryTeller has given me something no one can ever take away—memories of him. In some twisted way, if I die today, I can go happily.

Suddenly, I become conscious that StoryTeller has come to crouch in front of me. As I raise my head, I see him staring.

Shame fills me, and guilt, that I'd put him in the position he's in. "I'm sorry."

Rearing back, his eyes narrow. "What the fuck have you got to be sorry for?"

I shrug. "That you found my book? That you felt that you had to come after me? That you were forced to…" I wave my hand, not quite sure how to signify what I mean.

But he gets the message. "Forced to fuck you?" He sweeps back his long hair, holding it in a ponytail for a second, before again letting it swing free. "Fuck, Sheri. Wrong time, wrong fuckin' place, but it wasn't any hardship to give you my cock." He considers me carefully for a moment. "I thank fuck that I found that novel. I thank fuck that I found *you*. And I'm fuckin' grateful you're a thousand times more than I ever dreamed you'd be." He chuckles softly. "You're a biker's wet dream, baby. Far too good for the likes of me."

My mouth drops open. I don't know what he's talking about, or whether he's been surreptitiously taking something that I haven't seen. *Surely, he must be high?*

He reaches out his hand and cups my cheek. "You might have noticed, it didn't take any effort for you to get me hard."

And he'd made it impossible for me not to reciprocate. But then, I was faced with an apparition summoned from the pages of the books I enjoy.

He's still staring at me. "Don't know what you see when you look in the mirror, babe, but I know what I like. And I'm the lucky fuck that got to have you for the first time." He grins sheepishly. "Though I would have preferred to have you in my bed where I could take my time. But hey, that's for next time."

"Next time?" I squeak, my brows rising so high I feel them against my hairline.

"You didn't think I'd be satisfied with just one taste, did you?"

My mouth opens and shuts. My brain tries to remind me that he's a biker and not the man for me. That he'd only want me until he got tired of me. I'd be stupid to think anything else. He could even be thinking of passing me around to his friends. No real-life biker is going to be faithful.

Leaning forward, he brushes his lips against mine. When he applies pressure, my body takes over from my mind and I open my mouth, making no protest as he kisses me. I may even grab on to his t-shirt. I mean, what woman in her right mind would turn down such an opportunity?

He pulls back far too soon, but his eyes sparkle with promise. "When we get out of here, I'm taking you to my bed, and don't bother expecting you'll soon get out of it."

Oh my. Hell, parts start tingling inside me, and I know my cheeks flush. That would just compound the mistake I've already been forced to make. I cup his face with my hand. Such a fantasy is hardly likely to come to pass. We're still both prisoners of the Dominators and our future might be measured in hours. Why not allow myself to dream, when it's more likely a nightmare will come to pass?

Maybe I should make the most of every opportunity.

This time, it's me pulling him toward me, my lips crashing into his, my tongue invading his mouth, my hands gripping his hair. He moans into my mouth, and I reciprocate. His hands cover my breasts, and I'm going to Hell, but I start to respond to him when he suddenly pulls away.

Bereft, not sure what I've done wrong, I start to reach for him.

"Later." He sounds breathless as he looks at me with dilated eyes. "Hold those thoughts, babe. Can't afford to get distracted." His fingers rest against my cheek. "The Dominators will soon be back again." His eyes grow hard. "There's just one thing, babe. Never, ever, put yourself between me and a bullet again."

He's surprised me. "He would have killed you."

"Nah." His eyes creases for a moment, then he shrugs.

"You know you're wrong." I point my finger and jab him in the chest with it. "And where would that have left me?"

He sits back on his haunches again but captures my stabbing finger in his hands. His eyes get back that twinkle I so like. "So, it wasn't to save my life, but for your selfish reasons?"

"I, er, no, I…"

Again, he moves swiftly, pulling me into his arms. "I'm fuckin' with you, babe." He nuzzles the top of my head. Then he stands, rubs at his ear, and walks to the other side of the cage.

I, too, get to my feet and survey my surroundings. Whether it's now that I'm different, and unable, due to the stickiness in my panties—I never realised sex was so messy—to forget my changed status, but I'm looking around as if with new eyes, and watching the other women with more sympathy.

Of course, I knew the mechanics. I knew part A went into slot B, but now I know had StoryTeller not taken the care that he had, just how bad that experience would have been. And that's only looking at it physically, ignoring the mental scars it would leave.

If it had been Tats or Fang, or heaven forbid, Knuckles himself… It's a thought I can't bear to think about, and the women who've been at their not-so-tender mercies have all my sympathy.

"You okay?"

I turn to see Carole staring at me, and flush, knowing she had a front-row seat to the porn show I'd starred in.

I raise my head then drop it. Under the circumstances, I'm probably the best I can be.

Behind Carole's cage I see Kelly slowly pulling herself to her feet, then putting both hands on the bars of her cage. Though her voice is husky through all the tears that she's cried, it doesn't stop her words coming over clearly.

"You're no better than us now." A twisted smirk comes to her face. "Even he," she raises her eyes, and they land on the back of the man looking, for some strange reason, like he's speaking to himself, "won't be able to protect you. In fact, he's just made it worse."

A ball of horror starts to swell in the pit of my stomach as I realise she could well be right. StoryTeller might have protected me once from being raped, but he may not be able to again. And now they know for certain that my virginal status has been taken, I'll be fair game.

I swallow hard. *They could take me just to fuck with him.*

My eyes flick upward as I hear multiple footsteps sounding on the stairs. My heart rate increases, and I cast a worried glance StoryTeller's way.

He's heard them too. He ceases his murmuring with one last barked comment, and comes to put his arm around me, pulling me back from the front of the cage and putting me behind him.

It's Tats and Fang again. This time Limey is with them. Like before, they march straight up to the cage that we're in, ignoring everyone else. Tats and Limey both have guns trained on us, while Fang fiddles with the key in the lock.

Once the door is opened, Tats barks and beckons with his weapon. "Stand back and let her out."

"Over my fuckin' dead body," StoryTeller growls. "You hurt her, you can forget about getting your hands on the guns."

Tats barks a laugh. "Not going to fuckin' hurt her. We're

just going to give her more of what you did earlier and what she so obviously enjoyed. Now step out of the fuckin' way, else we'll take you out."

StoryTeller doesn't budge. "I thought you wanted the guns."

"If there are any guns." Tats eyes show a rare glimpse of intelligence as he regards the man who's protecting my body with his own. "Could be you were stupid enough to walk in here with nothing concrete to offer. In that case, it's no matter if you're dead, and better for us than leaving a fuckin' Soul alive."

"There are guns," StoryTeller protests. "Kill me and you'll have missed your chance."

"Seems we've got the stronger bargaining point. Let us have her. Sure, we'll rough her up a little, might not make her so keen to have your cock a second time, but hey, bonus, we'll probably keep you alive. Refuse to give her to us? We'll shoot you and take her anyway."

StoryTeller might not have been able to help me escape, but I can't criticise him for trying. No one else has ever bothered about me or made me think they'd care if I was dead or alive.

If only for a short time, StoryTeller had made me believe that I mattered to him. In that, he's given me something I never had before. He owes nothing to me, but I owe him.

StoryTeller's standing in front of me, his arms crossed, refusing to move.

Tats aims his gun lower. "I'll shoot out your fuckin' kneecap if you don't let her come to me."

"Stay where you are," StoryTeller growls, unfolding his arms and pushing me back, as if reading my mind.

Tats barks a laugh. "There's no fuckin' way you can win this, Soul. Not without ending up full of fuckin' holes."

The bastard in front of me shrugs as if being made into a sieve is of no consequence. *He'd die to keep me alive.* Swallowing hard, the realisation is dumbfounding.

"Last chance." Tats aims the gun more firmly. "We're taking her. It's just up to you whether you make this easy on yourself or not."

Fang palms his crotch. "Just get on with it, will ya? I bet she's got a tight little cunt and I can't wait to get in there. Maybe see if I can get her to bleed again."

As a roar comes from StoryTeller's throat, his body tenses as if he's going to leap for them, but there's nowhere to go. He's got two guns aimed on him. I come to the conclusion he's going to try anyway, and instantly realise I can't see this man, the only man who'd ever shown anything approaching care for me, injured or killed just to delay the inevitable.

Slipping around him in a move that takes them all by surprise, I launch forward, my action making Tats lose his aim as he reaches out to grab me, tugging me off balance, and using my momentum to push me to Fang who's waiting behind him.

I have a split second to decide whether to go to my fate meekly, or to fight like hell to survive. I'd prefer to die than have any of these men defile me, especially when I can still feel evidence of StoryTeller being inside me. As much as anything, I don't want that memory sullied.

Knowing this can be no halfhearted struggle, and that I'll need to put everything I've got into it, I tense my muscles. Taking advantage of Fang who thinks he's dealing with a weak woman, I wrench myself free of his hold, and continue my movement to aim a kick straight up and between Limey's legs, hopefully shooting his balls right back into his body cavity. It seems I'm successful from the howl.

But even as he goes down, I realise it's still two against one. Quickly I discount Tats as he'll have to concentrate on keeping

StoryTeller in line, but Fang wastes no time drawing back his arm. In a split second, I realise they've been brought up on a diet of fighting dirty, and my answer to violence has always been to run and hide.

I don't wait for the blow to land. Instead, I duck, then surprise him by aiming my fingernails for his eyes. He rears back as an overloud crack sounds from behind me and Tats comes crashing forward, his weight knocking Fang to the ground.

A hand grabs my arm. I swing around but it lets me loose immediately. It's StoryTeller getting me out of the way to clear himself some space. He doesn't waste time, launching himself onto Fang's back, twisting his head into an unnatural position and giving it a twist, his action accompanied by a sickening crack.

Limey, at last uncovering his manhood, reaches for a gun, but I throw myself forward, knocking his arm and deflecting aim so the bullet that was meant for StoryTeller plants itself harmlessly into the ceiling. Then he's by my side, taking the gun from Limey's hands. His actions are like poetry in motion as he raises an already bloody knife and in one swift movement, with no second thoughts or hesitation, he slits the Dominators' throat.

It's only then I notice Tats is making weak choking noises. One glance shows this is the second time StoryTeller's used the same method of attack, and presumably with the rival biker's own knife.

Tats quickly gives up his battle with life. After one last rasping breath, there's no other sound. For the first time since I've been here, no one's crying or wailing. There's an air of expectancy as time seems to stop, and all eyes, including mine, are on the man who's standing tall, gun in one hand, knife, its tip wet and scarlet, in the other, his face and clothes splattered with blood. Otherwise still as a tableau, his chest heaves from the exertion.

I'm stunned. The speed at which he disposed of our enemies happening so fast, it's as if my brain is needing a moment to process what my eyes are seeing.

With his eyes fixed on me, StoryTeller seems to be talking to himself. "Three dead," he says calmly. "Shot fired. Not sure if that warned anybody." He pauses, then adds, "Yeah, just about to do that now."

He nods as if in agreement with somebody, then his eyes find mine. There's something in his expression, as if he has admiration for me, but I did nothing. He did all the work. He sinks to his knees, uncaring he's kneeling in an ever-spreading pool of blood, and begins searching Limey's body.

When he finds keys, he tosses them to me. I'm proud that although unexpected, I don't fumble the catch.

"Open the cages. Let them out."

He waits only a second to check I understand what I'm meant to be doing, before starting to collect all the weapons from the bodies on the ground. He moves to position himself by the door as I start to undo the padlocks.

Carole steps out, her eyes hopeful and gleaming. She spits on Tats's body, then comes to my side. Kelly and Angie also waste no time taking advantage of their liberty, but MaryAnne and Leah need a little more encouragement. Leah casts worried glances toward StoryTeller as though he might be the Devil, not the man who's hopefully going to save us. MaryAnne is so lost in her own misery, I don't think it's sunk in that she's free.

"Stay together." StoryTeller gestures with a gun. "Get into the far corner and keep your fucking heads down."

Carole and I usher the women together, knowing while he's doing the best he can to protect us, we're still in the direct line of fire. I'm all too conscious there's only one man between us and the Dominators seeking revenge.

Once they're all huddled behind me, I raise my eyes and watch StoryTeller guarding the door. I thought he'd cut an impressive figure before, but now, armed and exceedingly dangerous, bloodied and fierce, he's nothing short of magnificent, a Viking warrior from times past. Only a few moments before I had doubts that any of us would get out of this, but with StoryTeller being a one-man freaking army, I start to believe we've a chance.

Three down. Four to go.

StoryTeller has managed to push home the bolt on this side of the door. A fact the Dominators find out when they try to get in. I hear angry shouts about *"what the fuck is going on down there."*

"I thought we had a fuckin' bargain," StoryTeller shouts back angrily.

"Tats? Tats, you there?"

"Tats won't be talking to anyone anymore," StoryTeller responds without any remorse in his tone. "I don't take kindly to being fuckin' double-crossed, Knuckles."

A more hesitant voice sounds. "Limey? Fang?"

"Sorry," comes the reply from the man who's not apologetic at all. "They can't talk right now." Then after a pause, he adds, "Or ever."

"You've just signed your fuckin' death warrant," Knuckles screeches. The words are accompanied by a heavy banging on the door. "You killed my brothers, asshole."

StoryTeller does that thing where he seems to talk to himself. After a moment, he nods and descends the stairs.

He approaches our huddle. "Stay together and keep out of sight."

I rise from my position among the others and go to him. "How the hell are we going to get out of this?"

If I'm hyperventilating, who could blame me. My adrenaline's going to run out sometime, and then I'll crash. But until then, I'm buzzing with energy. "What can I do?"

He gives me an admiring look and places his hand on my cheek. "You did good, babe. You know that? If it hadn't been you giving me that opening, well, things would be very different now. But don't worry, my brothers are close by, and they've got this. All we've got to do is wait for the cavalry." At my worried look toward the door, he chuckles. "Fucker's reinforced that door. Now what's keeping us in is keeping them out. We've just got to sit tight."

"How will your brothers know what's going on?" Carole must think it's a reasonable question to ask.

Again, his lips curve in mirth. Strangely, he pushes his long hair back over his ear, and leans close, pointing to something inside it.

As her brow furrows, he explains, "It's a bug. They can hear everything that's going on and I can speak to them."

They what? *His brothers can hear everything?* Oh my God. They know what we did. *How will I ever be able to face them?*

"Sheri?" StoryTeller must catch my expression, and I realise I'm distracting him from his job. And really, if his brothers can do the impossible and free us, I can take a little embarrassment. After all, I'll never see them again.

I try a weak smile to signify as far as possible, I'm alright. He gives a sharp nod. After his head has tilted to one side for a moment, he says, "They're coming in now."

I suppose there's nothing I can do but wait and worry. I return to the other women and let them know help is on its way. From the looks they give me, I'm not sure they believe me.

Suddenly gunshots sound from the floor above. Kelly and

Leah scream and clutch at each other, while Carole looks to me in dismay.

"They can't get in," I tell her. "It's StoryTeller's friends. They're here to get us out."

Heaven knows how many of StoryTeller's brothers there are. There's only four Dominators left as far as I can tell but it sounds like a full-fledged battle going on overhead.

Suddenly after another barrage of gunfire, there's an explosion that rocks the whole house.

"Goddamnit!" StoryTeller shouts, grabbing onto the banister to stop himself from falling down the stairs. He leaps out of danger, then, seeing the women flinch and scream in terror, he makes a visible effort to calm his voice. "It's okay. We're safe."

Safe? I eye the ceiling above us from which flecks of plaster are coming down, falling like the first flakes of snow in winter. I stand and cautiously make my way across to him. "What's happened?"

As he beckons me closer, with a wary eye on the women behind, I gather he doesn't want to alarm them. "Dominators fuckin' rigged the house to blow up."

My hand goes to my mouth. "Any of your guys hurt?"

He seems surprised that's the first thing I've asked. "Superficial cuts and bruises, and two of the Dominators have used the confusion to escape. But we've got a problem."

I raise my eyes to him, then twitch my nose. With growing horror, I realise what he's going to say next before he gets the words out.

"The fuckin' house is on fire."

CHAPTER FOURTEEN
STORYTELLER

Having told Sheri about our predicament, I turn my attention back to the voice in my ear.

"Knuckles must have had a plan for if they were ever under attack. He's set off explosives, hoping to destroy all the evidence. We got a couple of them, Brother, but Knuckles and one other have run. Skunk and Pothead have gone after them."

Much as I'd rather they were all dead, dealing with them is for later, once we're safely out. "Tell me more about the fuckin' bomb. What's our escape route like?"

"Not looking good, Bro. We're trying to clear a path in through the door and down to the basement, but flames are beating us back. We'll do what we can from this side and give you the go when we've got a chance of getting you out." There's a pause then Chaz says, *"You haven't got long. That fuckin' building is going to collapse."*

Fuck. I sweep back my hair with my hands. This wasn't how I was meant to die, burned to a cinder, caught like a cornered rat. Adrenaline courses through my body, but there's nowhere to run, and fuck all that I can do. I have to rely on my brothers to help.

A wheezing sound gets my attention. Turning, I see one of the women gasping to get air into her lungs. It's then I realise it's getting harder to breathe. The fire must be sucking up air into the floors above.

"Get blankets," I yell to Sheri, running into the cells and grabbing some for myself. I place them under the door where there's a gap.

Sheri, and surprisingly Carole, appear with a couple more, but as I study the doorway, I know our efforts are futile. The door isn't fixed tightly enough.

Still, I try to ram whatever we've got into the voids, hopefully keeping our meagre air supply from being decimated for a little longer.

"We haven't got long," I speak for my brothers' benefit. "Getting hot as hell down here."

"*Working on it, Bro.*" Chaz's voice comes over to me, sounding calm. "*We're removing debris from the front of the house. ST, when it's time to run, you'll be coming out hot.*"

That's an understatement. But when it's time, I'll be exiting that door, taking my chances. I'd rather let the flames have me, than suffocate. I'll go out fighting, just as I've lived my life.

Having to trust in the toil of my brothers, I turn my attention to Sheri. She's scared. Her eyes are flaring, and her cheeks are pale. Then, I can see no more as the overhead light goes off, and the only illumination is the orange tinge seeping in through the cracks in the door. Other women are screaming, one starts praying, but Sheri makes her way over to me.

She's afraid but keeping it together. "What can I do?"

Impressed as fuck with her, and not for the first time, I think fast, trying to find something positive as much as to keep her occupied. "See what water we've got. Tell the women to soak something, clothing, hell, whatever they can find, and be prepared to put it over their heads."

"We won't be able to run through that fire," Carole states, overhearing as she too comes up close.

"You've got any better ideas?" At least Sheri's trying to stay positive and take action. "This is our best chance, Carole." I have to get through to her as I need her help. I've noticed she's some de facto leader, and the others look to her.

Fuck. I've got women already traumatised, and I'm preparing to be a Pied Piper, expecting them to follow me to probably death.

"Carole, either we try to get out of here, or we die from lack of air and smoke inhalation, and that's if the ceiling doesn't cave in and crush us first." Sheri's summed up our predicament well.

"Or wait for someone to put the fire out." Carole doesn't seem to like anyone else taking charge.

It could have been a good suggestion, but I'm not sure how long we've got. This place is miles away from anywhere, and help won't get here soon enough.

I could get myself and Sheri out, leave the others to face which-ever fate they choose. But that's not the way I roll. Where there's breath, there's a chance.

"We've got a hose. Front door is clear, but that fire's taking a hold. If you're going to get out of there, best do it soon, Bro."

Again, Chaz sounds calm, unflappable, but his soothing tone doesn't help. Even he can't disguise that what he's proposing is risky as fuck.

It's easy enough to say. Go up the stairs, open the door, and run like hell. But I know from the roaring sound that fire means business, and the cracks of the building as beams fall, mean that time's running out.

"Gotta make a move, Bro." Though he successfully avoids

injecting panic into his voice, the message comes over loud and clear. It's now or never.

Sheri's back by my side. "They've all got something to cover their heads." She pauses, and while it's hard to make out her features, I think she's grimacing. "We ran out of water, so I emptied the buckets as well."

It's good thinking, but I don't know how the fuck she persuaded the women to cover their heads with piss-covered cloths. Still, I suppose, they've been kept in these filthy conditions for long enough that they no longer smell themselves.

As if reading my mind, she tugs at my arms and says calmly, with only a slight quiver to betray the fear in her voice, "Can we get out of here? I'm dreaming of a cold shower."

I can't help it. I pull her to me, slam my lips down on hers and kiss her as if my life depends on it. She responds with the same desperation, as if agreeing if this is all we have of our time, we'll make the most of it.

A crackle, a crash, make me jump away. In the dim orange glow, I meet her eyes, noticing her flaming red hair enhanced by the light. Taking a tie from my pocket, I gently pull her hair back, twisting it into a bun, and securing it at the top of her head. Then, with a spare, I do the same to mine.

She straightens her back and gives a small nod of her head as though acknowledging it's time.

I can't leave her like this. Curling my hand around the back of her neck, I tilt her head so she's forced to look into my eyes.

"Gonna get you that shower then get you into my bed." In case she doesn't understand what I'm saying, I add, "'Cause you're fuckin' mine."

A shudder goes through her as I promise a future that's out of my hands. Whether either of us survive the next few minutes is up for debate.

"When I open the door," I tell her. "You run, got it? Don't

look back, don't hesitate, just wrap that cloth around your head, cover your mouth and head for the door. My brothers will be there."

"Not before them," she responds, pointing back to where the women are hidden in the darkness. "They'll need some persuasion to run through fire. I'm not leaving any behind."

Can't she understand that that's my job? That I'll only be able to do it if she's safe? But there's no time to argue, and it's just one more sign this woman was meant to be mine. And she's going to be if I have any say in it.

But first, we've got to get out of here.

While I did my best to block the door, smoke has been filtering through the cracks and the air is getting denser by the second. I flick my lighter to get some light and can barely see across to the rear where the traumatised women are huddled.

I make a split-second decision. "Let's get the women, then Sheri, you go out first. Carole, can you make sure all the other women get out and I'll bring up the rear?"

"Uh-uh." Carole shakes her head. "Soon as that door opens, I'm out of here."

I can't see but I can imagine Sheri rolling her eyes. "I'll make sure everyone gets out," she promises. I see her head move toward the door, then, as if realising time is indeed running out, she disappears into the thickening smoke.

"Go help her," I snap to Carole.

But she doesn't move. "The air is better here."

I don't think it is, but the woman who seems to have held herself together better than the rest is not only as hard as nails, but selfish to boot. I have no means to force her to do what I want, so I wait impatiently, getting updates from the brothers outside. What I'm hearing isn't good.

I bounce on my heels, then, impatient as I hear no one moving toward me, use my lighter again to light the way over to where Sheri is trying to get the women organised. A couple are on their feet and ready, two more are still curled into balls on the floor.

"I can't get them to move," she confides, apologetically.

Assessing the situation, realising the time for cajoling has gone, and that Sheri's probably tried her best, I bark loudly, "Get on your fuckin' feet."

One girl whimpers and gets slowly to her knees and then stands. She gives me a wide berth as she moves closer to Sheri. I jerk my head toward the door, and Sheri starts to lead her away. I've kept the lighter for myself, but Sheri can easily find her way by the orange light coming through the gaps.

"Move," I snap, completely losing patience at the woman who's causing a delay which might mean the difference between life and death. When she still doesn't react, I'm sorry to say, I give her a gentle kick, just to show I mean business.

Instead of bringing her to her senses, her body falls sideways.

"Motherfucker!" I exclaim as I crouch on my haunches. Somehow, probably from one of the dead bodies I carelessly left lying around, she's got hold of a knife and has slit her wrists. There's blood pooling around her.

I feel for the pulse in her neck. It's there, just, but only a flutter. Closing my eyes and swearing in my head, I realise the chances of us making it out of here are slim as it is and carrying a near corpse isn't going to help matters. It's unlikely she'll survive, and the only sensible choice is to leave her.

But fuck. As I stand and turn my back, I hate that I can do nothing for her. The Dominators had successfully broken her. I hadn't missed it was her Fang had dragged away and returned after he'd had his fun with her. That must have been the final straw.

If he wasn't already dead, I'd kill him all over again. And this time, make his torture go on for fucking days.

This is why I wouldn't be involved in the Wretched Soulz if they saw women as commodities to be used and sold at their pleasure. Whoever she was, she didn't deserve the treatment she got at those sons of bitches' hands.

Though I've only got seconds if we're going to get out of here with a chance of staying alive to breathe fresh air, I feel like a punch in my gut. *If I hadn't found that book, Sheri could be the woman bleeding out here.*

"Motherfucker!" I scream loudly, smoothing my hands over my head, knowing that all over the country there are women just like her, used, discarded and thrown away as if their existence doesn't matter.

"What is it?" Sheri's back by my side.

Roughly, I pull her close to me. "She fuckin' killed herself. Got hold of a knife."

I feel her shudder and her intake of breath, then a different tension makes her muscles taut. "There's nothing more we can do for her. Let's get out of here."

She's right, and that should have been my line.

With that swift kick up the ass, I grab her hand and lead her to where the others are waiting. Bravely, Sheri wraps the damp towel around her head, leaving just a slit for her eyes. With one last lingering look on the woman I hope to see on the other side, I wrench away the blankets which had been inadequately blocking the gaps, immediately allowing for a thick cloud of hot choking smoke to enter under the door, and then pull the door open.

The roar of the fire amplifies and while Sheri bravely steps through with only the slightest hesitation, I have to physically push and prod at the other women to encourage them. Despite her earlier assertion, Carole falters halfway up the stairs and makes as if she wants to go back down.

"Be my guest." I, too, have a cloth covering everything but my eyes, though that gap is sufficient for me to glare at her. "You want to take your chances and go back down, I ain't gonna stop you."

She looks up at the flames I'm asking her to walk through, and then to the basement we so recently left behind.

"Go on." I gentle my voice. "I got you."

And then we're in the thick of it, burning beams cluttering the ground and glowing embers floating around. It's hard to hear, but I can make out men yelling.

"Go." I push hard at Carole, sending her forward.

She screams as the heat hits us like a physical force.

My lungs burn as there's no oxygen to inhale, just the fucking smoke that's trying to kill us. I keep my eyes trained to where I can see bodies moving ahead of me and wipe everything else from my mind except for putting one foot in front of the other.

I'm in some kind of trance when hands reach for me, unceremoniously dragging me out by my collar, away from the flames, away from the heat, away from the house and, eventually, finally, letting me drop to the ground.

There I lie, my lungs heaving, screaming for life-giving air. Once I start coughing, it's a while before I stop, but I'm not the only one. Rolling over onto my stomach, I anxiously look around, only relaxing when I see Sheri.

Is she curled over trying to recover? Fuck no. She's up and about and checking on everyone else.

My lips curve.

Yeah. She's my one. I've found her.

Now I've got to hang onto her.

CHAPTER FIFTEEN
SHERI

There were a few moments there when I genuinely didn't think we were going to make it.

I thought I knew what it was to be scared when the Dominators snatched me from the parking lot and transported me God knows where. But that was nothing compared to making myself walk through flames with the only hope that StoryTeller's brothers would be waiting on the other side to help me.

My arms and legs feel raw from the heat. I have a particularly nasty burn on one side when I'd avoided falling beams and careened into red hot pipework. I don't know whether my lungs will ever be the same again, but I'm alive. I'm out, and apart from the poor girl who took her own life, it looks like all the others have gotten out safely.

I know I'll have nightmares where I'll dream that I didn't make it, probably even PTSD, but for now, all I can concentrate on is that the burning house and that torture chamber of a basement are behind me.

For some reason I feel responsible for the women who were

with me, even though I'd been the last to arrive. I check on Carole. Like me, she's got a few burns, and is finding it hard to breathe, but she doesn't seem to have any immediate threat to her life. I look to the other women, sparing a moment and a comforting hug for each of them. Apart from the breathlessness, sore throats and minor burns, we all seem to have escaped relatively unscathed.

We're free. It takes a moment to sink in. Then, as I look around, seeing StoryTeller being hugged and backslapped by other men, for a moment I worry whether we've left one dangerous situation, only to land in another. *How do I know his club hasn't the same nefarious purposes?*

I tense as I see StoryTeller walking toward me. As he gets closer, he gives me a concerned, assessing look, then opens his arms. "Come here."

I'm emotionally drained, sore, hurting, tired, and running on fumes, but his deep voice still somehow has the ability to make the core of me start to throb.

My immediate impulse is to throw myself at him, but I hold back. Behind us the building is still burning, in its death throes for sure now, creaks, crashes and sounds like sighs as it slowly comes crashing down.

No one needs to tell me we got out by the skin of our teeth.

Everything goes through my mind in a flash—my abduction, imprisonment, StoryTeller appearing on the scene, the threats Knuckles had made, followed by the weird seduction and very public loss of my virginity, then, the break for freedom.

Out of the corner of my eye, I regard the man of my dreams. His hair has started to come out of the bounds of the bun that he'd put it in. His face is dirty and must reflect mine, darkened with soot, and red patches showing overheated skin. His clothes are tattered and charred, but he's still the most magnificent being that I've ever seen. It's that that makes me cautious. *He's too much of a man for me.*

In the broad light of day, he's given me hopes that normality is within my reach. I can return to my day-to-day life and keep him as a memory. Anything else that he offered had surely been only to keep up my spirits when all had appeared lost. He can't really have any special interest in me.

"Sheri." He uses my name as a command this time.

My body turns to him as if he's in control of it. I've automatically lowered my face toward the ground, but with one gentle finger, he raises it. His eyes roam my body but not in a lascivious way, and I immediately realise he's assessing the state I'm in. I give a small smile and nod to indicate that I'm okay, and that's the only permission he needs.

As if he's been holding himself back, he lurches forward, putting his arms around me and holding me close. His hands roam up and down my body. The feeling's so good, I suppress my wince and try to hide that he's found bruises and burns.

I can't help wrapping my own arms around him. If he's in pain, he's working as hard as I am not to show his suffering.

As well as the leather I'd smelled before, he now smells charred, but then, I do myself. It makes me remember what a state I'm in, how I haven't washed for days, and that the crotch of my jeans is stiff with the dried remnants of our combined juices. The implications of which I've tried to keep at the back of my mind.

But the way he's holding me shows either he's not got a sense of smell or just doesn't give a damn. I lean into him, wishing this could be forever, and not just a brief moment in time. Even if he wants me to stay around, it will only be until the vestiges of the last few hours have worn away.

He couldn't want me. Not boring Sheri Secord who'd never

amount to anything, too stupid to go to college or make something of herself.

And I shouldn't want him. He's not just not in my lane, he's on another road altogether. How would I ever belong in a biker world? I already know it's not like my fantasies. Well, except for the rescuing part that is. I can't deny the Wretched Soulz have saved us. I hadn't missed how they'd been desperately hosing the entrance with water and yanking us out of the way as soon as we'd appeared, getting so close as to put themselves in danger.

I feel him let out a shuddering sigh, then he pulls back, putting me at arm's length and again scrutinising my face.

He frowns. "We need to get you checked out."

"I'm okay."

"Nah, I think you're, *we're,* running on adrenaline, babe. That bump on your forehead looks nasty."

I can't even remember hitting my head, but now he mentions it, I do ache. "All I need is a shower."

He nods, leans in and gently kisses my forehead. "Just wait a moment then we'll get out of here."

Looking around, I can only see bikes. I'm not even sure I'd be able to get on one myself, and I'm certain some of the others are in no fit state to ride.

"How are we going to get them out of here?" I wave behind me.

"Them?" He turns his head in the direction I've indicated as though since getting out of the house he's not given the other women another thought. He frowns as he turns back. "Someone will see the flames and come to investigate, which is why we haven't got much time. We need to get out of here."

My brow furrows. "Hang on. You're just... leaving them here?" Again, I gesture behind me. "They need medical attention." *And probably years of therapy.*

He gives a little shake of his head as though he's confused. "Which they'll probably get." His eyes narrow. "What do you expect from us, babe?"

"ST? You coming?" a voice yells. "Skunk and Pothead are back, Knuckles and the other man got away."

"Be there in a sec, VP." He half turns to shout over his shoulder, then raises an eyebrow at me.

Once again, I gesture toward my rear. "You can't just leave them here."

Again, he looks like he can't understand me. "We're not in the habit of rescuing damsels in distress, babe. They'll be okay. I'm sure of it." His brow creases, then the lines fade away. "Tell you what, I'll wait until we're away from here, then give 911 a call, just in case the fire isn't reported. That do you?"

I don't know what I expected, but the bikers in my books would have had transport available to either take us all to a hospital or back to their compound. They'd have stood guard over them until the escaped Dominators have been caught and rendered unable to seek vengeance on their kidnappees. They wouldn't have ridden away and left them.

I start shaking my head and back away.

He ruffles his hair, then tries to approach me as I raise my hands. "What do you want? Babe, we're not social services. We need to get free of this place before we're caught up in this mess. Don't you think the cops will see our cuts…" he pauses, flinches, clearly remembering he's not wearing his, then continues, "well, those of the others, and won't wait for explanations until we're locked up. They're always looking for an excuse to throw away the key."

"You could make sure they get somewhere safe." But as I say it, I know I'm losing this argument.

I feel I'm being pulled in two directions. For some unknown reason, I feel an obligation to make sure these women are okay. Maybe it's because I hadn't been kept captive as long as they'd been, nor had been so traumatised. The closest I'd come to being raped was StoryTeller taking my virginity. And though it should be, that could never be placed in my box of regrets.

On the other hand, StoryTeller's offering me a way out of my boring existence. While I doubt anything he feels for me is anything more than that we've come through a shared experience, I've no doubt anything between us will only be fleeting. My soul longs to be with him, to step out of my comfort zone and jump into the world I read about.

But he's just thrown cold water on all my expectations. The Wretched Soulz aren't the warriors in leather, the tameable bears, like the bikers who populate the minds of the authors I admire. They can't be, not if they're prepared to walk away from this mess.

For once I want to amount to something and leaving Mary-Anne's body in the basement plays on my mind. While there's not much more I can do than offer support, I can hopefully ensure no other woman will get so distressed, that they'll find a way to end it before hope arrives. StoryTeller's proposing walking away without even telling them help will be summoned.

And I can't forget, Knuckles and one of his men are still on the loose, and who's to say they won't come back?

A lump rises in my throat as I prepare to give up on my future. "I can't leave them."

"Sheri?" His jaw drops.

I take another step back. "I can't leave them unprotected. Give me one of the guns you took from the Dominators, and I'll stay."

His eyes flare. "You'll what?"

"Go." I make a shooing motion at him, hoping he won't argue.

My resolve isn't that strong. Half of me wants him to pick me up, sweep me away and forcibly sit me on his bike. If he did that, I think I'd be swayed. I need him to leave before I change my mind, before I beg him to take me with him.

But wondering what happened to the women would be on my conscience all my life. I can't live with that, even if he can.

"You're giving up on us. On what we could be?" He sounds incredulous.

"ST?" his VP shouts again. And this time, his voice is accompanied by multiple engines starting.

I mouth the word but can't bring myself to verbalise it. *Yes.*

"For fuck's sake," he growls, then spins on his heels. He marches over to a stunning black bike parked a little way back from the rest. After a moment and a gesture toward the rest of the bikers, he runs back to me.

He passes me two items.

One is the gun just as I requested.

The other?

A book. I don't even need to look at the cover to know what it is.

Then, with a scowl, a final assessing look at my face, he leaves.

I stay rooted to the spot, watching them leave, not moving until the sound of the last engine fades.

A little voice inside is shouting at me. *What have I done?*

A tear comes to my eye, and I swallow back the sob, then I walk back to join the other women.

"They've gone," Carole states, unable to mask the disbelief in her voice.

"They've gone," I agree. I straighten my back. "They're going to call the authorities. Someone will be coming for us soon." I hunker down and join their group. "How are we all doing?"

Not well, by the look of it. Kelly is shivering even though the heat from the burning building can still be felt, and I'm worried she's going into shock. Angie has her head in her hands and is rocking, much like she did in the basement. I'm not even sure she knows that she's free.

A loud crash sounds as more of the house behind us falls down, and Leah jumps.

There's not much I can do for them mentally. I notice Carole cradling her arm. "You okay?"

"Are they really going to call someone?" she asks, instead of answering. "Are we really safe?"

It's then I notice how exposed we are, illuminated by the dying flames. "I think we'll be safer if we get to the woods. We only need to show ourselves when we know who's arrived."

Her eyes fall on the gun I'm holding in my right hand. She gulps, catches my eyes, and reads the unspoken message. We both encourage Angie, Kelly and Leah to come with us and get out of sight.

As we hide, I try to stop the shaking, knowing I'm still running on the aftermath of the adrenaline coupled with the thought we won't be safe until the authorities turn up. There's a large part of me that's crying out for StoryTeller. While he'd only been in my life a few hours, he'd made an enormous impression on it, and one I know I'll never forget.

I suspect there'll be times I'll regret not going with him, and I could really do with his comforting hugs right now.

But I made the only choice I could. I'm a good citizen girl, while he's an outlaw.

CHAPTER SIXTEEN
STORYTELLER

"What the fuck's wrong with you, ST? You've been like a bear with his paw caught in a trap since we got back." Iron observes me carefully, then his features soften. "That bitch really got to you, huh?"

I reward the sergeant-at-arms with a scowl. He just chuckles and slaps my back as we make our way into church.

I know I've not been the easiest brother to live with, but who could fucking blame me? The whole business with Sheri was fucked from beginning to end. It hadn't been the first time I'd applied the finders/keeper's law before, but definitely the only time I've ever felt any remorse. Normally, it was the bad luck of the loser, knowing if I hadn't picked the item up, someone else would have done. Or, in the case of the book, it could have ended up swept into the trash.

That a provenance could be associated with it, again, was something I'd normally ignore. If something was that precious, the owner should have taken better care of it.

The attack of conscience, the desire that had driven me to reunite book with owner, were out of character. And look at the result? I'd fallen for Sheri, but she'd left me without even giving us a chance. I should have learned my lesson years before—bitches can't be trusted. But once again, I let myself be swept away by a pretty face and some rounded curves.

The things I said, the promises I made, might have been in the heat of the moment, but I'd meant them. And she'd thrown it all back in my face.

I'd hated Fi when she betrayed me. That had been easy. But Sheri? I can't feel anything but admiration and respect for her, even though she'd walked away. I miss her. Miss that I lost my chance with her. And what I detest is that I can't get her out of my mind.

I wish I'd never found that fucking book.

Though even if I could wind back the clock, I wouldn't change anything I'd done. Sheri deserved to be rescued. It's not her fault that it's her face I see when I close my eyes at night, and her body I think of when I'm in the shower.

Compared to the woman I'd once wanted to be my wife, Sheri had been a breath of fresh air. Timid for sure, but with a backbone of steel, brave, and looking out for others rather than herself. She'd put herself in danger to protect me, and no woman has ever done that for me before.

She'd been a virgin. Maybe that's another reason I can't get her out of my head. The sex was good, and could have been better, had we had time and a bed.

I'd claimed her as my old lady to get the Dominators to give her back. I'd claimed her for real, when I saw the woman she was, and hadn't wanted her to slip through my fingers.

In walking away, she'd cemented her strength, and I admire her for putting others first.

The Wretched Soulz aren't in the business of rescuing women, nor mopping up after the mess that someone else had spilled. If the cops had caught us at the scene, they'd have tried to pin the whole fuckup on my club. That's how they work. Wretched Soulz, Dominators, and tens of other most wanted outlaw clubs, are all lumped in together. The pigs wouldn't have cared which patch was on our backs. All that would have mattered was that we'd been found with dead bodies and abused females. We'd have been in the penitentiary with the key thrown away because what does the truth matter? Any outlaw biker is fair game as far as they're concerned.

I fucking hated her in that moment when she turned her back on all that we could have been. I'd even offered to have her ride on my bike, when I've only ever before had one other woman up behind me. She threw it all back in my face.

Well, fuck her. Or that's what I'd like to say. It's been a few days and I still can't stop thinking about the vivacious redhead I left behind.

And now it's church.

Being a nomad, I'm not usually regularly drawn into the formalities of running the club and attending regular meetings. I know I'd be better able to move on if I could get back on the road. What I need is some wind therapy to wipe all the might-have-beens from my mind. But I'm still stuck here while Chaz has the ongoing problem to solve. All in all, I'm not currently a happy man.

Iron walks around the table and takes his seat to the right of Chaz, while I skulk to my lowly place at the opposite end, congregating with the non-officer members. Clasping my hands on the table, I avert my eyes to avoid being drawn into conversation. Even so, I remain conscious of Bull seating himself on the other side of the prez, then Beard, as treasurer, sitting down next to him. Claw's already in position, leaning back in his chair, speaking to Skunk a few seats down. Weasel and Legend join the rest of the officers, while Fire, Pothead and Legit take their places at my end of the table.

The door opens again and in walks Slugger. Chaz shoots him a look, then shuffles his chair over to make space. Iron stands, pulls up a spare seat and places it beside Chaz. Then we wait again while Slugger makes himself comfortable.

Chaz bangs the gavel.

It's our first proper sit-down since we came back from rescuing the girls, so I'm not surprised that that's what Chaz kicks off with.

"What's the fallout from the raid?"

It's Legend who responds. "From the police reports and identification of the bodies, it was the prospect, Handle, who was with Knuckles. They both got away clean." He jerks his chin toward Skunk.

Skunk, looking sheepish, takes over. "They took a shortcut and lost us as they knew the ground."

"Yeah, sorry, Prez." Pothead looks equally disappointed.

Prez just stares as though he's recalculating in his head. "We've two witnesses who knew that the Wretched Soulz were involved."

Slugger sits forward. "I've got my ear to the ground. Not sure whether Knuckles was running his own operation, or whether it was part of a larger network. So far, there's been no chatter about half of one of their chapters being taken out."

"You think Knuckles might have gone rogue?"

Slugger shakes his head. "It's a hope, but I haven't stayed alive this long by being optimistic. We act as if we've taken the whole fuckin' Dominators on and prepare for retaliation."

"Won't make much difference." Bull snorts. "The relationship between our clubs couldn't be much worse."

Now Slugger's head changes direction, this time moving up, then down. Then, his eyes focus on me. "It's him I'm most worried about."

Me? I frown.

Prez nods as if this isn't news to him. "Yeah. If they go after anyone, it will be StoryTeller, which is why we've got you this, Brother."

A brand-new leather vest, styled like the one I used to own, is sent down the table toward me. I turn it over. Frowning, I ask, "You run out of nomad patches? I don't mind waiting, Prez." The look in his eyes tells me this is no mistake. I groan. "You can't fuckin' mean this?"

Prez shrugs. "Under the circumstances, we reckon it would be best to keep you close to home." His voice drops an octave. "Put the damn thing on, ST."

I stare at the offending object, then stand, my chair rattling with the force that I used to get to my feet. Angrily, I slip into my new cut, feeling the unfamiliar stiffness of the untried leather. But it's not that that bothers me so much as the fucking rocker that's replaced my nomad patch. Now I've one that firmly states I'm a member of the Arizona club.

"Not what you wanted," Prez acknowledges. "But it's safe to assume you'll have a target on your back."

The VP backs him up. "Safest to stay where your brothers have your six."

"What do you know?" Fire calls out. "You might even find you like us."

I shoot him the finger, knowing this really isn't what I wanted, but understanding they've got my interest at heart. They just better sort out a new mattress and better fucking digs.

Me? A permanent fixture of the club?

Legend sends a wary glance my way, but I give a slight shake of my head to show I won't be kicking off against my new status. I'd be a fool to think I'd be safe out on the road. Knuckles knew I was a Wretched Soulz nomad, but he didn't know what chapter I was affiliated with. Staying close to home will be the safest. But fuck, it isn't what I want.

Prez moves on. "What's the latest on the women?"

Legend clears his throat. "The cops picked them up and took them to the hospital to get them checked out. Once they were registered, I was able to check into their backgrounds. Carole was a hooker taken off the streets. Seems she went straight back there."

That doesn't surprise me. She'd seemed better able to cope, probably as she already knew the worst that men could do.

"Angie and Leah..." Legend continues. "Were apparently good girls snatched one way or another. They're back with their parents."

And hopefully getting therapy. Tons of it.

"They need anything?" As it's Beard who asks and he's our treasurer, he'll be thinking of financial support.

Legend shakes his head. "They come from good families who don't seem to be hurting."

A spark of anger goes through me, remembering that Sheri had walked away thinking we didn't give a damn about the women we'd rescued. We do care, as Legend's checking up shows.

"Kelly?" I ask, remembering the final name.

Legend brushes a hand over his face, and he grimaces. "Not good, Bro." When his eyes meet mine, I can tell by his expression, her story won't have a happy ending. I raise a brow to encourage him to continue anyway. He obliges. "She checked herself out of the hospital, went home, and overdosed on painkillers."

Motherfucker! Standing, I walk to the wall and smash my fist into it.

What if I hadn't found that book? What if I hadn't followed up on tracing who owned it? Sheri might have ended up the same way as Kelly, dead, either through her own actions or because someone had killed her for pleasure. Who the fuck thinks they can take people, toy with them, use them, sell them, when they are living breathing creatures with their own desires and emotions? Damn Knuckles to hell and everyone like him.

"It's not your fault, ST." Legit stands and puts his hand on my shoulder, not reacting when my flinch shakes him off.

"I want Knuckles dead."

Slugger barks a laugh. "You're not fuckin' alone in that."

"Keep an eye out for him, Legend, yeah?" Prez suggests. Then to me, he adds, "We're not going out hunting, but I don't mind nabbing him if he comes close. Until then, we've got far greater fish we need to fry."

"What about Sheri?" Slugger asks while shooting me a look.

Legend shrugs. "Back home from what we can tell."

So she's getting on with her life while ignoring the fucking huge hole she left in mine.

"One interesting thing," Legend drawls lazily, but deceptively so that he catches my interest. "I got into the hospital records. Cops followed the procedures, but Sheri? Well, she refused to comply. Specifically, she refused the rape kit."

Chaz breathes out but doesn't have to say anything.

I was a SEAL. My DNA is in a database. If Sheri hadn't thought of that, then I could have been arrested and all that she and the others had gone through would have been blamed on my club.

Perhaps she hadn't completely forgotten me.

Whatever, she'd come to my rescue once again.

CHAPTER SEVENTEEN
STORYTELLER

TWO MONTHS LATER…

Reluctantly, I've come to accept having a base in one club rather than being out roaming the roads. It wasn't an easy adjustment to make, but I tried not to take my changed status out on my brothers, having realised that Prez was right. Knuckles would be out for my blood. One sight of me and he'd shoot first.

Not that I'm in hiding. I'm in plain sight, but I have brothers around me and am not as vulnerable as I would have been out alone on the road.

I try to enjoy the positives—the new mattress and bed for a start—club women on tap. But while Brandy, CeCe and Brea are fun to be with, there is no emotional connection, which means going back more than a few times soon gets repetitive and boring. Even the town girls coming for our parties hold little appeal.

Strange really. Mindless sex had never bothered me in the past, but that was before I met Sheri.

Maybe it was because I'd just had her the once, and not in the most ideal of circumstances, but she's still fucking with my head. When I'm with a whore, it's her face my eyes see, her gasps which reach my ears, and her body my hands and dick feel. But they can never replicate her taste or soft skin, nor the thought that I'd been the first man to touch her.

And the first, and only, time in my life I'd gone ungloved. Maybe that was what had made it so special and why she's still haunting my mind. Whatever the reason, in the past eight weeks, no one else has measured up.

I'd offered to bring her into my life.

She'd not given me a chance.

But what did we know of each other? I knew her taste in books, that her body was enough to tempt me even after time had gone by, but I know nothing of her likes or dislikes. Like-wise, to her, I'm a total stranger.

I try to convince myself that parting as we had was for the best. A relationship between us wouldn't have worked. But it doesn't stop me thinking about her, nor, in the dead of the night, using the memories of her to fuel my hand fisting my cock.

The gun deliveries over the border on behalf of the cartel had gone without a hitch, thanks to my planning, the smoothing of many palms, and more than a little good luck. Prez had appreciated my input, his gratefulness being double sided, as it made him more determined he didn't want to part with me now.

Regaining that nomad patch doesn't seem likely.

I'm hunkering on the ground, fixing my bike, when Legend walks into the garage. I glance up when I see the motorcycle boots and recognise the owner.

"Yo, Bro." Pulling myself up, I take a rag out of my pocket and wipe my dirty hands on it. "What can I do for you?"

He hands me a tablet he's holding. I give a glance at his face, then look down. Squinting my eyes, I see a grainy figure on a motorcycle, but am hard pushed to make an identification. I pass it back, raising an eyebrow.

"Knuckles," he tells me. Then taps the picture. "And this photo was taken in Austin."

I take the tablet again, and this time with that key, am able to confirm. My blood heats as I recognise him. "So?" He's miles from here. By the time I was mounted up and riding, the chances are he'd be miles away. Anyway, Chaz had said, we weren't to go hunting. Now if I were still a nomad, I could take off if I want. But I'm not.

Legend widens his eyes. "You forgotten so quickly, Bro? Austin is where Sheri Secord comes from. It's her fuckin' hometown."

I still. That puts a different complexion on things. "You think—"

He cuts me off. "I think he can't get to you, so he's going after her. He would if he believed she was your ol' lady."

Pinching the brow of my nose, I grimace. "Austin's a fuckin' big place." It's a bit of a stretch to think he's just cruising around looking for her. And that's if it's even his intention.

Legend shrugs. "I found her, Bro. We might not think much of the Dominators, but they've got experts who can work with info just as well as I can."

Jesus. He's right. Or at least, I'd be wrong to dismiss the possibility. If Knuckles is still looking for me, then locating the woman he thinks is mine would certainly get my attention if she really were my old lady. Turning, I start to pace, the thought of Kelly coming into my mind, or the girl who slit her wrists even knowing rescue was imminent, what happened to them being so awful they'd preferred to have died. If Knuckles takes Sheri for a second time, he's not going to hold back.

Something warns me if he can't use her to get to me, he'll make her wish she was dead.

My hands clench as I realise I've no option. I wouldn't be able to live with myself if something happened to her. And if Knuckles is planning to get my attention, I could turn the tables on him, and put a bullet in his head.

"I'm going to Texas," I tell Legend.

He half smiles. "Thought you might. Think you ought to clear it with Prez first though."

I should. Unlike when I was a nomad and could make decisions for myself, I now have to get permission. Not for the first time, I resent having the charter rocker on my cut.

"Oh, and ST?" Halfway out the door, I swing around. "I've got Sheri's home address, but not much else. Don't know her phone number to track her."

I raise my chin. Sure, that's a start, and hopefully closer than Knuckles has got. The thought I might already be too late spurs me to move faster.

As I approach Prez's office, my gut rolls as questions I didn't ask Legend start revolving in my head. Like, how long has Knuckles been in Texas, could he have already found her? And what will I do if Chaz doesn't sanction me leaving at this time?

I knock at the door. After getting no response, I spy Bull and ask him if he knows where Prez is, getting the answer he's outside. I find him with his head stuck under the hood of his precious car.

Clearing my throat, I try to get his attention.

Seeing I'm there, he swings around. As I open my mouth, he holds up his hand. "Legend told me you'd be coming."

Well, Legend hadn't told me that. "He tell you why?"

Chaz dips his chin. Closing the hood, he leans up against the Mustang and folds his arms. "It's been two months, ST.

Can't believe you're still strung up on the girl. And Knuckles being in Austin might be a coincidence."

As his eyes bore into me intently, I scramble to get my thoughts into some kind of order. Shrugging, I try to brush off my interest. "Don't want Knuckles to get his fuckin' hands on any of the women again. I'm worried he might be targeting her."

Equally offhandedly, Chaz responds, "If she's fool enough to let herself be taken for a second time, then that's on her head. That's if, she means nothing to you, ST." Suddenly he swings around, his laser sharp eyes piercing into me.

My mouth opens and shuts. The lie that Sheri means no more than any other bitch I've ever been with can't escape through my teeth. Even knowing Chaz will take advantage and mock the hell out of me, I decide to tell him the truth.

"She got to me." Placing my hand over my heart, I show him how. "Fuck knows why. I know nothing about her." Shaking my head, I let him know how much even I don't understand it.

"You fell for a woman once before, ST." He frowns. "And what a shitstorm that was. Cost us a brother and sent you out on the road."

Chastised, I look down at my feet. "Fi betrayed me just as much as Custer."

"Yeah, she did." He brushes back his hair from his face. "But whether she encouraged him or not, Custer shouldn't have gone there. That's why I had your back." He sighs heavily. "Don't want you bringing another bitch in to cause trouble."

"Sheri won't," I tell him fast. "She's not like that."

He raises a brow and scoffs. "You only knew her for five minutes."

"Yeah." I snort. "And what a five minutes they were. She had my back, Prez. She was willing to take a bullet for me."

"But she didn't choose you. She stayed with the rest of the bitches." Again, his hand brushes over his temples. "I was fuckin' there, ST. I heard you offer to have her on the back of your bike."

"And can you fuckin' blame her? At that point, all she saw was my cut—"

"Or not your cut, as by then you'd lost it."

My hands fist at the reminder, but I shrug the insult off. "She was scared, Prez. Acted out of instinct." Having thought about it over the past few weeks, I wondered who could blame her. Rumours abound about how women are treated in motorcycle clubs, and Knuckles hadn't done anything to reassure her.

"Fuck it, ST. You go running to Texas, she might not even give you the time of day. She could call the cops on you—"

"She refused the rape kit,"

Chaz rests his boot lightly on the car's bumper and leans on his knee. "Women, fuck, men as well, can let things fester. 'Specially when traumatic events occur. Time and distance may not have made her heart fonder. ST, we all know what you did to her, we fuckin' heard it. She might hate your guts."

"Don't you think I feel fuckin' guilty about that?" I snarl. "It's not an excuse that it was me or them, I did that to her. I took that one thing she could never get back."

Chaz raises his head, puts his foot back on the floor, takes a step forward and gets into my space. "And there we fuckin' have it. You feel guilty and think you need to save her again."

"Maybe that's it. Maybe it's more basic and I just want a chance to have another taste of her. Or maybe she's the woman I want in my life."

He grins at my outburst. "Honesty at last. After what happened with Custer, I didn't expect you to want to get close to a woman again."

"Neither did I," I admit freely. "But she's different, Prez. And if nothing else, I owe her my life."

"And then there's Knuckles." Again, his eyes pierce me. "You can't tell me you don't want your chance with him."

If I said I didn't, that would be a lie. "I want him in the ground." At the very least, he's got the deaths of two women on his conscience. Or should have if he wasn't a murdering-women-trafficking motherfucker. The expression on Chaz's face worries me. *If he tries to stop me from going...*

"I'm going to go, Prez. Just prefer it to be with your blessing."

He stills, his face hardening. "Might have been better if you hadn't admitted that."

I stand my ground stubbornly.

"You prepared to give up your patch? As that's kind of where you're going with that statement."

Give up my patch? He might as well ask me to give up breathing. "Fuck no."

The bastard laughs. "Then it's a good thing that I've already contacted Strider. Legend's got you on the afternoon flight to Austin, and Strider's agreed to let you have one of his loaner bikes. He'll have it waiting for you at the airport."

"You motherfucker," I tell him, as relief sweeps through me. All this grilling and he'd already had my back. I'm surprised at the lengths Chaz has already gone to, contacting the prez of the Austin chapter for a start.

Greeting my insult with just a grin, he continues, "Strider's happy enough to have your back if you get the opportunity to take Knuckles down."

Well that sounds like a fucking plan. I raise my fist and bump it to his.

CHAPTER EIGHTEEN
STORYTELLER

The timing of the flight means I have little time to prepare. I run to my room, throw a few belongings into a rucksack then get Shitface to give me a lift to the airport.

I go through the formalities, get on a plane, and am soon in the air. It's only a two-hour flight for a journey that would take me over fourteen hours if I were to ride. Not that the miles would put me off doing it, but I feel a sense of urgency. I don't like the feeling that the Dominators and Sheri are in the same town, however big a city it is.

If Legend can find her address, there's no pretending that Knuckles can't. I couldn't afford to waste any time.

With only a rucksack, I don't have to wait for my luggage to arrive, so am soon outside the terminal. First thing I do is to put on my cut, and quickly notice there's a man I don't recognise who's wearing colours the same as mine.

It's the signal I'm waiting for, and I head straight for him.

We might not have met each other before, but we're part of the same tribe. Back slaps and man hugs are obligatory. I light a smoke as he finishes his and follow him to where a bike's just been wheeled down off a trailer.

"What the fuck is that?" My eyes widen as I view the green monstrosity.

The man, usefully wearing a name badge which denotes he's called *Shout*, gives a snort. "We kind of acquired this in lieu of a debt," he tells me, with a glint in his eyes that doesn't give me warm feelings about what happened to the previous owner. "You wanted a loaner, this is about all we got."

Beggars can't be choosers. Although I'd prefer to have an American steel horse, I won't turn my nose up at anything with two wheels and an engine. I take the key he's holding out to me with sufficient grace and thank him.

"You want to follow me to the clubhouse?" he asks when I finish checking it out and putting the shit I brought with me into the saddlebags.

"Nah, Shout. I got somewhere I need to be. I know where the clubhouse is. I'll catch you there later."

"Sure thing, Bro." He slaps my back. I slap his and add my thanks for him coming to drop off the wannabe motorcycle, then he gets back into the cage and drives off.

Starting the engine which purrs rather than roars, I click on my phone and begin to listen to the tinny instructions being sent through my Bluetooth earplugs and begin to navigate the unfamiliar streets of Austin. Of course, I've hit it at rush hour, and even the benefit of being on two wheels and not four doesn't prove to be of much assistance.

Eventually I'm out of the traffic and heading into the suburbs. The sat nav takes me to an area that I feel slightly dubious about. I stop at the apartment block when the GPS tells me I've arrived. I sit on the bike, examining my surroundings. *Sheri lives here?* For a moment, I wonder, or maybe hope, that Legend has got it wrong. Though looking around I see no discarded drug paraphernalia, so perhaps it's not as bad as I first thought.

It does remind me, I know little about her.

I dismount and arm the alarm on the bike, not wanting to omit security in this neighbourhood. Then I go inside and take the stairs to the second floor. Checking the number, I knock at the door.

It's opened cautiously. I note the flimsy chain that I could break easily, and also that the person who's answered isn't the woman I want.

"Is Sheri here?"

"No," is the blunt answer.

Okay then. I swallow down my frustration. "Can you tell me where she is?" She might be at work, at a friend's...

I get an unfriendly response. "Why should I?"

Fair enough. I'm a stranger, and possibly not a very savoury looking one, with my long hair, tattoos, and that I'm wearing a cut. Belatedly I wonder whether I should have removed it.

"I'm a friend," I tell her, then, in the off chance Sheri might have mentioned me, I add, "My name is StoryTeller, and it's important I find her."

"I'm her housemate, not her keeper. I've no idea where she is."

It's like pulling teeth and I'm getting nowhere. "Any idea when she might be back?"

"No."

From the closed look, she's going to tell me nothing. And indeed, before I can ask anything else, the door is slammed in my face.

Frustrated, I bang my palm against the wall, then retrace my steps down the stairs. At the bottom, I call Legend.

"She's not at home," I tell him as soon as he answers. "You got any other info you can dig up? Where she works, perhaps?"

After asking me to hold on a moment, he comes back on the line with information. "Looks like she's got family close by. They might be able to tell you more. I'll text you the details."

Hopefully family might be more forthcoming than the housemate.

The traffic's clearing a little now as we're heading into the evening.

I pull up and park just past the property that I want and decide it might be expedient not to wear my cut. I fold it carefully and place it in the saddlebags, and for good measure, make sure it's securely locked away.

After loosening then retying my hair to neaten it up, I approach the front door.

I lean on the doorbell for a few seconds, trying to summon up words to say to the woman I haven't seen in two months. Should I start by explaining I'm here as she could be in danger, or do I keep that tidbit to myself?

Footsteps sound long before I'm prepared to face her. I glance at the door in expectation but when it opens, it's not the person I want, but someone far older.

"Can I help you?" the woman asks disdainfully, eyeing my jeans and t-shirt with obvious disgust.

"Who is it?" a man's voice calls from somewhere deep in the depths of the house.

"I'm here to see Sheri Secord," I get in fast before I can be dismissed as someone asking for a handout. "I'm a friend of hers."

"That figures," she says in a nasal tone. "She's not here." She starts closing the door.

Expecting the move, I have my steel-toe capped boot already positioned to wedge it open. "Do you know where I can find her?"

"Who is it?" the male voice calls again.

"Some good-for-nothing asking about Sheri."

Heavier footsteps now sound, and a man appears behind what is presumably his wife. He gives me just as contemptuous look as her. "What business have you with my daughter?"

"I'm a friend." A friend who's fucking worried about her. If she's out walking around, there's a chance Knuckles could get to her. "Just tell me where I can find her."

He shrugs. "We've no idea. Just told her to go get her problem sorted and not to come back before it is."

"It's damn inconvenient," the woman says. "I'll deal with this, Ted."

Obediently the man walks away, and I'm left with the woman who's glaring at me. "Is this your fuckin' fault?"

I feel like I'm falling down a rabbit hole and need to get some control back. "I don't know what the fuck you're talking about. I haven't seen Sheri for weeks. Now will you tell me where she is?"

"I don't care where she's gone as long as she gets it sorted. Sheri's a selfish brat, always has been."

My eyes narrow. Someone selfish doesn't give everything up for strangers, nor puts herself in line for a bullet. I'm quickly not liking this woman or the man I believe is Sheri's dad.

A growl comes to my throat. "Where's she gone?"

My menacing tone seems to get through to her as she steps back to put space between us. "Out of state, somewhere, anywhere, where she can get rid of the kid. She came here asking for help. I told her she couldn't come back until she got it fixed."

"Kid? What kid?"

She shakes her head as if I'm stupid. "She's pregnant."

My hand slams against the doorjamb. For a moment, I need support. Visions quickly go through my mind of how good it felt to come inside her ungloved. I knew at the time there could have been consequences but had thought the odds were on my side. Now I realise they weren't, and unless Sheri got a taste for sex and went with someone else after me, she's likely to be carrying my child.

Jesus. It's hard to keep a myriad of expressions coming to my face. Once I saw myself with a wife and a child, but betrayal and cheating had soon cured me of it. I'm a nomad at heart, a man who likes moving around all the time. How could I be tied down?

I doubt Sheri's any happier about it.

What a fucked-up situation this is. We didn't give in to passion. We didn't forget to take care. Both of us are totally blameless. Just another thing to be laid at Knuckles' door.

Sheri doesn't know I'm here. She doesn't know how to find me. I could disappear, leave fate to play out as it will, could go back to Arizona and continue my life as a single, unburdened man.

It takes one split second for me to think of running away and an equal time for me to dismiss it. Even if Knuckles isn't trying to get his hands on her, there's no way I could leave Sheri right now.

She must be in pieces.

Especially at it appears she's got no support. This woman, who I suspect is her mother, has sent her away to get rid of it. Maybe that would have been my go-to response were it not for the callous way she's talking about it. *Get the problem sorted.* Like there's no emotion involved.

If I know anything about Sheri, she'll be tied up in knots. It's her body, her baby, her life. Neither I, nor this woman, have anything to do with it.

It doesn't matter if I'm reeling with shock. Now's not the time to consider how I'm dealing with it. It's Sheri who needs my help, now more than ever. And Knuckles? Heaven help him if he hurts the woman bearing my child.

I see red. Moving forward fast, I push her against the wall and wrap my hand around her throat. "When did she go?"

Her face is turning blue, so I ease off to allow her to speak. "Earlier this morning."

"You got her phone number?"

A shaking hand reaches into her pocket and pulls out her cell. After getting her to unlock it, I snatch it, call up the contacts, and send her number to myself.

Scowling, giving the phone back and regretting I don't stoop to hitting women, I race to my bike, only pausing a moment to send Legend a text.

With her number, he can hopefully track where she is.

And while he's doing that, my best bet is to get to the airport.

"Hey!" Cut back on, I'm just about to start my engine when a woman comes running out of the house. Someone who looks like a younger version of the one I was speaking to just now. "You want to know about my stepsister?"

If she's talking about Sheri, I do. I again dismount and wait for her to come close to me. The introduction sounds right. This woman doesn't resemble Sheri at all. She's made up to the nines as if she was just going to go out.

I expect her to stop a distance away, but instead, she invades my space, almost pressing her body against mine as she says, "You don't want to waste time looking for Sheri. Why don't we get to know each other instead?" Her hand even comes up to cup my cheek.

I wrench it away, her touch feeling like bugs crawling over my skin.

"The fuck you saying?"

"Come with me," she purrs. "I know how to give men like you a good time."

I've a sneaking suspicion it's not me she wants, but she wants to keep me away from finding her sister. I think I've got the answer why Sheri prefers to live in a scruffy apartment rather than here with her folks.

"I can get a good time with a woman like you anywhere," I tell her, a sneer on my face as I mentally compare her to the club whores we have back home. "Now get out of my way so I can find a woman worth finding."

Her face reddens, and her eyes blaze. "You're making a mistake."

Ignoring her, I swing my leg over the bike, start the engine, and leave her in the wake of my exhaust.

CHAPTER NINETEEN
SHERI

Looking back, it's stupid how I didn't connect the dots, let alone read the signs, but then picking up the threads of my normal life hadn't been easy after what I'd been through. It had taken me a long time to get anywhere close to regaining my equilibrium after coming back home following my ordeal.

Agatha had tried to talk to me, to find out the details of what had happened, but I gave her the bare bones, just like I told everyone else. I was abducted, kept captive for a couple of days, and then miraculously released.

My dad and stepmom had professed their fake concern for me, even offering to have me stay for a few days. But I refrained, knowing it was only so my stepmom and stepsister could get mileage out of gossiping at my expense.

I couldn't afford therapy, so suffered my nightmares during the hours of darkness and tried to pull up my own socks during the days. If at times a bout of uncontrollable crying comes over me, I just take myself away and deal with it. There's no point in complaining about what had happened. I force myself to remember that the women with me had had it far worse.

When it gets too much to bear, I try to picture StoryTeller, sometimes wondering if I'd conjured him up out of my mind. I'd dreamed of a biker riding in to rescue me, which is exactly what had happened. The fantastical element so unbelievable I kept it to myself, treasuring the memories, thinking no one would believe them. What would a handsome biker want with a nobody like me?

The book? Well, that stays by the side of my bed. If I find it comforting that it had been in his hands, I keep that to myself.

I could have gone with him. But I did not.

Looking back, I don't regret making the decision that I had. Okay, so a fictional biker might have forsaken all others and taken me as his old lady for life, but the Wretched Soulz aren't a club summoned up from the mind of an author, and there's no happily ever after. Best he lives on in my dreams as there he can be the man I want him to be, one who has eyes only for me.

Just coping with my daily life has been enough. Firstly, I had to plead to get my job back after being absent without leave. Getting out of the apartment was a chore in itself. I flinched at every strange man I saw approaching me. For the first few weeks, I didn't venture out except to go to work. And even that space wasn't safe enough. I freaked when I needed to serve a table of men who'd walked in carrying motorcycle helmets, refused to take their order and hid out the back. I was fired.

Agatha came close to asking me to leave, but I assured her I had a small cushion in savings to tide me over until I found new employment. While I was still making rent, I could stay.

When I missed a period, I wasn't surprised, putting it down to stress. When I missed the second, I still wasn't worried. It hadn't been until my breasts started to feel tender that I put two and two together, then yesterday bought a pregnancy test which provided the confirmation.

"What the fuck is this?" Agatha had spotted the empty box in the bin. "You're pregnant?" She looked incredulous. She knew even before my kidnapping my social life was non-existent.

What could I do but admit the truth and say yes.

Her eyes had narrowed at me. "You said you weren't raped."

I nodded as that was the truth and what I had told her when I had gotten home. "I wasn't."

"So what the fuck was it then? You gave it away?" Agatha's hands landed on her hips. "You come back here with stories about how you were held captive and abused. Yet here you are pregnant, yet apparently not forced."

There was nothing I could say. I hadn't told anyone the whole story, about the man who rescued me, and definitely not about what I'd been forced to do in front of the other captives and my abductors. I hadn't come to terms with that myself, so how could I admit it to anyone else?

"It was all made up, wasn't it?" Agatha's face darkened. "You went off for a weekend with a man. Maybe it didn't work out, maybe you got more than you bargained for. Maybe you were even involved in some kinky kidnapping plan, then concocted a story to play on my sympathy when it all went wrong."

My mouth had dropped open at her accusation. It was so far from the truth. But still I was loathe to give her another explanation.

I might have been staying quiet, but Agatha hadn't finished. "You can't get a job. Your condition," she waved at my stomach, "won't help with that. I need to get someone else in to help me make rent."

It took a second to process what she was saying. "You're kicking me out?"

"You've got parents. Go get them to help you."

Not parents, just a dad and a stepmom who hated me.

I didn't have a choice. I couldn't blame Agatha for making sure she had someone staying with her who could pay half the rent, and with my dwindling savings, I wouldn't be able to do that for long. Add in my apparent new circumstance and well, I'm devastated and scared. Now I not only need a job to support myself but also a child.

I think I was in some sort of trance, shock perhaps, since seeing the appearance of those two telltale lines. Instead of thinking it through, I acted like a child and ran to my dad.

I caught him alone, threw myself at him and cried. He'd been stunned, but had hugged me, telling me everything would be alright.

Until my stepmom had returned from her shopping trip. A short conference between them and suddenly my previously pro-life father was telling me I needed to take care of my problem. He'd stuffed some money in my hand and told me to go and not return until I'd rectified matters.

Which is why I'm now at the airport, wondering where I should go. Or rather, I'm sitting outside it, not even knowing where to start.

I discard one tissue in the convenient bin next to my seat and take another from the pack, seeing I'm fast running out. My thoughts are a complete jumble, and I can't focus on any plan. The one certainty is I can't go home. Or only after I've done what my sperm donor wants.

It's getting harder and harder to think of him as my father. While my mom was alive, he seemed a good enough sort. Quiet, of necessity as my mother was the backbone of the house. How he's changed since Mom died and Charmaine entered our lives.

This morning had been such a whirlwind, I'm not sure which way is up. I'm not even sure why I'd driven to the airport except for perhaps I needed some direction once I'd gotten into my car.

I've barely had a chance to process I'm pregnant.

Now, with the background noise of planes taking off and landing, I'm taking some time to myself.

I am pregnant, with the baby of a man I've only met once in my life, and that was under the most horrific circumstances. A man who I walked away from, because he represented everything that was wrong with the world, even though he'd rocked mine during that short period of time.

He hadn't made me feel worthless. For those brief hours, it was as if I'd mattered. It's probably only my imagination, but for once, it was as if someone had seen me.

He'd offered me a chance of escape, a chance to be with him. I'd turned him down as he was the same as the Dominators who'd taken me—an outlaw who surely couldn't be trusted to keep his word. He'd have used me, then I'd have been discarded once he'd really gotten to know the real boring person I am inside.

I'd been scared to take a chance. He'd been pressuring me to leave with him, and at the time, it was easier to stay with the women to whom I could relate, the ones who'd been captured with me.

My mind goes back to that hour or so after the bikers had gone. We'd hidden, all scared out of our minds. The rumbling of engines hadn't brought relief as we'd assumed it was Knuckles bringing more Dominators back. It was only when the fire truck had arrived and we saw the flashing lights of the police car, that Carole and I had stood and revealed ourselves.

After that, it was all a blur. The medics soon had us in the hospital where I suffered the ignominy of being prodded, poked and questioned.

The cops had gotten me back to Texas, taking me straight

to my parents' home. My dad had seemed relieved to see me, but my stepmom had berated me about causing them worry and refused to believe anything other than I'd been careless to get myself kidnapped.

"Sheri."

I might not have heard it for two months, but I still recognise that deep tone, almost a purr as he says my name. Swinging around, I shade my eyes from the glare of the setting sun, unable to believe that it's not my mind summoning up a fantasy. But unless my sight is deceiving me, StoryTeller is really here.

I open and shut my mouth, not sure what to say. Questions like how the hell did he find me, go through my head.

Without being invited, he sits beside me. Even though there's not a part of us touching, I swear I can feel the warmth from his body. Familiar scents that I remember from before wash over me. I don't know why it is that I immediately feel comforted, and not so alone. Which is crazy.

When I'd first seen the lines on the pregnancy test, my first thought hadn't been to contact him. How would I have known where to start? All I knew was his road name, and that he was a member of the dreaded Wretched Soulz. I didn't know where he lived, was based, or where he'd come from.

And he knew even less about me.

As the sun beats down, dappled light flickering through the overhead trees, neither of us seem to want to start a conversation. On my part, how do you tell a man you've only met once that you're carrying his baby? I suspect he'll run a mile as soon as he knows, and I selfishly want to enjoy his presence just a while longer.

Eventually, though, I can contain myself no longer, and have to ask, "Is this a coincidence? You seeing me here?" It has to be. I can think of no other reason.

He chuckles softly. "No. I knew exactly where to find you." He glances over his shoulder at the terminal behind. "You waiting on catching a plane?"

In truth, I don't know what I'm doing. "I could be waiting on someone to arrive."

"Yet you're not," he contradicts, confidently.

I shoot a quick glance at him, wondering whether he's a mind reader. My hand has the urge to rest on my stomach, I make a conscious effort to keep it away. *Has he a right to know about the baby?*

The only responsibility he has was that he provided the semen that got to my egg. He'd done the deed under duress. He'd probably have not willingly wanted to touch me had he not been forced. So why should he be lumbered with my problem when it couldn't be described as his fault?

Knuckles wouldn't have let him stop to put on a condom.

My mind veers between thinking how much I should tell him and questioning why he's suddenly appeared. The statement he knew exactly where to find me suddenly echoes in my head.

"How did you know I was here? And why did you bother to come find me?" My eyes narrow, particularly as his body movements show he's intent on remaining sat next to me on the bench.

I shift along an inch, making sure nothing of our bodies is touching.

StoryTeller's lost none of his appeal over the intervening weeks. He's like an apparition from one of the books that I read, miraculously come to life as though he's just stepped straight from the pages. He's so goddamn handsome I can barely imagine the words an author could use to adequately describe him.

Me? Well, I'm the non-descript girl who fantasises about

having such a man look at her once, let alone twice. So why he's actively seeking me out is a mystery.

I didn't fail to notice the sideways glance that he gave me as I moved away, nor the strange look of uncertainty that crossed his face. Is he regretting what must have been an impulsive decision to come say hi? After all these weeks, I'm certainly not sure what he'd have to talk to me about.

He clears his throat. "I went by your house."

I startle as his statement suggests he was actively looking for me. But that wouldn't have led him here.

"Agatha didn't know where I was going," I blurt out. I hadn't known myself. Not until I'd driven around and found myself at my parents' house.

"She didn't. So I went to your parents' instead."

Overlooking how he could have discovered either address, I let my head drop into my hands. "You spoke to my stepmother?" Rubbing frantically at my temples which have started to pound, I worry just what he could have been told.

"Yeah," he admits. He shakes his head. I catch the movement out of the side of my eye. "I also met your stepsister. She's a piece of work, isn't she?"

I intake a breath sharply. Normally men fall at her feet. There are not many that see straight through her. She's beautiful, slim, and everything that I'm not. Perhaps StoryTeller isn't so shallow as to not look further than what's on the outside.

I ask what matters to me most. "What did they tell you?"

Now it's his turn to rub at his forehead. "The reason why you're sitting outside the airport, wondering what the fuck to do next."

Suddenly I understand what a deflated balloon feels like as my bones turn to jelly, and I fold in on myself. "It's got nothing to do with you." Though I try to be forceful, my voice sounds tremulous.

"Like fuck it doesn't," he says under his breath, but loud enough for me to hear. He moves his body so he's facing me, and one of his hands reaches up, gently touches my face, and gently forces me to look at him. "If it wasn't for me, you wouldn't be in this position."

"If it wasn't for you, I'd probably be dead." Or wishing I was. I shudder at the memory which still has the power to give me nightmares most nights.

"Look," he starts, his voice gentling. "You don't need to be dealing with this on your own." I go to open my mouth, to say any decision is mine, but he stops me by placing his fingers over my mouth. "Let me say my part, yeah?" After a second, I incline my head before raising it again. "What's happened wasn't planned, hoped or wished for. But if it wasn't for me, you wouldn't be in this spot. I'm not the person who'll have to cope with the outcome and carry this burden for the next," he does a quick calculation, "seven months."

I don't correct him to the accurate six and a half, and just say, "And eighteen years after."

"Unless you go for adoption." His face is unreadable as he offers the option. Then his eyes crease and a faraway look appears. "Or I take the kid and bring it up."

That gets me looking at him sharply. "You want this baby?"

He shrugs. "I've known about it for an hour or so. Hell, Sheri, I don't know what I fuckin' want. There are options, that's all."

I've not known about it for very much longer.

Suddenly his hand is on mine, squeezing my fingers gently. "Whatever you want, Sheri, I'll be beside you." He swallows, then offers, "You want to deal with it, I'll help you. You want to keep it? I'll support you in whatever you decide."

That would be simple enough. He's not the only one to not know their mind.

It's then he notices what I'm holding in my other hand. He prises it open, taking the notes out of my fingers and counts them rapidly.

"A thousand dollars?" He snorts. "That's all you got?"

"It's what my father gave me," I explain. I choke. It's not enough for anything and I know it. Maybe an airline ticket to get out of Texas, but there won't be much left for anything else.

When he swears violently and says something decidedly uncomplimentary about my folks, I'm not inclined to correct him.

CHAPTER TWENTY
STORYTELLER

The moment I saw Sheri with that luscious cascade of red hair flowing down her back, my cock had shown a natural interest that I'd needed to force with the whores. It seems I hadn't built her up in my imagination over the past couple of months. She appeals to me just as much as when I'd first seen her.

Standing back, I took the chance to examine her while she was oblivious to my presence. Two months ago, I wanted her enough to call her my old lady. What do I feel now? Leaving aside the fact that it appears that she's carrying my child, do I still want her as much? Was I influenced by the emotion that she saved my life? Now with a clearer head, was I seeing her any differently?

The answer was a resounding no. Here, on neutral turf, not held captive at another man's whim, Sheri's even more than I thought when I'd first seen her.

I'm eyeing the pitiful amount of money her father had given to her and I'm overwhelmed with disgust at how her family treats her.

I'm not poor. Sure, not all I own has been made legitimately, but that doesn't bother me. I've more than enough to get her situation resolved if that's what she wants, or, conversely, enough to support both her and a baby.

A baby.

Once upon a time, I thought about having a family, but those dreams died when I walked in and found Custer with Fi. A lucky escape, maybe. I'm not sure how a kid would fit in with my lifestyle.

I clasp my hands between my knees and gaze out without really seeing. Around us people are bustling around, some coming, some going, very few standing still. Reaching into my cut, I take out my cigarettes and tap one into my hand. Without thinking, I idly offer one to the woman at my side who scoffs and turns away.

"Sorry, didn't think. Do you mind?"

She shakes her head as though in the scheme of things a little smoke is nothing. Nevertheless, lighting up, I stand, and make sure I'm downwind.

I'd like to say the nicotine hit clears my mind, but it's no help at all. After a few more drags, I stub the damn thing out and throw the end in the container that's nearby. Returning to Sheri, I sink to my haunches and take both of her hands in mine.

"When did you find out?"

"This morning."

Taking a deep breath, I sigh. "That's no time to make any decision. What d'you say you come with me, we'll get something to eat, then find somewhere for our heads to lie tonight." If she thinks that means I'm going to be taking her to an anonymous hotel, well, I haven't actually told an untruth. I know the general location, just not the room they'll be putting us in. I've got the feeling that if I tell her outright, I'm taking her to the Austin Wretched Soulz' compound, she'll refuse to go. It's probably not one of my best ideas, I've been there before, and it's not for the faint-hearted nor the uninitiated. I have a feeling one step inside is going to make her want to run a mile in the other direction. But I can't ignore that Knuckles is somewhere hanging around, and I need brothers around me if I'm going to protect her.

"I don't want to go home."

And that's the last place I want to take her, having met both her housemate and her stepmom.

"Come on." I stand, offering her my hand.

She stares up at me. "Where are we going?"

"To eat."

She doesn't stand nor make any move to leave. "This is my problem, not yours."

I breathe deeply, trying to keep my patience. "When will you get it into your head that I'm involved as much as you? You didn't impregnate yourself."

"I may have gone with someone else—"

I snort. "No way."

"You saying the sex with you was too good for me to get it anywhere else?" she challenges. "Maybe you got me hooked and I wanted more. Or," her eyes spark, "I wanted to see what a real man was like."

A guffaw bursts out of me. I love this woman's spirit, and how she's not afraid to take me down a peg. "Seriously, babe, you didn't get all my best moves under the circumstances, but I'm happy to give you another demonstration if that's what you want." I wink at her, realising what I'm passing over as jest is actually my end goal. I let the amusement slide off my face. "Babe, you went through a traumatic experience. I doubt you'd have jumped into bed with anyone else."

"Only 'cause no one would want me." I have to strain my ears to hear her words.

"What the fuck?" This time I brook no argument and pull her to her feet, forcing her to stand in front of me. "What the fuck are you saying, Sheri?"

She tries to pull loose, but I hold her hands tight. A growl gets her throwing out, "You've seen Agatha and my stepsister..."

"Stop it," I instruct sharply. "Sure, I've seen them. What of it? It's you that I fuckin' like." And that's the truth of it. Since I met her, nobody else has caught my eye. Sex with the sweet butts has left me unimpressed.

This time she manages to pull her hands free. Once she does, she places them on her hips. "Why are you even here anyway?"

Fuck. With all the drama about finding her pregnant, I'd put the reason I came to find her to the back of my mind. As I rake my hands through my hair, I wonder how to tell her. What if the shock scares her too much? Is it too early for it to hurt the baby inside? Is there some way I can protect her without admitting she's in danger?

My eyes flick to the left as I respond. "No particular reason. I was in Texas—"

"Bullshit." Again, there's challenge in her eyes.

My mouth quirks with the ease at which she calls me out. Under her intense stare, I guess nothing but the truth is going to work. But when I try to form the words, I realise I don't want to frighten her. A strange thought enters my head, and I half-turn to try to talk some sense into myself.

That doesn't work. Fate seems to have wound its fingers around me, bringing me to this time and place. *I'm at the fuckin' airport.* My unpacked bag is still on the back of my borrowed bike.

My mind is filled with the phrases I need to formulate my lie. When I turn back, I'm wondering how to say something that will convince me as much as her.

"Come back to Arizona with me."

"Arizona?" Her eyes crease.

I realise she might not have noticed the patch on my back, so I turn so she can see it, then give a verbal explanation as I turn back. "I was nomad, but I'm now based at my home chapter."

Now her eyes have opened wide. "You want me to go to Arizona with you?"

"Why not?" I challenge her. "From what I've seen, you've not got a lot here."

"Because I'm pregnant with your baby?" She stares, then gives a shake of her head. "I don't even know what I'm going to do."

"I said, the decision is up to you, but I've got a responsibility to support you while you're making it."

"This is ridiculous." She throws up her hands. "I don't know you. And, you're a biker."

On both counts, she's not wrong. But I can't leave her here where Knuckles could get his hands on her, especially not now. My conscience, such as it is, won't let me.

My initial words haven't worked, and I'm not sure how else I can verbally convince her. As I drag my hair loose from its tie, then restrain it once more, I have a flashback to when we were held in that fucking cage. I persuaded her once, maybe I can use the same approach again.

Ignoring where we are, that passengers are filing past, I strike fast. Closing the distance between us, I curl my hand around her neck and pull her in tight. I swallow her gasp as I firmly place my lips over hers. As she tenses, I graze my teeth against her mouth until she opens and lets me inside.

Fuck, her taste. Just like it happened to me the first time, my dick starts to stir.

I'm not a fan of kissing, but it seems that I am with her. I can't get enough. Her tongue tangles with mine, twisting, sliding together, and fuck me, those sounds coming out of her mouth. She's pushing herself into me as though she can't get close enough.

I swear I feel electricity spark between us.

When my need for air becomes too great, I pull away, cradle her face in both hands, and stare into her eyes. She moans, cups her hand around my head and pulls me down for another taste.

Once again, I'm swept away.

There's chemistry between us, there's no denying that. Maybe our bodies speak volumes more than anything that comes out of our mouths.

This time it's she who pulls away for air. As we part, our eyes meet.

"Fuck, babe. You do things to me. Take a chance. Come with me."

"I'm pregnant," she reminds me.

"I know. Whether you want the baby or not, give me a chance, Sheri. Come back with me."

CHAPTER TWENTY-ONE
SHERI

The last half hour has had my brain spinning, well, the whole morning come to that. Ever since seeing those two lines appear on the test, to stupidly going to my dad, only to basically get thrown out of my childhood home.

Then for StoryTeller to turn up like a knight on a white horse, already knowing the problem reconnecting with me would cause. If he'd walked away, I wouldn't have blamed him. But he didn't. He came looking for me even with the knowledge of what that might entail.

At first, I was suspicious that he, too, would pressure me to have an abortion, but he seems pretty adamant whatever course of action I take would be up to me. Then, there was that out-of-the-blue offer to go to Arizona with him. When words didn't persuade me, he'd tried with a kiss.

We'd met again as two awkward strangers, when he pulled me into his arms my body recognised him as a kindred spirit, a lifelong partner or friend. There's no denying there's a connection there, though it could be on the most basic of levels.

He's a biker. He belongs to a notorious motorcycle club,

and I've no idea what kind of home he could offer to me. But what have I got to stay here for? A housemate who only tolerates me as I help her make rent, and a parent who's shown his comfortable life and happiness are far more important than mine.

It should be the stupidest idea in the world to go off with someone I really don't know, but I'm carrying his baby. And while I wouldn't have chased him down to tell him he's a potential father, now he's turned up, I can't block him out of any decision I make.

He's studying me, his hand reaching out, touching my hair, pushing a wayward strand away from my eye. His touch so gentle, I want to lean into him. His stance so strong, it makes me want to give him all my problems and have him deal with them.

In many ways it's an attractive proposition, getting out of town for a while, getting some space in which to make my life-changing decision. I doubt he's offering me anything permanent, just the time to get my head sorted out.

But he's a biker. I shudder as the image of the Dominators come into my mind. What if the rest of the Wretched Soulz are more like Knuckles than StoryTeller? How do I know they don't mind sharing women around?

People are passing around us while we're sat in our own bubble, all oblivious to the problems I'm wrestling with. How I wish I was one of them, just getting on with ordinary life.

He gives me time, not pressuring me. Stealing a sideways glance, I remember that StoryTeller came to Texas to find me. Can I read into that he'd missed me as much as I missed him?

I need more time before making such a momentous decision. "You offered me dinner," I start, not quite meeting his eyes. "And suggested we find somewhere to stay for the night."

"I did," he confirms, with a spark of interest.

"Can we start there?" My voice now contains eagerness. "We never really had the chance to get to know each other before."

An easy grin comes to his face. "Sure, you're the local. Anywhere particular you recommend or want to go?"

I shake my head. At the moment, any decision seems beyond me.

He holds out his hand, giving me the choice whether to take it or not. I do, immediately comforted by the feeling of his warm fingers surrounding mine. It's been a very long time since I've felt that anyone was on my side.

As if on my wavelength, he bends his head to speak into my ear. "We were a good team."

He leads me to the parking lot where a bright green motorcycle is parked. I don't know what I had in mind, but I'd pictured him riding something bigger. One thing I do know, the word Kawasaki written on the side means it's not a Harley.

"It's not mine," he tells me. "It's a loaner from the local charter."

Anxiously, I look into his eyes. "I've never been on a bike before. Can we take my car?" I thought if ever I was in this position, I would leap at the chance to find out what it feels like to be cuddled up behind a biker. Now I'm faced with it though, my mouth has gone dry. Most of the Harley's I've seen have somewhere comfortable for the passenger to ride. This one has no backrest, and the pillion pad, allowing for his taller height, would put me at the same level as him. It looks dangerous.

"Hey, you let me be your first time, now let me be your first ride." He winks at me.

Casting my mind back, I can find no recollection of any of the women I read about, doing anything other than loving riding up behind their man. Maybe there's something I'm missing. While it seems a scary prospect to me, I too will enjoy it if I give it a try.

"Here." He pulls a helmet out of the saddlebags attached to the bike. It's one of those skull cap ones which looks more for decoration than to actually protect anyone.

"Is that a spare helmet?"

He shakes his head. "I haven't even got one for myself. It's not necessary in Texas. But someone must have left it there."

"It's sensible and recommended," I tell him primly.

Ignoring me, he swings his leg over the seat, then reaches out his hand. "Some risks are worth taking, and I'm a safe rider. I'll drive carefully."

He better. When reading books, I've been entranced by the description of the freedom they feel when riding, of being one with the scenery and with the elements. I'd always thought I'd like to try that for myself, but now I'm faced with the chance, I'm not sure I want to run with it.

To delay as much as anything else, I ask, "Do you often take women on the back of your bike?"

He tenses and the amusement fades from his face. He looks away from me and into the distance. Just as I'm wondering whether he's going to answer, he turns back.

"I've only ever taken one woman on the back before, and that was the woman I was engaged to."

"You're married?" I knew there had to be a catch.

He's quick to respond to my expression of shock. "Fuck no. Luckily, I found out about her before tying the knot, and that was five years ago." His closed expression suggests he's not going to say anymore.

"But no one between her and me?" I ask, hoping for confirmation.

"No one I've wanted to ride behind me."

Maybe the etiquette I've read about in books is wrong, but I don't think StoryTeller would let me on the back of his bike, even if it is a borrowed one, unless he was at least considering giving a serious relationship a try. I take it as an indication that perhaps I should do the same.

I honestly am nervous though as I at last take his hand and inelegantly swing my leg over the seat behind him. Being ungainly, I manage to kick him in the back, but he just chuckles and inches forward, giving me more room. The seat is hard, and there's nothing to support me. There are tiny handles to each side, but I don't see how the hell I could hold on to those.

Patting my thigh, he says, "Hold on to me tight."

He starts the engine. With a yelp, I wrap my arms firmly around him, feeling his tight chest muscles under my hands. When the bike starts to move, I'm tense and terrified. My helmet bangs into the back of his head when he pulls up at a junction. I shout an apology, but he just laughs.

Not wanting to knock him out, I try to keep my head rigid on my shoulders, while keeping my hands locked around him as every moment, I feel I'm in danger of sliding off the back, the weight of the backpack I'm wearing only making matters worse.

I'm regretting every moment of this ride, and when he pulls up outside a fast-food restaurant, I say a quick prayer for having survived.

Placing my hand on his shoulder, I can't wait to get off this bike. The seat is so high I stumble as I hit the ground and would have fallen if it weren't for his quick reaction and the hand that holds me up.

"You okay?"

I am now. Placing my hand to my heart, I will it to stop beating so fast. Incapable of using words right away, I give an up-and-down nod of my head which could mean anything.

He grins. "I make all your first times exciting."

I suppose that's one way to describe it. His playful comment makes me roll my eyes but as I stand back while he walks the bike back into a space to park before getting off himself, I wonder what I'm getting myself into. There's no doubt in his head we'll be sharing a bed again soon, and I can't help but wonder if I'm going to be enough for him. It was obvious from the positioning of my hands while we were riding that he's all muscle, whereas I carry a fair amount of flab.

Blissfully unaware of the thoughts flying through my mind, he takes my hand and leads me into the restaurant. It's basic fare, but a burger will do for now. There'll be time in the future to start eating healthier. When I get out my purse to pay, he responds with a scowl, making me hastily put it away.

I ask for a milkshake while he gets a soda, then we go to a table and wait for our food. Luckily it comes quickly. I feel ravenous and quickly pick up my burger and start to eat. It's actually good and after a couple of mouthfuls, I lick my lips.

It's then I look up and see him staring at me, his own food held halfway to his mouth. There's a quirk to his lips and amusement in his eyes. Embarrassed, I chew, swallow then replace my burger on the plate.

"Fuck, woman. You even eat sexually." He shifts himself in his seat, then he catches my expression. "Talk to me," he demands.

I glance at him then turn my head away. "You're making fun of me."

"What the fuck? Sheri, I have no idea what you're talking about." His eyes crease as though in confusion.

I should be on a plane right now or doing something to sort out my life. I'm not sure what made me come with him, and no idea why I got on his bike. I hadn't missed the way the waitress eyed him up when she delivered our food while none of the men here have looked at me twice.

Taking a deep breath, I turn to look him straight in the eye. "I know nothing about you, StoryTeller—"

"Jake," he offers quickly. "When we're alone, I'd like to hear you call me Jake."

I tamp down the pleasure at him giving that to me. "Jake," I say, obediently. "I know nothing about your club. The only real-life bikers I've seen have been the Dominators."

"We're nothing like them," he snarls.

"How would I know?" In reverse to his vehemence, I gentle my tone. "Jake, you must know what you are. You're the type of man who'd excite any woman you meet. You're handsome, built, you ride a motorcycle and wear a cut. You've got the confidence which comes with having a club around you. I bet you have women falling at your feet."

His agreeing smirk that he can't keep off his face shows me I'm not wrong.

I give a small shake of my head, unable to stop a tear dribbling from my eye. "I can't trust you. What do I know of what you'll do to me if I go with you to Arizona? At best, I'm no more than a flash in the pan and you'll quickly get tired of me. Or maybe you'll share me with your brothers."

"Fuck that," he growls. Leaning across the table, he takes my hands and jerks them. "You're right. You don't fuckin' know me. If you're mine, you're mine. Ain't no one else who's going to be touching you. And why do you think I'll get tired of you?"

"Look at me. I can't be anything like the normal women that throw themselves at you."

He huffs a short laugh. "You're not. And don't you think that might be why I'm so attracted to you? Because you're different?"

"Different?" He's got that right. "Try boring and plain."

He moves around the table, coming to sit at my side, and cups his palms around the sides of my face. "Darlin', you're fuckin' gorgeous."

My watering eyes widen, and I try to push him away, but he refuses to move. "You must need glasses."

His eyes flare. "What the hell are you talking about?"

I know he's seen her, so I bring up the comparison. "My stepsister is gorgeous. I'm not."

"Your stepsister is a piece of fuckin' work, as I told you before. I wouldn't look at her twice." He mouths words as if he's trying to bring himself under control, and when he speaks again, it's more softly. "What's all this about, Sheri? Why is it so difficult for you to accept that I want you?"

Because no one ever has. I thought I said the words under my breath, but I must have been louder, or his hearing is excellent.

"No one has wanted you? Look, I'm struggling here. Help me understand." His eyes stare into mine.

Unable to bear his scrutiny, I fix my gaze on the table. "My parents decided on only having one child. They had a boy they were delighted with. Trouble was, he was diagnosed with a rare and acute form of leukaemia. They tried for another baby who'd be a match for bone marrow treatment, so along came me."

As my voice trails off, for a moment lost in the memory, he prompts me, "Did it work?"

"No," I reply, simply. "I was a match, but he died anyway. I could never replace him." I swallow hard. "I didn't know why my mom was never loving with me. Dad was okay, but Mom? Well, she was the boss in our house, and he wasn't allowed to get close to me. She blamed me that the treatment for Adam didn't work."

"Fuck that," he swears. "You were a child."

But not enough for my mother. "She'd wanted her son. She ended up with a girl."

"And you grew up with that hanging over you?" His eyes fill with disgust.

Moving my head negatively, I explain, "No. I didn't know until I was nursing her through cancer. It was only then she told me, and everything made sense." I think I'd rather not have known. "Then when she died, Dad, who'd left home two years before when she got sick, came home with a new wife and her daughter. My stepsister made a point of taking my boyfriends, and then, because I didn't get on with my stepmom and it was awkward, my dad asked me to leave the house."

"Sheri, babe." He moves closer, putting his arm around me, using his strength to hug me close, and pressing my cheek against his chest.

I feel his heart beating, but that doesn't stop the wail coming from me, "No one's ever wanted me, so why should that change now?"

"That's simple," he tells me, squeezing me tight. "Because you've never had anyone like me in your corner before."

I feel like I've been through an emotional wringer with my confession. I'm worn out, tired, scared of the future and wary of the man who's currently cuddling me. *Can I trust him?*

All my life I've been let down by people who I should have been able to trust.

StoryTeller's, no, *Jake's* hand is slowly stroking up and down my arm, his warmth surrounding me. It would be so easy to relax and pass my happiness over into his hands. It would be all too easy to give in.

My thoughts are invaded by the ringing of a phone. It's his, not mine. I feel cold when he moves his body away, leaning back to give himself room to rifle through his jeans.

"StoryTeller... Prez. Yeah... No, I'm at a restaurant... He is, yeah?" There's a longer pause while he listens to the indistinct voice I hear on the other end of the call. "Yeah, I didn't think... No, no disrespect..." Throwing me an apologetic look and holding up his hand as if telling me to wait, he gets up and walks to the door of the restaurant. Turning, I see him outside. He's listening to someone avidly, his face going through a myriad of expressions until finally he sighs, kicks at a stone and ends the call.

He enters again, immediately putting his phone back in his pocket, then he sits back beside me. As he half turns to face me, he gently moves my head to face him.

"You asked me before why I came to find you." I did. I swallow as it looks like I'm going to get my answers now. His slight wince is off-putting. "First, Sheri, I haven't been able to forget you. But you walked away, and I was being stubborn about that." He chuckles softly. "You ask any of the brothers at home and they'll tell you what an asshole I've been. So, when I had an excuse to come find you, I didn't think twice. Then, when I saw you again..." His cheeks puff and he blows out air. "Well, that's when I knew I wasn't going to let you go a second time. And I meant it, I'm going to be here to support you. Whatever you want to do."

"So what was the excuse?" I ask him.

Pulling my head into his chest, he kisses my hair, then tightens his arms around me. His shuddering breath prepares me to hear something bad. "Knuckles has been spotted in Austin."

I feel the blood drain from my face. "Knuckles?" Due to my mom's illness, I didn't finish my education, but I've never been accused of being slow. That Jake is here means there's a connection between the Dominator and me. "You think he wants me?"

Jake shakes his head. "Possibly. But I think it's more likely he wants to use you to get to me. He only knows me as a nomad and not the chapter I'm from."

"So you've done exactly what he wanted you to do. Came to me." I flick my eyes toward the window of the restaurant as if he might be waiting out there. "Jake. If he was watching me, waiting for you, you could have walked into a trap."

"There you go." He rolls his eyes. "Thinking of someone else." My lips purse, but then he explains, slowly as if to a child, "Knuckles wouldn't be waiting for me to come to you. He's more likely to force the situation and take you. He'd predict I'd come to your rescue, like I did before."

"But he can't still think I'm your old lady." I scoff. "I mean, we're not living together."

"Nomad." He points to his chest. "Or that's what Knuckles still thinks I am, and that I'm on the road all the time. It's unlikely I'd take an ol' lady with me." He sees me frown as I wonder whether he'd be able to commit to staying in one place now, and he reaches for my hand. "Sheri, I've been in a relationship before. She fuckin' betrayed me, went with one of the members when I was still a prospect." I stare at him, feeling uneasy at the animosity which accompanies his words, and the faraway look in his eye as briefly he seems stuck in the past. With a shake of his head, he comes back to me. "I went nomad from the day I was patched. Couldn't stand to be in the club which I felt had disrespected me."

"Because of the member who betrayed you with her was still there."

His eyebrow rises, and there's a quirk to his lips, when he explains, "No. He kind of left the club."

Do I want to know how? I decide that I don't. Or maybe it's safest I refrain from pushing for details.

"Chaz, my prez," he continues. "Well, he made the most of

me. Turns out I made a good travelling enforcer. I was happy on the road." Again, he seems lost in thought. "Until that business with Knuckles got me grounded. Lost my cut, as you probably remember, and when I got a new one, it had the Arizona patch on it." He gives me a quick grin. "Fuckin' killed me knowing my freedom was gone."

And there's my worry. That Jake won't be happy staying in one place. He's been travelling too long.

"But now I know fate works in ways we don't understand." His shoulders rise and drop. "If I didn't have my place in my home chapter, I'd have nothing to offer you."

I state my fear. "And that's why this would be a mistake. You'll blame me for tying you down."

"No," he exclaims, both of his hands cupping my cheeks. "When I was a prospect, I was, as I said, in a relationship. I wanted it all—my patch, but along with that, my own family, my own picket fence." He grins as if knowing how crazy that sounds for a biker. "When Fi betrayed me, I lost all those dreams, thought all that was beyond me. But then I met you..." He leans forward and kisses me. It's as though there's a wealth of emotion in that caress, as if he's using his lips to tell me things his mouth isn't ready to articulate yet.

Can I believe him? "You want that dream with me?" I ask when he lets me take in air.

His grin widens. "Seems like I do." Leaning forward, he gives me another of those kisses that make me go weak. My toes once again curl, and I lose all sense of where we are. All I'm conscious of is the man that I'm with.

When he releases me, I remember where I am, and glance around, hoping no one is staring at me. While I see nothing to worry me, I do notice there's a group of people coming in the door and that our table is probably needed.

"What do we do now?" I ask, remembering he'd suggested finding a place to stay and hoping that's still in the cards.

"Babe, that phone call earlier... That was my prez reminding me I need to show my face at the Austin clubhouse. They lent me a bike for a start."

I'm glad that green monstrosity wasn't his. "When do you need to go?"

"There's no time like now."

"Okay." I feel disappointed that his plans have changed, but I suppose if his prez tells him to do something, he has no choice. "Can you drop me off at a motel or something?"

"You fuckin' what?" Rather than angry, Jake looks perplexed. "You're coming with me."

I gesture no. "It's not even your own club, Jake. You have no idea what these men are like. And what if you want to go with a sweet butt? I'll only cramp your style."

His eyes widen. For a moment, he looks confused, then he laughs. "I presume you got your info from the fuckin' books you said you always have your nose in."

So what if I have? They conned me, though. They painted a rosier picture than real life.

"I won't be going with any sweet butt, babe. Not now I've got you at my side."

I'm not sure I believe him, but I think of another objection. "What am I going to do if you're called into church?"

"Church?" He outright belly laughs now. "You've certainly got all the lingo. Look, Austin isn't my club, babe. I doubt if I'll be sat round their table." He runs a hand over his long hair, holding it back in a ponytail for a moment before letting it drop. "I can't deny the Texas lot are a rough bunch, and you might see things you'd rather not. But no one is going to lay a hand on you." All mirth has gone from his face as he takes my hand, squeezing it tightly. "Don't forget the reason why I'm here, babe. Knuckles has been seen around, which means there's no way in hell I'm leaving you unprotected."

There's one thing he knows nothing about, and my last bastion of hope now. "I'm not a sociable person, Jake."

Raising his hand, he sweeps hair back from my brow, and he stares at me for a long moment. "I think it's time you come out of the shadows, babe."

CHAPTER TWENTY-TWO
STORYTELLER

Come out of the shadows, I'd told her.

It's obvious she's been hiding all her life. That story she'd told me made me feel like I'd been punched in the gut. No wonder she doesn't know her own value. What fucking parents would admit they had her, just as an abortive attempt to save the favoured child? That's fucked up. Her stepmom sounds like a selfish unfeeling bitch, and as for her stepsister? The only thing I'd ever give her is a piece of my mind.

Sheri's fucking gorgeous, yet hasn't got a clue how attractive she is. There's a spark I see in her. I think she's got a backbone, a side of her that life had her too cowed to allow to come out.

Can she cope with my Texan brothers? I fucking hope so. If not, it doesn't bode well for our future. It's not as if I've any choice. I've been summoned to their clubhouse, and, if nothing else, I've got to take back that borrowed bike.

I wasn't being unfair when I reminded her Knuckles was

around. He's in the same city, and that's too close as far as I'm concerned. At the clubhouse, surrounded by men wearing the same patch as me, she'll be protected, and I really don't want to let her out of my sight.

"Come on." I stand. As I've still got hold of her hand, I pull her up with me.

"I don't know about this."

"Trust me." Placing the helmet on her head, I tighten the strap. When I see her eyeing the pillion seat with distaste, I can't blame her. Once she gets on my Fat Boy, she'll have all the comfort she needs. "Just hold on to me. I promise I'll take it easy."

Once on the bike, I make sure the passenger foot pegs are still in place and, this time, encourage her to step on the left one to give her a boost up, making it easier to swing her leg. The bike dips as she settles on it, and I hold it steady, taking a moment as I'd done before to adjust to the extra weight. When I start the engine, her hands come around my waist in a death grip. Easing out the clutch, I pull away as smoothly as possible, having regard for my precious cargo and her precarious perch on the back.

I've travelled through Texas a time or two over the years, and this is far from the first time I've stopped off at the Austin clubhouse. While the route's not that familiar, my memory serves me well enough, and I'm soon heading in the right direction that will take me to my destination.

We leave the city, heading into the outskirts and a more industrial area. This time in the evening, I notice it's fairly deserted. I'm concentrating on where I'm going, and the feel of Sheri on the bike, noting she's not relaxing, even though she must be growing more familiar with riding. Suddenly there's a sound I recognise, and the breath of air whistling past my ear tells me a bullet has missed us by inches.

Fuck.

Turning my head, I see a Jeep approaching fast.

Hoping to hell Sheri will hang on, unable to warn her, I twist the throttle so hard it almost makes the bike sit up and beg. In my mirror, I can see the Jeep accelerating to keep up, and a darn pistol barrel visible out of the window. I throw myself left and right, zigzagging the bike, then take a corner almost at a right angle to the ground. Sheri's scream echoes in my ear, but I haven't time to explain and slowing down is not an option.

I take routes around the factories, turning right then left, hoping not to come across a dead end. For once I'm grateful I'm not on my own bike. The one thing the Kawasaki's got going for it is the manoeuvrability and quick turn of speed. On my Harley, I wouldn't be so agile.

At last, when I reach the main road again, I risk taking the direct route to the clubhouse. Ignoring any speed limit, I lay on my horn as I approach the gate, and luckily see it's being opened quickly for me.

I tear through, go around the clubhouse and brake hard at the back, in my mirror seeing the brothers swinging the gate closed behind me.

"Hey, ST. Way to make an entrance," Shotgun, their VP, drawls as he comes up to me. His eyes quickly go to the woman who's still hanging onto my back. Now I've stopped, I can feel her hyperventilating. "Let me help you off, little lady."

Loosening her hands, I watch her slump against the man who's picked her up, lifted her off, and put her on her two feet. But she doesn't stay vertical long. Within seconds, she's bending over and vomiting.

"Sheri," I cry out, going beside her, and pulling back her hair.

The partially digested dinner she'd just eaten is now on the ground. She retches a couple of times and wipes her mouth with the back of her hand. She pauses for a moment before she straightens. Then, ignoring the men surrounding us, launches at me.

"You delinquent bastard! You could have killed me! What the fuck did you think you were doing?" Stunned, I simply stand as her hand slaps my chest, then does it again and again, punctuating her words. "I don't know how I managed to hold on. Or was that your plan? If you didn't want me riding behind you, you just had to tell me, not do all those twists and turns, trying to make me slide off. Have you any idea how fucking terrified I was?"

"Lady—" Shotgun tries to get her attention.

Ignoring him, she continues to shout at me. "You're a dick, you know that?"

"Christ, she's scary," Shout says quietly in a whispered aside.

"Woman!" Shotgun tries again, a little more forcefully. When she still doesn't pay him any mind, he walks behind her and wrenches her backpack off.

Stunned, fear flares in her eyes as she turns her attention to him, trying to retake possession of her bag. But he holds it out of her reach, then turns it so the rear is facing her.

"You are fuckin' lucky to be alive," he roars at her. "And that's all thanks to StoryTeller's riding."

My eyes narrow, then widen as I see what he's pointing to. Sheri stares as well, her face draining of blood. Now it's me who's feeling sick to my stomach, and me who's retching, bringing my recently eaten burger up. *She could have been killed.* I'd told her never to get between a bullet and me again, but that's what I've done. Put her straight in the path of danger.

Did I draw Knuckles to her? Would she have been safe if I'd never turned up? I vomit again, thinking how close I'd come to losing her.

When my stomach is empty, I stand and try to make amends. "Sheri," I start, my voice full of pleading, of apology, but then find I can't summon the words to tell her how fucking sorry I am. There's nothing that will express this anguish inside.

But she's not even looking at me. Instead, she rips the backpack out of Shotgun's hand and studies the hole with a perplexed expression in her eyes. Then, balancing it on her stomach, she pulls it open. After a moment looking inside, she brings something out, her stunned face meeting my incredulous eyes.

I can't believe what I'm seeing. In her hand, she's holding that book that brought us together, but it's not pristine anymore. Instead, there's a neat round desecrating the cover. When Sheri upends her pack, holding the contents in, but shaking it, a bullet comes harmlessly dropping out.

"Well, I'll be fucked." Strider, the Prez of the chapter, has been watching the proceedings.

Buzz, his sergeant-at-arms, bursts into laughter.

Sheri just stands, holding that MariaLisa DeMora novel in her hand. Troubled, I see her already pale face going completely white. Worried, I close the distance between us and I'm only just in time to break her fall as she faints clean away.

While I'm still trying to get a good hold to lift her up, Strider comes and grabs the back of her shirt and raises it.

"What the fuck?" That's my woman he's touching.

With a dismissive snarl, he continues examining her back. "Haven't you ever taken one to a bullet-proof vest?"

Fuck. Yeah. I have. But unless I drop her down, I have to rely on his eyes. "What's it like?" She must have been so terrified of my riding, she hadn't felt the bullet hitting.

"Not too bad, but she's going to have a bruise. Bring her inside."

Turning, he beckons to me to follow him, while calling out for a prospect to come and clean the forecourt up.

We enter the clubhouse, which is much like any other I've ever been in, only the positioning of the bar and the grouping of tables and what entertainment facilities there are serve to distinguish one from the other. Up behind the bar is a flag showing our insignia—two wraiths holding onto each handlebar while a skull gives a rictus grin underneath.

Strider indicates I should place her on a seen-better-days couch, then cups his hands around his mouth and yells, "Jasmine?" When a sweet butt's head pops up from behind the bar, he continues, "Grab a bottle of water and look after her, will you?" He gestures to Sheri in case there was any doubt what he meant. When Jasmine approaches, he bends his head to hers, and presumably offers further instruction.

I crouch down by her side, but Strider puts his hand on my shoulder and squeezes it almost painfully. "My girl will take care of her. You're coming to church."

One look toward him shows he won't be budged. With a grimace and silent apology to Sheri, who looks like she's starting to stir, I shoot a warning glare toward the woman called to watch over her.

In return, Jasmine gives me a pleasant enough smile and says, "I'll take care of her. You go do your man thing."

Reluctantly, I follow the other men who are walking after Strider.

There are a few spaces around the table, understandable as this meeting was called out of the blue, but the main ones are there. Strider, obviously, sits at the head of the table, Shotgun to his left and Buzz to his right. Tequila, the enforcer, is next to him. Shout gestures for me to take a place at his side, and another man, Mex, whose name needs no explanation, also introduces himself.

The rest assume I've already met them, so I just offer a chin lift in return to theirs. If I need to know their names, I'll look at their cuts.

The door closes after the last man enters, and this is someone who Strider greets by name.

"Data. What you got for us?"

As he's carrying a laptop, I assume Data's their go-to tech guy, but then his name probably gives it away.

Data sits, then looks around seriously, finally settling on me. "We've got the approaches lined with cameras just for situations like these, like where we need to know who's gunning for us." Seems fair, so I raise my chin once more. He continues without needing prompting. "Got a good shot of the driver and passenger—he was the one doing the shooting." He opens his laptop and turns it my way.

The man holding the gun is definitely Knuckles. My hands fist as I realise just how close I'd come to losing Sheri. *If she hadn't been wearing that backpack...* My stomach rolls once more, and I look for the nearest bin in case it decides to rebel. For once in my life, sitting around the table has become a chore. I want to be out with my woman, checking on her.

"That's Knuckles," I confirm. Data rolls his eyes, showing my comment was totally unnecessary. I wouldn't have been in Austin if someone from this club hadn't recognised him.

"How the fuck did he find us?"

Strider snorts. "Fucker may be crazy but he's not stupid. He wasn't after your woman but after you, ST. All he needed to do was get himself noticed for you to come into town, then sit back and wait for you to come to him."

Buzz throws me a look of disdain. "He's probably been hanging around, waiting for you to bring her to us. And, ST, that red mane of hers sticks out like a fuckin' sore thumb. You didn't think to disguise her?"

Sounds like I've done a whole lot of no thinking at all. Shooting my chair back, I stand, walk to the wall, and beat my fist against it. Trying to kick my brain into gear after realising my carelessness came too fucking close to getting her killed, I reach for any answer I can come up with.

"If he didn't see my patch, I can take her back to Arizona. Just need to get her to the airport."

"And if he did?" Strider barks. "You've been flying under the radar as he thought you were nomad. If he saw your rocker, then you're taking a heap of trouble back to your club."

And Chaz is really gonna appreciate that. He's already told me he won't get into a war to take out one Dominator.

Shotgun takes out a packet of cigarettes. It's a signal for many to copy him and light up. I do the same even though I've had thoughts about giving up. *Because of the baby.* Right now, though, a nicotine hit might make me think clearer.

Strider's been watching with his head resting on his chin. He waves to indicate I should return to my seat at the table. When I do so, he suddenly grins. "Seems like Knuckles might have the idea you're stupid, Brother. He might be on to something."

My eyes narrow and I glare at the Austin prez. My mouth opens to deny that I'm how he describes when I realise it was my rash and senseless actions that had put Sheri in the position of getting hurt. *If we'd taken her car, she'd have been better protected.* But, oh no, I'd wanted her behind me on the bike, even though it wasn't the best suited to break in a new passenger.

She's gonna hate me. Will she ever forgive me?

A loud rapping gets me looking toward Strider again. "You back with us, ST?" His mouth quirks. At my nod, he continues,

"Yeah, so Knuckles probably expects anything from you right now. So he wouldn't be surprised if you take your woman back out on your bike—"

"Not going to fuckin' do that," I growl, thumping my fist on the table in emphasis. "I almost lost her today. And she's fuckin' pregnant. Ain't going to be risking her."

"*Pregnant?*" Strider exclaims. He leans back in his chair, and chortles. "Oh, this is fuckin' good, Brother."

If there's ever a time I wanted to be able to reclaim words I've just spoken, it's now. "She, I, only just found out. Nothing's yet been decided." I shrug as if contradicting that her status is anything important.

Tequila speaks, his voice deep and growly. "Seems like our Arizona brother has doubts about us." He meets my eye, and his hand slaps the table so loudly it makes me jump. "Seems he's jumping to conclusions without hearing us out."

Strider's nodding in confirmation. "Think Knuckles might have the way of it. He's a few cents short of the dollar."

I want to jump in and defend myself, but I'm feeling pretty damn stupid right now. Instead, I look toward the enforcer.

In turn, Tequila nods across at the small Mexican man. "You fancy wearing a wig, Mex?"

Taking his cigarette away from his face, and staring at the glowing tip for a moment, Mex laughs. "I'm small, but I ain't that small. But yeah, I'm up for hugging the hell out of ST over there. Long as the getup includes body armour."

Suddenly a conversation starts, one from which I feel excluded, but only because of the brotherhood between these men, that having ridden together they communicate and understand each other without spelling it out for a newcomer. Slowly, though, the gist comes over.

This club, which owes nothing to me, is going to have my

back to take out a Dominator, and possibly draw down blow-back on their charter.

Chaz, my own prez, wouldn't take on my war. But even there, Strider seems to read my mind and have the answer.

"It wasn't worth bothering with Knuckles when he was an annoying gnat buzzing around without having a target. Arizona would have had your back, Brother, if he'd come for you head-on." He shrugs. "Now he's brought his war to Texas. We're happy to teach him a lesson."

An opportunity to take down a Dominator and get rid of the threat of Knuckles for good? That makes me sit up and take interest. I listen carefully to the plan Buzz has come up with and find nothing to argue about—a baited trap with only me and the Texas brothers putting themselves in danger, Sheri protected by staying back here in the club.

As Strider wraps up the meeting, I feel more optimistic than when I entered the door. Now I can't wait to get back to Sheri and check that she's alright. But as I eagerly leave my seat, Strider beckons that I should stay back.

Reluctantly, I wait until the room is vacated with the exception of the president and myself.

Strider lights a cigarette and offers them. I decline. He sits back in his chair, blowing out smoke lazily, while I'm on edge.

"She's pregnant from that debacle with Knuckles?"

Debacle. What a way to describe it. I indicate to Strider that I might need to take him up on his offer of a cancer stick for this conversation. Smirking, he slides the pack down the table to me. I take one out, shoot the pack back, then use my own lighter. Looking down, I tap my fingers on the table.

"Knuckles was torn between taking her story that she was a virgin and mine that she was my old lady."

Strider snorts. "Sounds like the beginning to one of your stories."

Breathing in smoke, I huff it out. "Yeah, fuckin' unbelievable. But it's the truth I'm telling you. I assumed she was lying to get them to keep their hands off, and Knuckles, too, was of that opinion."

"You going to give me the full narrative or cut this one short?"

Seeing as I want to get out to see Sheri, I give him the concise summary. "It was either him or me, so I did the deed." As I pause, he raises an eyebrow. "She wasn't lying."

"Fuck me."

"Yeah." I meet his eyes, then sigh. "Clearly, Knuckles wasn't handing out condoms. You called me stupid, I probably am. I didn't give any thought to what the outcome could be."

"But your swimmers scored a goal the first time."

It's not a question, so I don't answer, only explain, "Only found out today. And she only did the test this morning, so it's all pretty new."

"She want it? Do you?" Strider sits forward. "Bringing a kid into the world we live in shouldn't be done casually. You're a fuckin' nomad, ST."

I tilt my head back as if to indicate the rocker. "Arizona, remember?"

"Pah." He waves his hand dismissively. "You're a nomad, here." He thumps his hand over his chest. "Unless you can change, ST, you're setting that woman up for a world of hurt."

"I think she could be enough to change me," I admit. Then agree, "But I need to be sure. And so does she."

"She want the baby?" he asks again.

"I don't think either of us considered being parents."

He gives a half-smile. "I've got the solution if you want it." His eyes close for a brief moment. "One of the whores got herself into a predicament. She wanted the medication to sort it, and we got hold of some stock. Seemed a good thing to have handy."

I suppose an MC can get drugs of all sorts. I frown, thinking over what he's just offered. Turns out, if Sheri doesn't want to be pregnant, she won't even have to leave the state to sort it.

I can't understand why I'm unhappy with that.

CHAPTER TWENTY-THREE
SHERI

My head hurts and I feel dizzy, and for some reason, I feel I've been kicked in the back. I start to come back to myself just in time to see Jake walking off with a load of men wearing similar leather or denim cuts, the only difference being where his says Arizona, theirs say Texas.

So much for him caring for me. He doesn't seem to give a damn that I could have been killed. No wonder I fainted from the shock.

I start to stand, placing a hand on the dirty arm of the equally filthy couch where I've been abandoned, when a pretty woman, maybe a couple of years older than myself, approaches. She hurries her footsteps when she sees me trying to get upright, and by placing a gentle hand on my shoulder, encourages me to sit back down.

"Strider told me to watch out for you as you weren't feeling well. I gather you took a bullet to the back."

I gasp, and fruitlessly try to look behind me, placing my hand, worried about seeing blood.

"Oh no," Jasmine cries out. "Not literally. It was stopped by your pack, but you've got a bruise you're bound to feel."

Indeed I have. While she's been explaining, it's all comes back, and the blood drains from my face again. I'd thought Jake had lost his mind. Turns out, he was trying to protect us. *Someone shot at me.* I shake my head in disbelief. *This is not my life.*

"Do you want a glass of water?" She glances toward the bar. "Or something stronger?"

I could really do with a shot of tequila but remember before the request leaves my mouth that I can't drink now. And, unless I do something about my situation, won't be able to for another six and a half months. *At least.*

"Water will be fine," I request at last, needing something to take the remaining taste of vomit from my mouth.

After bringing me back a bottle with dew on the outside, indicating it's fresh from the cooler, she sits beside me, showing she's taking her babysitting duties seriously.

"So," she starts, after I've taken a good few swallows of the cold refreshing water. "You came in pretty hot. Must have been pretty damn scary."

I shudder, replaying it in my mind—from hanging on for dear life, not knowing why Jake was riding so erratically, to finding that bullet hole in my backpack. Nausea threatens me again as I realise if I hadn't been wearing it, had the contents not been in the right alignment inside, I could be dead. For some reason, that makes the life I'm carrying seem precious.

I'm going to drive myself crazy thinking about it when I can't talk it out. But Jake's not around to ask whether it was really Knuckles who was after us and if so, how he could have found us. Nor whether it was me the bullet was intended for or if it was Jake he was trying to take out. Or, indeed, whether there's another enemy gunning down members of his club.

"Where's Jake gone?" I ask, hoping he'll soon be back. At her puzzled look, I amend, "StoryTeller."

"Oh, the men are in church. They're discussing what happened to you."

Church. The meeting Jake said he was unlikely to be invited to, but under the circumstances, I suppose it makes sense. It irks, though. It was me who had stopped a bullet, but I'm excluded from what's considered the domain of men.

"Are you an old lady?" I ask, wanting to get my mind onto something else while I'm waiting to get answers. Getting annoyed when there's no one to direct my anger to won't help.

Jasmine gives a pretty little snort. "Nah. No one's given me that title."

"So, you're a sweet butt?"

"Sweet butt?" Her eyebrows rise. For a second, I'm afraid I've offended her, but then she laughs. "It's complicated, honey. I'm not one thing or another. But when I have sex, it's always with Strider."

"The prez?" I frown. "And it's just a sexual relationship?"

She chuckles again, showing my questioning isn't offending her. "I'm not in his bed for anything else. And won't be unless he pulls his head out of the sand."

"You want to be more?" In my books, sweet butts always want to become old ladies.

Her eyes go to the meeting room door where the men had disappeared. "Whether I do or not is part of why shit is so complicated." She gives herself a little shake and turns sideways, hoisting her bent leg up on the couch so she can face me. "So, you and StoryTeller. Are you an item?"

Turning the tables on her, I reply, "It's complicated."

She flops back on the couch. "Isn't it always? Tell me how you met him, and how long you've been together."

She's nice, friendly, and there's no reason for me to keep

anything secret. As I haven't been able to discuss my situation with anyone else, I decide to tell her everything, starting from the beginning—how I was kidnapped, and what led Jake to me. When I've finished, her mouth has dropped open.

"That's so damn romantic. A book? He wanted to give it back and ended up rescuing you from a trafficker?" She fans herself. "Girl, stuff like that darn near burns my panties off. No wonder you stayed with him."

I lean back, then jerk forward. My back is certainly sore. Jasmine notices. "Here." She takes something out of her pocket. "Strider said you might need painkillers."

I eye what she's holding cautiously. "What is it?"

She shrugs and grins. "The good stuff, baby. Oxy."

Holding up my hands, I ward her off. "I can't take anything."

Her sharp eyes land on me, and the side of her mouth turns up. "No alcohol, no drugs. Is there something you're not telling me?"

She's easy to talk to, so I find myself opening up. "Yeah, I'm pregnant."

Clapping her hands together, she says, "Congratulations. I'm so happy for you." Then, seeing my expression, tempers her words. "Or isn't it something you want?"

"I don't know," I admit. It's the truth. I don't know how I feel, but something has driven me to refuse a strong drink or painkillers. Is my brain doing my thinking for me? Acting practically when my emotions haven't caught up yet? If I really was going to *sort it* as my father had instructed, surely, I wouldn't be worried about causing harm to what I know is just a simple clump of cells.

The way I'm thinking is scary. How the hell could I cope with a baby? I don't earn enough to keep myself alive, let alone have another depending on me.

Jasmine must be able to read some of the thoughts going through my head as she pats my hand, and leans in, speaking confidentially, even though there's no one within hearing.

"If you don't want it, I can get that shit to sort you out." When I turn to her sharply, she admits, "I've been where you are. Strider got the tablets for me, and I know he got extra in case it was needed again."

She's aborted a baby? She took the sensible way out. Maybe that's really the choice for me. "How did it make you feel?"

"You're asking me if I regret it?" She grimaces. "Hard to say. It was Strider's, and I was pretty damn sure the last thing he wanted was a baby." I think she's got more she wants to say, so I wait. "I don't know. It was quick, easy. One day, the test showed two little lines, a few days later, it was as if it had never been. Only…"

As her voice trails off, her eyes seem to glaze. After a moment, I prompt, "Only?"

Her shoulders rise, then fall. "Strider's been different with me."

"Is he worried about the same thing happening again?"

She gives a half-grin. "No, we made sure. He gloves up and I'm on the pill. But…" Again, she leans in, saying quietly, "Though he didn't say anything, I do wonder whether some part of him wanted the baby." She seems to shake herself. "But that's crazy, yeah? Wretched Soulz prezes don't want kids, or not with anyone but their old lady."

StoryTeller is very much a Wretched Soul. The chances of him wanting to be lumbered with a child are probably below zero. And now I've been offered an easy way out.

I don't have time to contemplate further as the meeting room door opens and the men file out.

I come quickly to realise I'm in the middle of a biker club, surrounded by tough-looking men I don't know. Anxiously, I look for Jake, but he seems to be the only one who hasn't come out. I try to tell myself these are Soulz and not Dominators, but still my adrenaline spikes.

What if they think I'm a sweet butt Jake's brought along to share?

At least I've got... No. Even Jasmine has abandoned me, getting to her feet and disappearing behind the bar, leaving me sitting alone on the couch. Trying to shrink back, I pray no one pays me any attention. But almost before that thought runs through my head, a tall bald-headed man is approaching me. I recognise him. He was one of those outside when Jake and I rode in.

My mouth goes dry as he looms over me, wondering how to reply if he demands I service him. But when he speaks, his words aren't at all threatening.

"How are you, sweetheart? You got over your shock yet?"

What do I say? Anxiously licking my lips, I politely respond, "I'm getting there."

"How's your back?"

It feels bruised, but it's the least of my worries. Perhaps if I say I'm in tons of pain, he won't try to take advantage of me.

"I'm Shotgun," he tells me, pleasantly. "Your man is just having a chat with the prez. He'll be out shortly." Having given me the explanation, he seems to lose interest in me, his eyes flicking around the room. When he spies the door opening and a couple of scantily dressed but well-proportioned and very attractive women walking in, he grins. "Ah. You'll have to excuse me."

Well, of course he didn't want anything to do with me. Not when he's got the likes of them. Strangely, I'm both relieved, and annoyed.

No one else bothers me. I'm left alone to watch. Most of the men exit the meeting room and go straight to the bar. Jasmine's rushed off her feet, trying to get drinks in all their hands, but she has a smile on her face, and a comment and laugh for almost every man.

Music starts to play from a jukebox, and the conversations grow louder to compensate. Balls start to clack on the pool table, and I watch some men settle down to a game of cards.

Shotgun clearly hasn't wasted time. He's now on another couch with one of the newly arrived women on his lap. She's writhing on him as though giving him a lap dance. I can't seem to draw my eyes away as he encourages her up, undoes his zip, pulls her panties to one side, then pulls her down, impaling her on his dick.

Blushing, I force myself to turn my head. To the other direction, it's not much better. One of the other men has a woman on her knees, his cock disappearing between her lips. The way she's hanging onto him doesn't look like she's being forced.

The air becomes thick with cigarette smoke, the smell of beer and the odour of sex.

I'm a redhead, and I'm certain my face is glowing red. Staring at my hands seems the safest option, so I'm startled when the couch dips and someone sits at my side.

Jumping and pulling away, I turn, only to find it's Jake, and he's wearing a look of concern.

"You okay?" Interrupting my answer are raised voices, and the sound of fists on flesh. Scooting over, I throw myself into the protection of Jake's arms. "It's only a couple of brothers assing around," he assures me, then, seeing I'm shaking, stands and pulls me up by my hand. "Probably a good time to get out of here."

I expect him to go toward the entrance, but instead, he

leads me deeper into the club. We pass a few closed doors, one open which looks like an office, and then out the back. There's a block of rooms here, similar to what you'd find in a motel. He extracts a key from his pocket and opens the first one up.

It's a functional room, bare apart from a bed. A door leads into a small bathroom. I suspect it's been set up for visitors like us, but only as some place to lay your head. Or, fuck.

My heart rate speeds up. *What does Jake expect? And what do I want to give him?*

"Make yourself at home," he instructs. "I'm going to get your pack and my shit from my bike."

With that, he's gone, and my nerves make themselves felt. Visions appear in my head of the casual sex I experienced in the clubroom. Jake's a biker like them, used to free sex, and tonight there's no doubt we'll be sharing a bed.

He's a full-blooded male. And me? Well, I'm only just one step away from being a virgin. I know both my inexperience and my naked body will disappoint him.

Last time, he hadn't seen me naked. Of course, he can tell I've junk in my trunk, but I don't work out, I like my food, and my stomach is far from flat. My breasts, while perky, are small and out of proportion in my view. I haven't been able to hold on to a man in the past against my lithe and sexy stepsister, so why should it be any different now?

Waiting for him, my confidence falls to an all-time low. *He's going to be so disappointed.* I know his rejection will affect me more than most, and not just because I'm pregnant with his baby. When he finally re-enters, I'd almost ready to bolt.

Nervously I eye him, my heart rate increasing as he steps close. His eyes grow dark, his pupils dilate. I notice his lips slightly part and what looks like an anticipatory flush comes to his cheeks. I don't need to look down at his crotch to know he's turned on.

While my brain screams that he'll soon turn away, my body automatically prepares itself. My breathing speeds up, my heart thumping in my chest. My panties grow damp, and I feel my nipples jut out against the material of the shirt that I'm wearing.

I shiver under the intensity of his gaze, then question the quirk to his lips as instead of approaching, he moves behind me.

"Stay still," he instructs, as I start to turn to follow him.

I do as I'm told, startling when I feel his breath against my neck. I suck in air as his lips gently meet my skin, his head dipping down so he can taste me. His touch is so light goose-bumps form. He sucks gently on the pulse point beneath my ear, then raises my hair so his caress can trace across the back of my spine, and then applies the same attention to the opposite side.

For a moment, the touch of his mouth is our only connection, and my heart rate increases as my skin becomes super-charged and heated. I'd expected him to start by ripping my clothes off me. His gentle approach has me discombobulated and off balance.

When I tense, he says, "Just relax and feel. This time, I want to do things properly. I want to see you."

His words don't help me at all. Seeing me could end this passion. When I feel his hands at the bottom of my tee, I cover them with my own.

"Let me."

Knowing resistance is futile, my hands first drop, then at his gentle insistence rise so he can extract me from my shirt. The cool air-conditioned draft has my overheated skin pebbling, or maybe it's the anticipation, or fear of what he'll think of me.

Still to my rear, he unclips my bra, pushing the straps down my arms. His hands come out to cup me, his fingers finding my nipples, newly sensitised thanks to my pregnancy. His touch makes me inhale air and lean back against him.

"Perfect," he whispers, alternating between toying with my nipples and weighing my breasts in his hand.

"Too small," I contradict, but at the same time, unable to stop the moan coming from my lips, as sensations like small electric shocks go from my nipples to my core.

His fingers move down, his palms pausing over my far-from-flat belly.

"I love this," he says.

"I'm fat."

"If I wanted hardness and muscle, I'd fuck one of my brothers." He snorts.

My breath catches. He can't be gay, but bisexual perhaps. "Would you?"

"That thought turn you on? Wanna see some man-on-man action?" He chuckles into my ear as I'm wondering whether I would or would not. "Sorry to disappoint, darlin', but I don't swing that way. Though, if you're interested, maybe I can hook us up with some brothers that do. Only to watch though." He rests his fingers on the pulse point in my neck and laughs again as I feel my skin flush. "I'm selfish and I want you to be all mine."

My breath catches as he slips his fingers into the waistband of my jeans and applies pressure on my mound.

"I'm going to see you naked this time," he warns, as he diverts to undo the button, then draws down the zipper. After he pushes them off my hips, I kick my legs, so they fall to my feet, then flick off my sandals and let my pants drop to the ground.

Turning me around, he leisurely inspects my body, his eyes

moving up, then down. A grin slowly appears on his face, and his eyes look heated. It might be wishful thinking, but I see nothing in his expression but appreciation and desire.

CHAPTER TWENTY-FOUR
STORYTELLER

Attraction can be a strange thing. What appeals to one man might not appeal to another. And any one man's ideal can be blown out of the water when elements he might not have considered before are packaged together in a particular way.

Sheri's a perfect pear-shape—small-breasted, but wide hips. She's utterly beautiful with it. While she's rounded and curved, her skin is so soft and smooth I can't keep my hands off her.

When I re-entered the room, having gotten our stuff, it was blindingly obvious that she was nervous. Her slight shiver and tremors reminded me that, for now at least, she's carrying my child inside her, and I can't just fuck her in my normal style.

I'd taken her virginity with no thought other than to get the job done and over. This time, I want to show her what it is like to be with a lover. We've no audience, no need to hurry.

She stands in front of me, wearing plain white panties, but with her blazing red hair streaming over her shoulders. she's the most enticing woman I've ever seen. Me, StoryTeller, who's fucked more women than I can remember, swallow hard, as I realise there's never been a time before when my performance has mattered so much.

She's so insecure, and that's all down to her fucked-up family. I vow going forward it will be my job to convince her that no one else matters, and that she's special to me.

When her mouth turns down, I realise I've been staring too long, and she's losing her confidence all over again. It's time to worship her body, to show her just how much she's come to mean to me.

Moving fast, I pull her toward me, slam my lips on hers, use my tongue to apply pressure, then, when she opens, sweep it inside. Just like our other kisses, this one has all the blood draining straight to my dick. I groan, and she moans as our mouths mate.

My dick's insisting I move this along, envious of my tongue being inside her. I pull back with little kisses applied to each side of her mouth, then lifting her bridal style, place her in the middle of the bed.

I pull those white panties off her, and spread her legs, holding them parted when she tries to lock them back together. Then, I lower my head.

Her gasp of shocked surprise suggests no one's gone down on her before. Her movements, and those sexy little sounds she's making, soon show me what she likes and dislikes. I might have done this a time or two before, so I'm not surprised that before long, my head's being trapped between her thighs and all her muscles are tensing. And there it is. When she comes with a scream, her back bowing off the bed, it's my name on her lips.

The last time I heard that was a lifetime ago, before Fi cheated on me.

Sheri's not Fi, I already know that. The two women

couldn't be further apart. Even her taste seems to be sweeter as I lick and nibble, bringing her down from her height, then ramping her up and over it for a second time.

When her breath seems to steady, I raise my head to look into her eyes, loving the stunned disbelief I can see there. *Oh yeah, babe, it gets even better.* I rise onto my knees and line myself up.

It might not be the first time I've taken her bare, but it's the first that I've been able to watch myself doing it. Seeing my naked dick disappear into her tight pussy almost has me blowing on the spot. I throw back my head, trying to focus on something different, but it's so damn difficult with her cunt squeezing the hell out of my cock. Mentally issuing her an apology that there's no way in hell I'm going to last long, I ease myself all the way in.

"Jesus. You feel good," I tell her, knowing immediately the memories of the last time had led me astray. I'd remembered it being good, but this is out of the world fucking fantastic. Never, ever has being inside a woman felt this way before.

It's not just physical, it's a mental connection. It's the trust she has in me.

I'm a biker. I like to fuck, but as I pull out and back in with slow determined movements, I know this isn't fucking, this is making love.

Raising her hips slightly, I swivel my hips, watching her expressions to show when I'm hitting that magic spot inside, loving the way she bites her lip and how the flush on her cheeks darkens. The sounds that are coming out of her mouth encourage me on.

I resist the urge to start bucking and hammering inside her, wanting to prolong this as much as I can. She feels so amazing, skin on skin even better than I remember it being before.

Although it's not a foregone conclusion she's going to keep it, the idea that she's incubating my child is a massive turn-on.

My spine tingles and my balls swell. I keep my pace slow but groan, trying to hold back my own pleasure until hers is done.

She's holding her breath, her head's thrown back, her mouth opens and she gasps, then *thank fuck,* she's there. I don't have a chance. Her internal muscles clamp down and I let myself go with a roar.

Christ. This has never felt so good before.

It takes me a moment for my senses to clear, for the blood to return to my head. My eyes are squeezed closed, but when at last I'm able to fill my lungs with air, I raise my eyelids once more.

The satisfied smile on her face is beautiful. There's a glow to her skin, a red tint that extends down over her breasts.

I feel something inside me, a pressure in my chest, which makes me lean over her and before planting a kiss on her swollen lips, makes me utter the word, "Mine." Then with another wave of possession, I place my hand on her belly and repeat, "Mine."

Her eyes go wide. I don't know what reaction I was expecting, but it certainly wasn't for her to shove me away, roll off the bed and start reaching for her clothes.

"Babe?" I kneel up in my naked glory and reach out to grab her arm. "What are you doing?"

"You've had your booty call. Now I've got to get on with my life." She wrenches loose and bends to put on her pants.

"Sheri." I stand, shaking my head, trying to understand. "What the fuck's gotten into you?" *Booty call?* I just fucking told this woman she was mine. A claim I don't make lightly.

For an answer, she finishes dressing, picks up her backpack

and swings it over her shoulder. Then, she makes a move to the door.

I'm there before her. Blocking her way, I pick her up fireman style, and throw her back on the bed, covering her with my body and gripping her hands over her head.

"Fuckin' talk to me, woman."

She struggles but I'm not going to let her go. One moment, all seemed to be fine, we were lying in post-orgasmic bliss, and the next, she's like a wild animal trying to get free. I feel like an ass when tears fill her eyes, but I'm not going to let her leave. Especially not when there's a man out there trying to kill her, me or us both.

"Talk to me," I demand again.

She stops fighting at last but relaxing only so she can turn and spit the words into my face, "You're a biker."

My eyes crease, but I keep the smile off my face. I shrug to show I've no idea what she's talking about.

"I'm... me."

What she says doesn't make sense.

Her eyes close briefly, showing her frustration. "You told me I was yours, but for how long? You're soon going to get bored. I saw those bikers out there," she waves vaguely in the direction of the clubroom, "having sex in the open and no one cared. Well, that's not going to be me. I can't give you that."

"Been there, done that. That's not what I want."

"StoryTeller—"

"Jake."

"Jake!" She throws up her hands and huffs. "I'm a normal girl. I didn't even like riding on the back of your bike—"

I pull her to me, holding her cheek tight to my chest, wanting to correct all her misassumptions. "Let me speak, huh?" I give her a second, but she doesn't object. "For a start, that wasn't my bike. You'll like mine, I promise." I know I'm babbling, words spilling out of my mouth in an attempt to persuade her. "And I'll keep you safe. You can't know my mind, Sheri. You haven't been where I am. You weren't there the last couple of months when all I could think about was a fiery redhead who I let walk away." I tighten my hold on her. "I jumped at the excuse to come see you. And when I did, I was fully prepared to be disappointed, to see you weren't the woman I'd built up in my dreams. Instead, I found you were everything I remembered, and more. I'd be a fool if I let you go again." Softening my hold, I nuzzle my lips against her hair. "And I won't, especially not if you're having my baby."

"I don't have to," she tells me. "Jasmine offered me—"

"No." I had one reaction when Strider suggested his easy access to abortion pills. Now it's coming from her, my visceral response is heightened. I know it's not fair for me to insist she has my child, when it's her that will have to carry it and suffer any lasting effects of the pregnancy, and any of the risks that might come along with it. But in my mind, it's all too easy to picture a redheaded baby, a son or a daughter.

After Fi, I'd given up my hopes of being a husband, of being a dad, but fate has intervened and put the opportunity within grasp.

Sparks fly from Sheri's eyes. "What the hell do you mean, no?"

I'm a scary motherfucker, I've perfected that persona. It keeps me safe on the road. But this woman challenges me at every turn and will never back down. It's her spirit I absolutely love about her.

Love.

The emotion slams into me as memories flash past my eyes, so fast, one image rolls into the next. I thought Fi was it for me. I thought we'd have forever, but it wasn't just an illusion, it was something I was forcing myself to feel. I'd felt obligated to act a role in that relationship.

For the first time, I wonder whether Fi had known I wasn't giving my all even though I'd said the right words to her. Words I now know rightly belong to someone else.

I'd had months to get to know Fi before I told her I loved her. I've only known Sheri a short time, but what I feel is one hundred percent sure. And though telling her might risk ridicule, it might just be enough to keep both her and my child by my side.

Laying my soul bare isn't something I want to do lightly. This woman doesn't know it, but she's got the power to destroy me. And there's no guarantee, or even hope, that my sentiment might be returned.

I'm still holding her close, breathing in that perfume that's all hers, my nomad bones telling me that I'm home, and wherever she is, is where I'll want to be for the rest of my life. I no longer have to be out on the road, travelling in search of something that's always out of my reach. Because here, all down to a book that I found, I've got everything I'll ever want in my arms.

"I've one last argument," I tell her, my voice deepening with all the emotion I feel. In case she backs away, I tighten my arms around her. "I've never felt this way before, Sheri, even though I once thought I had everything I wanted within my grasp. But it's you I've always been waiting for. It's you that I want. More than that, it's you that I love."

I risk easing my grip and pulling away, catching her gaze to ensure she can see the intensity in my eyes.

"I love you."

CHAPTER TWENTY-FIVE
SHERI

He loves me?

My first reaction is to scoff, to deny it, to say that emotion doesn't happen so fast. That love at first sight, or so darn close to it, is a myth that doesn't exist in real life. But I know that impulse to reject his declaration is tempered by my past, by the thought I've never come first in anyone's eyes.

It might be wishful thinking, but instead of instinctively pushing him away, I swallow back my immediate repudiation, and take a moment to drink in the expression in his eyes. It's like he's baring his soul to me, his dilated pupils like windows letting me see right down to the man inside.

It makes me hesitate, makes me wonder if for just once in my life, someone can put me first.

I don't deny his words, but I test them. "Is it just because of the baby?"

Still not unlocking his eyes from mine, he cups my face so gently as he softly replies, "I came for you before I knew about that."

"You came because you thought I was in danger." And he'd been right. At my reminder, a shadow crosses his eyes.

"I came because I could no longer stay away. The knowledge that Knuckles had been seen anywhere near you was the kick up the backside that brought me to my senses. I'm going to do everything I can to make you safe, darlin'." His eyes darken. "And I'll succeed, even if I lose my life."

I developed feelings for StoryTeller the first time I met him, though it was a bit of hero worship at the time. While sometimes I feel mortified that I let him inside my body in such horrific circumstances, I know it was my attraction to him that had turned me sufficiently on.

I'm worried that it's because I spend my free time reading books which romanticise bikers, that my judgment might be flawed and I've allowed myself to fall for him too fast. But if he's really putting down what I think he's offering, how can I walk away from him? Even if I'm dubious about how he lives his life.

"How would this work?"

Immediately, he's on my wavelength. "First, we get rid of Knuckles, then, unless you really want to stay in Texas, I take you back to Arizona with me." He pauses and shakes his head as if amused at himself. "We'll find a house we both like and where we can raise Junior." He moves one of his hands and caresses my stomach, the words and his action making me melt.

"Is what you do for the club dangerous?"

He sighs heavily and leans his forehead against mine. "I can't tell you it's not, but I'm also not a risk taker. Can't tell you we do everything legal because we do not. But we don't go out of our way to make waves and bring in plenty of money doing work you'd approve off."

I pull out of his arms, and this time, he lets me move away.

I like Jake, more than like him. I'm fascinated by his way of life. But I've always been a cautious person. Going with him would be a leap of faith. What have I got to stay here for? I've no job, and no family to speak of. And, truth be told, I want to keep this baby. It might not have been planned, but it's part of us both.

"Say you'll be my ol' lady."

I take a breath, shake my head at the magnitude of the decision I'm making, then jump off the edge of that cliff with just a simple, "Alright."

Jake's shout of delight has me laughing. Within moments, I'm naked again, and shortly after, he's sinking inside me, using that cock that it wouldn't take much for me to become addicted to. Then, sated at last, he pulls me into his arms, and we fall asleep.

I sleep restlessly. The noises from the clubhouse seem to go on until late in the night, and I'm constantly disturbed by the loud music or the heavy footsteps and voices walking past our door. Eventually, I must drift off, only to startle awake without knowing what had awakened me.

The one difference to the past couple of months is that while my sleep had been uneasy, it hadn't been haunted by nightmares, a factor I put down to the man who spent the dark hours snoring softly beside me.

I owe everything to Jake—my rescue, not once but twice. Without him coming to Austin, maybe Knuckles would have taken me again. I'd never have survived a second time.

Jake turns over onto his back enabling me to see his impressive erection tenting the sheet. All of a sudden, I want to do something for him.

While I've never done this before, I don't let my nerves get in my way, nor question whether I can compare to the many girls he's had go down on him. I slowly move my body, trying not to wake him, taking the sheet down as I go. Then, swallowing at the size of him, take his cock in my hand and press my lips to the head.

He murmurs, but a glance into his eyes shows he's still asleep. Knowing he's not yet conscious gives me the confidence to carry on.

Precum is leaking from the tip. It's salty, neither unpleasant nor something I would seek out, but I get a certain sense of power from tasting his essence. That he's not sentient of what I'm doing encourages me to experiment. His cock seems to have a mind of its own, and the little twitches and changes in the velvety hardness are the signs whether I'm doing it right.

I'm concentrating on trying out different actions, like sucking him as far as I can inside my mouth, hollowing my cheeks and applying suction, when I hear his voice. It sounds husky and an octave lower than normal, and almost as if he's in pain.

"Don't stop. For fuck's sake, don't stop." His fingers tangle in my hair, making the strands tingle as they pull at my scalp. "Oh fuck, Sheri, that feels so damn good."

Seems that although I'm an amateur, what I'm doing is hitting the spot. It makes me feel powerful, so I redouble my efforts, taking him deeper until it makes me gag.

Immediately he uses the grip on my head to pull me away. "Need to be inside you. Hands and knees, babe."

So far, we've only done it missionary style. I have no idea the difference this position makes nor how much deeper he can get inside me as I press my forehead to the bed. Now it's me who's groaning, encouraging him on. My hands scrabble at the sheet, trying to get a grip, something to hold on to, to anchor me, to keep me in this realm, because as my orgasm approaches like a runaway train, I'm certain its power is going to make me pass out.

I scream, as he roars, "Fuck's sake, babe, you're strangling my cock. I fuckin' love it." He reverts to gentle pumps as I come down from my high, then he pulls out, but only to roll me over so I'm now on my back.

Grabbing my legs, he bends them up, making me feel like a pretzel. With a wicked grin, he slams back inside.

My man's got stamina.

He resumes pumping in earnest, and it doesn't take long before my muscles are tensing again, and another powerful orgasm rolls over me. I'm incoherent as I both try to encourage him on and beg him to stop as I can't take much more. But he has no mercy, allowing me a brief recovery before using that roll of his hips to get my body singing again.

It's my third orgasm which takes him over. He lets out a deafening roar, a declaration of *mine*, as this time I can do little more than whimper.

When his dick ceases twitching inside me, he bends his head and takes my lips. "Fuckin' love you, woman," he declares.

There's no point in me not saying what I'm feeling. "I love you, too."

He beams as if I've just given him the winning ticket to the lottery. Then he pulls me into his arms and holds me tightly. For a moment, we say nothing more.

Then, leaving me sated, he goes to the bathroom. After I hear the toilet flush, he returns with a cloth which he proceeds to clean me with. His hand lingers for a moment on my pussy as if to keep his cum from running out.

"Fuckin' love that you've got part of me inside you. Fuckin' you bare, best fuckin' feeling ever."

"Lot of fuckin' in there," I respond, having recovered sufficiently to sass with him. "But I've gotta tell you, it's too late to try to keep it in there. Your swimmers have already succeeded."

The gleam in his eyes shows me he needs no reminder, as he places his lips to my stomach. "Fuckin' love you too, kid."

I swear if it would be possible to get pregnant again, my ovaries would burst from his action.

A loud knock comes on the door, disturbing our tender moment. I sit up and hide my face in his chest. The sex was so unbelievable it had almost made me forget where I am. Now it all comes back with clarity.

"What?" he yells at the door.

"Strider says get your ass up. Said you might as well as with the noise you're making, none of us are getting any sleep."

"Asshole," Jake calls back, while I know my whole body is flushing.

Will I ever be able to show my face?

Jake, it seems, takes it differently, slapping my ass with a look of pride on his face, and telling me we've got to get moving.

He dresses first, then throws my backpack my way. I take it into the bathroom and have a quick shower so I don't smell of sex, even though it's too late to hide what we've been doing. Once I'm ready, he leads us out into the clubroom which is teeming with men. One, the small guy called Mex, is fooling around, wearing a red wig. Seeing me, he comes over and flicks his fake hair over his shoulder and grins. He starts making fake kissing noises and pointing toward Jake.

"What's going on?" I ask, while simultaneously, Jake tells Mex sharply, "Get out of here."

He takes hold of my arm and leads me to a corner. He gives an uneasy grimace. "Kinda got to fill you in now that Mex is making an ass of himself. We're going to set a trap for Knuckles."

I'm quick to catch on. "With Mex pretending to be me?" I eye the short guy who's still prancing around. He's got about a hundred pounds and a few inches on me. The wig might help, but surely their plan will never work.

Then I realise the real downside to this. "And you're going to be playing yourself?"

"Babe, I'll be safe." He tries to reassure me. "The brothers here will have my back."

I'm worried about losing him and entwine my hands into his shirt. "Please don't do this. I don't want to lose you. Can't we just disguise ourselves, get to the airport and disappear?"

"And worry about Knuckles turning up when we least expect him?" He pinches the bridge of his nose. "Look, babe, I'm not one for hiding. And Knuckles signed his death warrant when he came after you yesterday. I'm not risking him being able to take another shot."

"So, you think Mex will fool him?"

Jake shrugs. "Hopefully. It's worth giving it a try." He jerks his head toward where Mex is still cavorting, taking the wig on and off. "He'll be wearing a vest and will be armed. All we need is for Knuckles to take the bait, and then we'll turn the tables on him."

"You ready to go, ST?" Strider yells out.

I grab at Jake's cut, realising he must have known about this last night yet hadn't said a word to warn me. Or worry me. At the apologetic look in his eyes, I realise this was how he'd planned it—spring the surprise on me and leave me no time to make a complaint. Or not, I think, without causing him embarrassment, viewing the men turning from the playful ones they were last night to being all business like now, They're bustling around, checking weapons and wearing serious looks on their faces. If I created a fuss, trying to hang on to my man, he wouldn't thank me for it. Not in front of the brothers.

Jasmine comes over to me, linking her arm through mine. "Smile," she says, quietly. "Send your man off with a kiss and leave the remonstrations until the job is done."

"You know what they're doing?" My eyes go wide as I turn to her.

"Not a clue. But it's club life. The men will do what they have to, and the least worry we give them the better."

I can see by the set of Jake's jaw that nothing I could say will stop him so I suppose she's got a point. The last thing he wants is to ride into danger worrying about my temper flaring at home. But when Jake comes cautiously over to me with a look of uncertainty in his eyes, I pull him to me, crashing my lips on his and invading his mouth with my tongue.

He responds and quickly takes over. Despite the situation, my arousal flares. But there's no time for that now, so I pull away, putting my lips to his ear and snarling, "You better come back to me in one piece, okay?"

His intense stare that makes it look like he's trying to memorise my features does nothing to comfort me, but then it's replaced by a cocky smirk as he retorts, "And you better keep up your strength for when I return."

And then he's gone.

The room empties of most of the men except for Mex who lingers. Catching my attention, he blows me a kiss and gives me an approximation of an effeminate finger wave before disappearing out the door after the rest.

It strikes me then how brave he is. It was me, riding pillion, who got shot yesterday. I might be worried about Jake, but the others are putting themselves in just as much danger.

I catch Jasmine's eye, see her swallow, and recognise her resolve.

This is my first experience of life with a biker.

CHAPTER TWENTY-SIX
STORYTELLER

Although I gave off an air of confidence while explaining my upcoming absence to Sheri, I'm not stupid and I know what we're planning to do comes with no guarantee that it will succeed, or that we'll all survive.

As Strider comes up to me and slaps my back, I indicate Mex with my cigarette. "He loco?"

"As a coot." Strider laughs. "But he's a solid guy."

A solid guy with a death wish in my view. You have to admire him putting himself in the risky position he's accepted, at my back, just where Sheri was when she was shot at yesterday. Of course he'll be wearing a bullet-proof vest and a helmet to resemble her, but it's still fucking dangerous.

Not for the first time, I'm struck how Soulz will pull together for anyone wearing the same patch, be it a nomad or someone from a different charter. A lump actually forms in my throat as I think of the dozens of things that could go wrong.

Strider wishes me good luck then pulls himself into the cab of a truck. He waits for a couple of his brothers to climb inside, then the prospect opens the gate and they're off.

Other brothers get into a variety of other vehicles and follow. They're going to be waiting at various intervals as we're banking on Knuckles making his move. We're pretty certain Knuckles was forewarned of my arrival in Austin, and that suggests he's got access to someone who can hack into the airlines' systems. Just in case, Data's already booked flights for me and Sheri, so as long as we're right, Knuckles will be on the lookout for us leaving this morning.

When the compound is empty, Mex, wearing the red wig, struts out of the clubhouse and, after waiting for me to get astride the loaner bike, launches himself up behind me, making the bike sink and almost throwing me off balance. I have to fight to keep it upright.

Once I've got it straight, I turn and give him a glare. "Asshole."

He just laughs and blows me a kiss.

I start the engine, and he puts his arms around my waist. *Okay. He's supposed to be Sheri.* Then the fucker moves his hands down dangerously close to my cock.

"What the fuck?" Again, I spin around.

"Just giving you the full ol' lady experience."

"Keep your fuckin' hands to yourself. Else you and I are gonna have a problem," I snarl.

"Spoilsport," he murmurs, but raises his arms to a more respectable level.

I kick into gear, release the clutch, twist the throttle and we're off. To be honest, I'm grinning at the audacity of the man riding at my back, rather than overly worrying about Knuckles. I'm hoping he will put in an appearance today, else I'll be spending more time riding with Mex at my back.

He's nothing like Sheri. I try to keep my weight forward, but he's holding me close, and there's no comparison between a man's junk and a woman's snatch. And if I never have to feel a cock pressed up against my ass again, it will be far too soon.

Trying to keep my attention on the road and not the asshole sitting at my back, I turn out of the compound and take the direct route to the airport. Although I saw all the club vehicles pull out through the gates, they're obviously hiding up well as it's only from time to time I notice one. At one point, it seems to have been so long since I last had a friendly face in sight, that I start to think they'd abandoned me.

I'm wary when a blacked-out SUV suddenly comes up behind me fast, and Mex's tap to my shoulder shows he's as worried as I am. But it's just an impatient driver, and I show him my middle finger as he zooms past.

I'm starting to think this is going to be a bust when this time a white truck appears in my rearview.

At this speed, I'm unable to warn Mex, so hoping he hangs on, I kick down a gear and twist the throttle. One thing about the Kawasaki is how fast it responds, getting into the spirit of the chase by giving me the speed that I need. From out of a parking lot zooms the truck driven by Strider, and another which I know had been taken by the VP.

Soon, they have the white truck boxed in.

I haven't made a study of how the Dominators work, but Knuckles seems surprised that he's surrounded and heavily outnumbered with guns. Neither he nor Handle, the prospect who's stayed with him, make any pretence of going for their weapons as Strider pulls them out of the truck.

Instead, Knuckles tries words to get out of his predicament.

"Kill me and it will be war."

"And killing me wouldn't have started one?" I challenge, rolling my eyes.

"Get them in the truck," Strider states. "We'll sort this out when we get back."

Within moments, both Knuckles and his sidekick are trussed with ropes and zip ties and thrown in the back of the truck Strider's driving. Mex goes back to stand by my bike.

"Hey," I tell him. "No need for that now. You can hitch a ride back."

"Oh, don't be like that, ST. You know you loved my arms around you. I won't tell your woman if you don't." He winks. "Don't deny you liked what I was doing." He mimes jerking off.

Tequila and Buzz crack up laughing. While they've got Mex distracted, I go to the green monstrosity, and before he can reach me, start it and take off down the road.

Asshole. But as I ride, I'm smiling.

It's a short journey back to the clubhouse. As soon as I get inside, Sheri heads straight for me, the relief on her face easy to read. I nod my thanks to Jasmine for taking care of her for me, then hide her face in my chest as Strider brings Knuckles in.

"You don't need to see him," I tell her. "Just know you'll never be bothered by him again."

"ST?"

Turning, I see Strider pausing and waiting for me. "I'll be back," I reassure Sheri. "Just hang out with Jasmine for a while, yeah?"

Her eyes widen, then a resolved expression comes over her face. "You go deal with business."

I steal another kiss, then depart.

I follow the brothers through the clubhouse, out the back and along a pathway. It leads to a concrete building. I walk in, expecting some sort of torture chamber, but instead, I find the club's gym. Around the edge are mats and different types of equipment, and in the middle is a boxing ring.

Strider appears at my side, putting his arm around me. "Think you might enjoy this, ST. Reckon we'll let you get up close and personal with the man who kidnapped your ol' lady."

I don't mind beating the hell out of Knuckles, I'd planned on it anyway. I was more afraid he'd be killed outright, and I'd lose my opportunity. But as Data sets up a tripod with a phone set up on it, and Knuckles is brought forward with his hands and feet now free and uncuffed, I start to get an uneasy feeling.

Strider pulls me forward. "I've spoken to Scorpion," he starts, mentioning the leader of the Dominators, akin to our Slugger. His name gets Knuckles' interest. "He asks we don't kill Knuckles without giving him a sporting chance. If he dies in a fair fight, there'll be no retaliation."

Knuckles looks dubious, and glances around at Strider's men. Then his eyes land on me, and he points in my direction. "I'll fight him," he says. "I've no beef with the rest of you. Ain't none of you been wronged except for him."

I hide my grin. It's far from the first time my fighting skills have been underestimated. To suggest I'm nervous, I even shift uneasily, and cast a wary glance toward Strider.

"Agreed," the Texas prez states. "You and ST in a fight to the death." He gives a twisted grin, and his gaze encompasses all the assembled men. "Scorpion reckons Knuckles here can handle himself."

"Fifty on StoryTeller."

I swing around to see Data nodding my way. At least someone's got confidence in me.

Tequila is giving a measured eye to Knuckles, measuring him up. "I'll match that on the Dominator."

Strider's grin widens as others get into the bidding. He approaches me and again slaps my back. "You going to put on a show for us, ST?"

I'm confident in my skills, and if he knew me, he would be as well. But I can't help but feel put out that I'm not certain he's sure which way this is going to go. Surely, he isn't intending for Knuckles to just walk out of here should he get the better of me?

Shotgun steps up and offers to wrap my hands, but I give a look at Knuckles and shake my head no. My opponent has a glint in his eye as he leers at me. He shakes out his hands, letting the light catch the rings that he's wearing.

I shrug. I wanted a bare-knuckle fight—in more ways than one—so I can't complain. Reaching into my cut, I extract a few little surprises of my own and start adorning my fingers. This is going to be no polite affair. This is going to be bloody, and one of us is going to die. It won't be the first time I've stepped into a ring, knowing it might be my last.

Strider steps up into the middle of the ring. "No bouts, no scores, no breaks. Once they get together, the fight continues until there's only one man breathing. Everyone got that?" He turns to stare into the camera and then casts his eye toward Data. "You better make damn sure that thing's recording as there won't be any second takes. Or, not with the same participants." He breaks off and everyone laughs.

Knuckles joins in, clearly thinking the joke's on me, particularly as I don't crack a smile. But far from being worried, I'm already sizing him up, judging his level of confidence and trying to guess his style.

He's got no fear, that's for sure, which means he's no stranger to a fight. Like most of my ex-opponents, he'll misjudge me to his cost. I'm pretty sure I can take him on with one hand tied behind my back. Not that I'm going to offer, of course, I'm not looking to commit suicide.

I assess how I want this to play out. Will I take my time and humiliate him, causing maximum pain, and consequently entertainment for the men who are still busy with money changing hands? Or do I go in straight for the kill?

The benefit of the latter approach is that I'll be back with my woman faster and fucking her with the leftover adrenaline from the fight.

Someone rings a bell. This is it. Time for deliberation is over.

Knuckles jumps into the ring and stands, bouncing on his toes, gesturing cockily to me, *bring it on.*

Gladly, I respond, letting my confident swagger do the talking for me. I slide between the ropes and stand still, not wasting any energy except to shrug my shoulders to loosen myself up.

Strider steps into the middle and holds his hands out to his sides. "No holds barred, boys," he says, as if we were in any doubt. "Now show us what you've got."

I expect Knuckles to rush straight for me. It's what a man does when he wants to show off, taking his opponent down with the first blow, showing what he's made off. It's slightly concerning that he holds himself back, suggesting he's perhaps a more experienced fighter than I thought.

We start to circle each other, to an increasing impatient chorus from our audience. I feint, he blocks, and then again, we move apart. I'm assessing every movement he makes. *Is he favouring his right? Is he slightly less balanced on that leg?* One thing's for sure, he's as focused as me, and I wish I'd been able to find out more about him. *Was he in the services like me? What experience has he got? Has he just got street skills, or has he been trained like myself?*

It's time to find out. Looking like I'm going to punch with my right, I let my equally powerful left fist fly. I've caught him out as he blocked the wrong side, and, with the impetus behind it, have winded him for sure.

But he recovers fast, coming at me with a sharp right, then

left, then a kick which would have emasculated me had my evasion not been fast.

As his momentum slows for him to gather his breath, I don't give him the chance and launch myself forward once more. Using a roundhouse kick, I go straight for his head, then when he crashes to the floor, I let him have the full force of my knuckle dusters in his face.

From somewhere he produces a fucking knife which would have sliced into my stomach had I not been so fast. Instead, it takes a chunk out of my arm.

There weren't many rules, but this was a no weapon fight. Fuck knows where he got that knife from. His cheating makes me see red. Ignoring the possible damage to my hand, I grab hold of the blade and tear it away. It flies to the far side of the ring and Knuckles staggers to his feet and starts moving as if to reclaim it.

I kick his legs out from under him, seeing him go down like a log. I take the split second he's winded to recover the knife for myself, then throw my full weight on him, twisting his head up and back, baring his neck to me.

"Kill him. Kill him." A chant starts from the small crowd.

I have no desire to linger, but I want Knuckles to know I hold his life in my hands. I let him see both the blade and the intention in my eyes.

He might be my enemy, he might have captured my woman and worked in a trade I dislike, but in that moment, I have respect for him as he shows no fear, only an acceptance, and while he could, he doesn't waste breath begging for his life.

I take a firm hold of his head, bare his neck, and slice across with the blade.

His body jerks and he gurgles. His hands come up to

scrabble at his neck, but he knows there's no hope and his eyes lock with mine as his life drains away.

When he's gone, I pull myself to my knees, holding my hand to my damaged arm.

"Anyone got a needle and thread?" I ask.

"I'll sort you out."

As I slide myself down from the ring, I glare at Mex. "Not in the mood to be fucked with, man."

"Hey." He raises his hands, looking as hurt as a man with a smirk can. "I was a medic."

"He'll see you right," Shotgun reassures me. "Though I advise a stiff drink. He's not known for being particularly gentle."

"Fuck you, VP," Mex retorts, but his grin, under the circumstances, is chilling.

"What about the prospect?" I ask, as much to delay being alone with the guy who's going to be stabbing me where I already hurt.

"Leave him to me," Buzz says. "I'll damage him a bit, then we'll drop him off."

"And remember to send that video to Scorpion," I remind them, as Mex looks impatient to lead me away. I want the Dominators to know Knuckles had had a fair fighting chance, and, due to his cheating, it was actually me at a disadvantage.

"Go get sorted," Strider tosses, seeming to lose interest in me. "Leave us to sort this mess out and deal with the trash."

CHAPTER TWENTY-SEVEN
SHERI

Once I'd seen Jake come back unharmed and Knuckles and the Dominator prospect being dragged through the clubroom, I'd breathed a huge sigh of relief. I wasn't sure what would happen to Knuckles, but I had confidence whatever it was, he wouldn't be coming after me anymore. I wouldn't be shedding any tears if they killed him. Without him, the world would be a far better place.

It's over. I can get back to normal. Except, my new normal appears to be that I've hitched my wagon to that of a biker and am pregnant with his child. On top of that, I've agreed to relocate to Arizona.

Jasmine, clearly knowing how to predict the men's needs after doing whatever they've gone off to do, is behind the bar getting drinks lined up, ready for when they return. I sit nursing a soda. Now I've seen Jake safe and sound my racing heartbeat can return to normal, and I can picture a future with him in it at last. My mind whirls with all the changes that have happened recently. I'd question I'm doing the right thing by agreeing to go away with him, but honestly, what have I got to stay for in Texas? I'm growing a new life within me. Maybe it's time for a fresh start. I'd hate myself forever if I never gave Jake a chance.

My lips curve. Maybe he will turn out to be like one of the panty-melting, home-loving, bikers in the fiction world I love, and might settle down to give me a happily ever after.

He promised he would.

I want to smack myself around the face sometimes. It's not his fault that I find it so hard to believe he could ever put me first. I'm loading him up with my own insecurities and that's my burden to bear.

He's shown me enough of himself to know that I'd be a fool to not grab on to what he's offering with both hands.

"You want a top up?" Jasmine approaches with another soda for me, which I gratefully accept.

"How much longer do you think they'll be?"

As I ask, she rolls her eyes. "Minutes, hours, who can tell?" She grins easily. "But when they come out, I warn you, it will probably get wild."

Even her warning doesn't bother me. I've seen enough of these men to know they are not like the Dominators. Sure, their partying can get a bit much for my inexperienced eyes, but I can't forget they all took a risk to take Knuckles down. And while I was worried, they've been nothing but respectful and friendly to me.

Jasmine sits down and takes a welcome breather, leaning back and closing her eyes. I sit quietly, allowing myself to picture a life with Jake and a redheaded child. I'm daydreaming when a voice interrupts.

"Hey. You. You're wanted."

Hearing a voice, I look up, then around, suspecting it's Jasmine being summoned. When I see the eyes of the speaker looking my way, I point to myself. "You talking to me?"

"Yeah. This way."

I glance over at Jasmine who I've noticed is listening, but she just inclines her head as though to say I should go along with it. So I stand and make my way over to the man who indicates I should follow him. I feel a bit on edge until he stops outside the door where Jake and I slept last night. When he opens it, I step inside.

"Fuck. Be careful, will you?" Jake is exclaiming as I walk in.

"What's going on?" I ask, my heart rising into my throat as I try to analyse what I'm seeing. "My God, Jake. What's happened?" Jake is sitting on the bed, his top half-naked, blood covering his chest—he even has some on his face and hair, and more, looking fresher, freely running down his arm and soaking into a towel lying underneath. Mex is hovering over him with a needle and thread.

"Jake?" I exclaim, trying to assess how badly he's hurt.

But neither of them acknowledges my presence.

"Don't be a baby," the small biker tells him with a snarl.

Jake flinches away. "I'd do better to sew myself up than the hash you're making of it."

He doesn't sound like he's at death's door. Moving closer, I get a better idea of what's happening. Jake has got a nasty-looking gash along his bicep which certainly does need stitches, and though there's lots of blood, he has no other obvious wounds. One stitch has already been put in, and as Mex is holding the needle, I assume he's the one who's done it. It's also clear to see that Jake isn't enamoured of him doing anymore. Though, clearly, his wound needs closing.

"Want me to give it a go?" I tentatively ask.

"Fuck, darlin'." Jake looks up, his brow furrowed and his

eyes creasing. "I didn't want you to see me until I'd washed the blood off."

Mex, however, dramatically sighs and hands me the implements he's holding. "Have at it. He's a real fuckin' baby."

"Whoa." Jake sees our interaction and holds his good hand up. "Mex might be a butcher, but, Sheri, baby, have you any idea what you're doing?"

"I sew my clothes," I tell him drily. "How much harder can it be?"

His eyes narrow until they become slits. "You're not squeamish?"

Looking at the needle I took from Mex, I check it's threaded, then eye up the gash. There's one stitch in already so I get the idea what I need to do. Knowing I'm going to hurt him however gentle I am, I start talking to distract him.

"No, I'm not squeamish." Though I have to admit, pushing a needle through skin is very different to a piece of material. I bite my lip as I concentrate, pulling the thread through and tying it off as Mex indicates I need to. "I've cleaned up more puke, vomit and even blood then I ever wanted to when nursing my mom."

"The mom who didn't want you." Jake flinches but doesn't object as I tackle the next stitch. He comments, "You're good at this," while Mex huffs.

"It made me want to be a nurse."

"Why didn't you?" Jake tries to swing round, but I position him where I want him again.

I snort. "I didn't finish school, remember? No GED, and definitely no chance of college."

"She'd make a fuckin' good nurse. Be good for the club," Mex tells Jake, looking at me thoughtfully.

Concentrating, I don't give much thought to the meaning behind his words. Jake goes quiet as I put the next few stitches in. The only sign he's suffering is that he holds his breath and looks away as I press the needle in and pull it through. By the time I've finished, I sit back and even I'm impressed by the line of neat sewing. Hopefully it will heal and not leave too unsightly a scar.

"How about instead of looking for a job in Arizona, you get your GED, then go to college and study nursing?"

Jake's suggestion takes me by surprise, and I look at him sharply. "I'm pregnant."

"So? No one said you need to rush it. But from where I'm sitting, you've got a talent for this. And Mex is right. Helping clean up cuts and scrapes could be a useful skill to have around the club."

My mouth opens and shuts. At first, I want to say I probably won't be any good at it, but then I remember how I nursed my mom, how the doctors trusted me to take care of her, and how I learned so much medical jargon just by being around her and the hospital so much. If I had a skill, I wouldn't be a waste of space and I could have something to offer for which I'd be appreciated.

The hard work doesn't bother me, nor the thought of trying to juggle a pregnancy and college. Something does though. "But that would take money."

Jake's got an answer for that. "I already said I'd support you. And I bet the club would contribute if you were going to practice your skills on us."

"I don't know."

"Mex. Get out of here." Jake speaks to him without taking his eyes off me. Mex smirks but gets up and leaves. As soon as he's out the door, Jake takes hold of my hand, tugging me so I fall into his lap. "It's you and me, babe. Whatever you want to do, I'm going to be right there with you." He pauses, then cups my face in his hands, making sure I'm looking at him and taking in every word. "I know you've never been put first, but I swear, Sheri, I'm going to love you like you've never been loved before." My eyes go wide as I realise that wouldn't be hard. But he hasn't finished. He continues earnestly, "You impress me at every turn, babe. You're so damn brave, and what you did just now? You didn't turn a hair at stitching me up. You were made to be a biker's ol' lady." His eyes get a spark in them. "Marry me, babe."

Marriage? Although everything in me screams out a yes, I decide to mess with him. "I kinda like my last name."

He snorts. "Only names that bother me are the one that comes out of your mouth when you're screaming it, and my road name which I worked fuckin' hard to earn. Don't give a fuck about anything else, if you want, I'll take yours."

I'm floored. Stunned. Honestly at a loss for words. Truthfully, I'm not wedded to the name I inherited. It's not served me well up to now. Once I'm capable of speaking, I let my mouth curve. "Sheri Cameron does have a nice ring to it."

"Fuckin' straight it does." Using his good arm, he pulls me to him and crashes his mouth down on mine. I respond, though I'm aware that I'm cuddling a man whose body is sticky with drying blood.

"This isn't all yours." Feeling uncomfortable, I pull back, indicating the discolouration that's now also on my clothes. If this amount was his, he'd be unconscious or dead.

"Not all mine," he confirms, his eyes hardening.

It's an obvious assumption. "Knuckles?"

His eyes narrow. For a moment, he says nothing, then imparts, "You'll never be bothered by him again."

"Did he hurt you? Did you kill him?"

"Sheri, don't ask questions I'm not going to give you answers to."

That response won't wash. "I deserve to know. He shot at me—"

He doesn't relent. "What you don't know, can't hurt you."

I huff. "So what you're saying is that I'll never know what happened."

"You don't need to. Just trust me."

I suppose this is life as an old lady. Either I trust him, or I don't. I suppose if I'm ever asked, I can truthfully say I haven't a clue what happened to Knuckles. But is this how I want to live?

Jake touches his hand to my face. "I promise you, Sheri, I won't keep you in the dark for the sake of it, but there will be some things you'll be better off not knowing. I won't be an ass, and I'll keep those to the minimum, okay?"

What can I say? He's trying to meet me halfway. I take it as a sign he's going to give this relationship a chance. All he's asking is for me to have faith in him.

I stare straight into his eyes. "I trust you."

He gazes into my face for a moment, as he reads the sincerity in my promise. Then his lips start to curve, and his eyes flick over me. "You've got blood on your clothes. Best get out of them, babe." There's a glint in his eyes that I have no trouble interpreting and don't need to look at this crotch to see he's aroused.

He's covered in blood though. My nose twitches with disgust. "You need a shower."

With a shake of his head, he pulls himself up and in a husky voice objects, "I need you."

"Clean."

Despite my rebuttal, he reaches for me. "It might be fucked up, babe, but there's something sexy about fuckin' you, wearing the blood of our enemy."

He's right. It is fucked up. I should be shocked, horrified.

Instead, my stomach muscles contract, suggesting I'm turned on by the very idea that should turn me off. A smirk appears on his face as he guesses I might be coming around to the idea.

"Take off your clothes," he demands. Forgetting he's injured, he tries to reach for me. "Fuck!"

"You shouldn't use that arm," I tell him primly as he rolls onto his back clutching his bandaged left arm with his right.

"Yeah. Just found that out," he grunts. "But I fuckin' need you, babe. How about you do the work?"

He's already half-naked, so it's only a matter of moments for me to remove his boots, then he helps by raising his hips so I can remove his pants. I lick my lips as his deliciousness is revealed and have to pinch myself as I remember this man just proposed to me. I look again at the blood drying on his chest.

This man just killed for me. He might not have come out and said those exact words, but it's all I can believe. He wouldn't be this relaxed if he'd left Knuckles alive.

"Seems like you have me at a disadvantage," he drawls, his eyes half-lidded, but looking at me in anticipation, as though I'm a tasty treat he can't wait to try.

Holding his gaze, I take off my top, then stand and kick off my shorts. His tongue comes out and moistens his lips as I unhook my bra and then slide my panties down.

"Come 'ere." His voice is deep and hoarse. "Hold on to the headboard and sit on my face."

For the next hour, he proceeds to give me an education as I follow his instructions, finding nothing to object to as we try cowgirl and reverse cowgirl as well. Finally, completely sated, we at last shower together. While keeping his arm dry, I sponge off the blood, then one handed, he does the same to me.

I help him get dressed then take the last of my clean

clothes out of my backpack. As I'm putting them on, I notice him staring at me.

I'm overwhelmed by a wave of emotion. This man has done everything he can to keep me safe. He's even, I'm convinced, killed for me. He says he loves me and wants to marry me. What more do I need him to prove he's all in?

Nothing, I answer myself. "I love you," I tell him.

I HAVEN'T much to pack up in Texas. Jake borrows an SUV from the club so he can take me to the apartment I shared with Agatha to put what I want to take with me in a suitcase. She was there, and her mouth dropped open once she realised Jake and I were together. After her shock, though, she genuinely appeared to be happy for me. We parted as friends, more than perhaps we'd been in the years we'd lived together.

After one more night in the Austin clubhouse and a round of goodbyes, back slapping for Jake and hugs for me, we leave early the next morning to catch a flight to Arizona.

I think I'm more excited than apprehensive. After getting over my initial shock, the brothers in Austin had grown on me, and the final night there had been quite a laugh. I'm hoping Jake's true brothers will be much the same.

Once we land and get through the airport, Jake's quick to spot a man waiting for us. He introduces him as Shitface, and I can't hide my smirk. Seems he's a prospect, and the name is just one of the burdens he has to bear.

"That poor guy," I whisper to Jake, as the prospect's putting our luggage in the back.

He laughs. "Nothing to do with me."

All too soon, we arrive at the clubhouse, where there seems

to be a reception committee waiting for us. It transpires I'm the first old lady in the Arizona Charter, so a bit of a novelty.

"ST." A serious and, if I'm honest, scary-looking man approaches. He links hands with my man and pulls him in for a man hug. "Good to see you back, Bro."

"Prez." Jake greets him warmly. "This is Sheri."

It's the first of many greetings, and I know I'm going to be hard pushed to remember them all. There's Bull, the VP, Iron, the sergeant-at-arms, Beard, who I might remember as he has a beard going down to his waist, who apparently looks after the money. Claw is the enforcer, and Weasel the road captain.

Then I'm introduced to the rabble, as Jake calls them, getting a few middle fingers raised in response. There's Fire, Pothead, Skunk, and Legit. Legend gets a special welcome. He's their technology guy, and apparently helped Jake to find me. For him, I have an extra special finger wave.

After we've had a drink with them all, Jake leads me down a corridor. I pause, taking a moment to view all the pictures on the walls. There are numerous men on their bikes, far more than I've met.

"Past and present?" I ask, as I examine them all.

"Past, present, locked up or dead." He frowns as he takes a moment to eye one in particular and I gather this one, at least, was not a friend.

His arms come around me as he stares at the face beaming back from the wall. At first, he's tense, and then he relaxes, and his hand moves to rest on my belly.

"Life's come full circle," he says quietly. "And this is where I'm meant to be."

EPILOGUE
CHAZ

THREE YEARS LATER...

"Daddy, Daddy."

Both of us turn toward the shrill voice, and I smirk as StoryTeller's face completely softens as he holds out his arms, letting his two-year-old daughter, Maria, run straight into them. After giving him a hug, she steps back and allows me to see what she's holding scrunched up in her hands.

I suppress a snort as she raises a clumsily made daisy chain. Recognising her intention, StoryTeller lowers his head, letting her place the circle of weeds on his head.

"Daddy's got a cwown."

StoryTeller glares at me over her head, an unspoken threat in his eyes which has me grinning and miming zipping my mouth. In a gentle voice he thanks her, pulling her onto his lap.

Oh, how the mighty have fallen, I think to myself, smothering a laugh. But I can't help but be happy at the way things have worked out for my brother. He'd been in such a bad place when he first went out on the road, I'd worried he wouldn't come back from it. But he'd coped, survived, and proved himself. My concern then had been he'd developed too much of a taste for the open road and would never be happy at home.

All it had taken was the love of a good woman to sort him out, and Sheri is certainly that. She's not only provided him with a reason to put down roots, but she's also had a positive influence on the club.

The clubhouse has changed beyond all recognition since ST brought her back, the touch of femininity, the tempering of behaviour, the now matching couches and chairs. Add in the additive enthusiasm for the life of his child who, it has to be said, we've all fallen in love with, and the atmosphere has changed from that of a frat house to one truly belonging to family. We've also gained a nurse who's happy to stitch us up, and who's now studying to be a paramedic.

Of course, we haven't changed all that much. We've not gone soft, and we still know how to party. We just tend to wait until Sheri and Maria have gone home before letting loose.

I think a few brothers are envious of ST and that he's found a woman of his own. Not me, of course, I'm too old and jaded to look for my own golden snatch.

"Storwy, Daddy, storwy."

The childish voice gets my attention back on the pair at my side. When ST settles Maria on his lap, she sticks her thumb into her mouth.

"Yeah, Daddy," I tease him. "You got a story to tell?"

He manages to show me his middle finger while stroking her hair. Otherwise ignoring me, his eyes focus on his daughter. "What story do you want, sweetheart?"

"The one about the magic book," she replies without hesitation, twisting on his lap as though getting comfortable for the long haul.

Now I do snort. "I think I know this one." I laugh at him, getting to my feet. "I'll leave you to it."

"Later, Prez." Then all his attention is back on his child. But as I walk off, I hear the beginning. "Once upon a time, there was a handsome prince who found a magic book that belonged to a princess—"

"The princess was in twouble, and the prince had to rescue her."

Yeah. I chuckle. It's not the first time Maria's heard that story. I wonder how long it will be before ST starts giving her the grownup version of how her mom and dad got together, and if they'll ever admit how she was conceived.

Magic book, my ass. But it's strange how everything worked out, and actually no wonder that Maria's named after the author. If Sheri hadn't lost that particular book and if StoryTeller hadn't found it, the ending would not have been so happy. Yeah, life can bite you on the ass sometimes and take you in directions you never wanted.

That damn book with the bullet hole in it is framed and has pride of place in their house.

"Hey, darlin'." I raise my chin toward Sheri, who's walking toward me, studying her as she approaches. My recollections had reminded me of the nervous woman who'd first arrived, and who'd gradually found confidence, her self-worth and her place. I doubt any of us would want to go back to the time before ST had brought her home.

"I seem to be missing a man and a child." She grins at me.

"It's story time." I jerk my head toward the picnic benches in the yard behind the clubhouse. More acquisitions since she moved in.

"It's bedtime." She rolls her eyes.

"For ST or Maria?"

"Chaz." She snort-laughs, then winks. "Both, if I'm lucky."

I walk off chuckling.

The sun is beginning to set as I get on my bike and ride to the auto shop which we own, and where we build customised bikes as well as provide the usual sales and maintenance service for all models. We've got quite a reputation, even if some people only like coming to us to be able to boast with their friends how they're not afraid to walk on the wild side.

Despite the success of our business, my mood sours as I draw close.

You'd think with what people know and rightly believe about the Wretched Soulz MC, that the last thing they'd do is steal from us. But for the last couple of weeks, bits and pieces have been going missing. Not huge things and not really valuable, just nuts, bolts, a battery cover and the odd bottle of engine oil. Insignificant, and as such, it took a while for us to notice anything had been disturbed.

Once Claw became suspicious, he'd done an inventory to check. What he found was that while we maintain and service all models of bikes, everything stolen was for a Harley.

We're Soulz, it's our territory. We've got lax about security, relying on our reputation to keep people away. Legend was pulled in to replace old or broken cameras and install new alarms. He was due to finish today, and tonight, I'm going to be here in case anything goes down.

Nothing like catching a thief red-handed.

It's been a while since my fists have seen some action so I'm looking forward to deploying them tonight. I'm really hoping our light-fingered guy will put in an appearance.

It must be near midnight and I'm on my third beer, when Legend suddenly exclaims, "There. Look."

Placing my bottle down, I sit forward as a shadowy figure seems to be approaching the security fence that's meant to keep everyone out. It's hard to tell much. The figure's upper body and head is shrouded in a hoodie, and their face hasn't yet been caught on a camera.

"I'll call Claw." Legend reaches for his phone.

"Nah. Hold off a moment. If it's only one, we can take them on ourselves."

"Will you fuckin' look at that?" Legend's eyes widen as he points to the monitor.

My jaw drops as I watch the man lithely scale the telegraph pole close to our fence, then secure a rope to it and swing down and over the high steel fence. The rope stays dangling there, and obviously, it's that that he intends to use as his means of escape.

"Guess that's the answer as to how he's been getting in." I'm already out of my seat. I may be impressed with the athleticism of our thief, but he's still got a lesson to learn about stealing from the Soulz. "Nah, you stay here, Ledge. I can handle one asshole like him." Or if I can't take the not-very-tall and definitely not-very-built figure who's been robbing us, then it's time to hang up my motorcycle boots.

I've honed the ability to move silently over the years. If I don't want you to know I'm near, you won't, not until I've gotten up close and personal. Moving through our darkened building that I know like the back of my hand, I emerge into the yard. There's the thief who's somehow not only managed to open our storeroom door but also defied the new alarm Legend had fitted.

I push the *what the fuck?* question to the back of my mind. It's not important for now. What's more critical is that I end this, and before the thief gets more confident and starts stealing things of higher value.

Stealthily, I come up behind the fucker who's rummaging through our boxes of spare parts, muttering softly as though they're looking for something in particular that's not immediately at hand.

Taking my gun out of my cut, I ease off the safety with an audible and unmissable click.

With a speed I wasn't expecting, instead of freezing, the thief comes straight for me, kicking the gun out of my hand and planting a fist in my stomach.

A split second is all it takes for me to think, *game fucking on.* No one's going to get the better of me and definitely not on my turf. Turning the tables, I go on the offensive, using every dirty street-fighting trick I ever learned.

But my opponent has clearly gone to the same school, and for a moment, we're evenly matched, despite that I'm far bigger in size. We both land and block kicks and punches. I'm breathing heavily when at last, luck's on my side and I get the upper hand.

I sweep the feet from under my assailant, and he lands heavily on the ground. I come down on him, my fist raised to punch a direct hit on his face only to pull it at the last moment.

"You're a fuckin' bitch," I gasp. To prove it, I sweep the hoodie back off her head, revealing her face.

"Get off me." She keeps struggling.

"Give it up. I caught you stealing from us." And I'm going to make her pay. I don't care if she's a woman, thieving is thieving whatever the sex.

She refuses to give in, unfortunately managing to attract the interest of my cock, and I harden as she writhes beneath me. I wouldn't be a man if I didn't suddenly have ideas about what retribution she could make.

"Yeah, just keep that up." I can't help the leer coming to my face.

But in the light of the streetlamp, I see her brave expression change, and her face pales. All the confidence she had while fighting me seems to have fled. Abruptly, she stills as she becomes aware of the effect her movements have had on me. She swallows heavily.

Fuck. I'm no rapist. Her palpable fear at the position she's in makes me guilty I got any enjoyment from feeling her curves.

"I'll let you up, but you run? I'll catch you and make you regret it," I warn her. When I see the little nod of acceptance, I lift myself away, regretting losing the softness of her body beneath me.

Free, she warily pulls herself up. When she's standing, she brushes herself off, wincing as she must catch one of the bruises I left.

Par for the course, sweetheart. You left some on me too. Reluctantly, though, I have to admire her and her fighting skills.

She's about five foot ten, a good eight inches shorter than me. I'd mistaken her silhouette for that of a man as she's got the smallest tits I've ever seen. Her ass is tight and high, and her waist tiny and pulled in. My cock, which should have stood down now her proximity has gone, jerks as though telling me he likes what he sees.

I should ask what the fuck she's doing stealing from the club, whether she's got a screw loose, or a death wish. But what actually comes out of my mouth is, "How the fuck did you learn to fight like that?"

She breathes in deeply, pulls back her shoulders and looks me straight in the eye. "The better question would be who forced me to learn to protect myself."

Okay, I'll buy it. "Who?" I shrug to show I really don't give a damn.

Air leaves her in a sigh. "Maybe it was the foster dad who thought he had a right to put his hands down my panties. Maybe it was the boyfriend who thought he could sell me to his buddies. Or maybe it was the cop who thought he'd exchange the fictional speeding ticket I supposedly earned for a sexual favour."

"Am I supposed to be impressed? Or devastated on your behalf?" I take a step toward her. "Maybe it would have more effect if I hadn't just caught you stealing red-handed."

As her eyes meet mine, she reclaims the distance I'd just closed by taking a step back. I see the moment she catches the expression in my eyes—the hardness, the scowl that warns everyone not to cross this particular MC prez.

"Who are you?" she finally asks.

"Me?" I reply nonchalantly. "I'm your worst fuckin' nightmare."

ACKNOWLEDGEMENTS AND AUTHOR'S NOTE

I am beyond lucky to be a signing author at Motorcycles, Mobsters and Mayhem in May 2023, and hope to see some of you there.

When offered the chance to join in with the collaboration Mayhem Makers with many other amazing authors, I jumped at the chance. The only stipulation was the book should mention the signing in some way. I think we've all come up with some very imaginative ideas.

I've long been toying with the idea of writing about the Wretched Soulz MC, a slightly grittier club than the Satan's Devils. Many of the characters have actually had cameo appearances in my other books. This is the first book, but there will be more Wretched Soulz coming along. Instead of focusing on one club, I've decided to focus on the presidents. I mean, who doesn't want to eventually learn more about RIP in Colorado?

Very grateful thanks go to MariaLisa DeMora who agreed to let me take liberties with both her and her book in Story-Teller's Tale. If you haven't read any of her books, I highly recommend them.

Special mention must go to Sheri Secord for allowing me to use her name.

As always, I have to thank all the beta readers who encouraged me, Sheri, Jo, Tami, Tera, Alex and Zoe, to my long-suffering editor, Maggie Kern, and to Darlene Tallman for proofreading.

The fantastic cover was done by CT Cover Designs.

Finally, last as always, but definitely not least, thanks to all of you, my wonderful readers who've taken a chance on this book. If it wasn't for your encouragement, I wouldn't keep writing. I have recently received messages and emails telling me how much you like my books, and I love reading everyone. A positive message inspires me to write more.

This book, like all of my works, has been to beta readers, through editing twice, to a proofreader and then to ARC readers, but there could still be the odd typo that's crept through. Please message me if you've found anything so I have a chance to correct the book. I love to hear from readers, even if you're pointing out something I've got wrong.

If you've enjoyed this book, please consider writing a review. Reviews are essential to us authors, and I appreciate and read them all.

Manda

COMING SOON

Book 1 of the Presidents of the Wretched Soulz is coming Summer 2023

Fighting Fire with Fire (Wretched Soulz MC)

As President of the Arizona charter of the Wretched Soulz MC, I spend my days keeping money in our coffers, our enemies at bay, and my brothers out of jail. With a reputation to uphold, I can't show any weakness. Men who cross me do so at their peril and won't live to tell the tale.

But what do I do when it's a woman who steals from my MC? A crime that would put anyone else underground.

Treat her just like a man. But she's not a man.

I'm the Prez. I'm in charge. Men jump to my commands. But not Queenie. She stands up to me, challenges me, hell, even gets the better of me when we fight hand-to-hand.

Despite my best intentions, she intrigues me.

I'm relieved when I find she isn't invincible, that she has her own demons. But I've enough battles on my own hands, do I want to take on hers too?

Iron, my sergeant-at-arms, thinks I should make her my old lady. But what would I do with a woman who fights me, verbally and physically, at every turn?

Changing her though, moulding her. That does hold some appeal. Hmm.

OTHER WORKS BY MANDA MELLETT

<u>Blood Brothers – A series about sexy dominant sheikhs and their bodyguards</u>

Stolen Lives (#1) Nijad and Cara

Close Protection (#2) Jon and Mia

Second Chances (#3) Kadar and Zoe

Identity Crisis (#4) Sean and Vanessa

Dark Horses (#5) Jasim and Janna

Hard Choices (#6) Aiza

<u>Satan's Devils MC - Arizona Chapter</u>

Turning Wheels (Blood Brothers #3.5, Satan's Devils #1) Wraith and Sophie

Drummer's Beat (#2) Drummer and Sam

Slick Running (#3) Slick and Ella

Targeting Dart (#4) Dart and Alex

Heart Broken (#5) Heart and Marc

Peg's Stand (#6) Peg and Darcy

Rock Bottom (#7) Rock and Becca

Joker's Fool (#8) Joker and Lady

Mouse Trapped (#9) Mouse and Mariana

Blade's Edge (#10) Blade and Tash

Heart Mended: A Satan's Devils MC Novella

Truck Stopped (#11) Truck & Allie

Satan's Devils MC Boxset 1 Books 1-5

Satan's Devils MC Boxset 2 Books 6-8

Satan's Devils MC Boxset 3 Books 9-11

Satan's Devils MC - Colorado Chapter

Paladin's Hell (#1) Paladin and Jayden

Demon's Angel (#2) Demon and Violet

Devil's Due (#3) Beef and Steph

Devil's Dilemma (#4) Pyro and Mel

Ink's Devil (#5) Ink and Beth

Devil's Spawn (#6)

Satan's Devils MC - Next Generation

Amy's Santa (#1) Wizard and Amy

Hawk's Cry (#2) Hawk and Olivia

Twisted Throttle (#3) Throttle and Gwen

Satan's Devils MC - San Diego Chapter

Being Lost (#1)

Grumbler's Ride (#2)

Avenging Devil Part 1 (#3)

Avenging Devil Part 2 (#4)

Satan's Devils MC - Utah Chapter

Road Tripped (#1)

Stormy's Thunder (#2)

STAY IN TOUCH

Email: manda@mandamellett.com

Website: www.mandamellett.com

Sign up for my newsletter to hear about new releases in the Satan's Devils and Blood Brothers series.

Facebook reader group: https://www.facebook.com/groups/mandasbadboys/

ABOUT THE AUTHOR

Manda's life's always seemed a bit weird, starting with a childhood that even today she's still trying to make sense of, then losing her parents in the late teens. Going from the tragic to the bizarre, who else could be unlucky enough to have had two car accidents, neither her fault, one involving a nun, and another involving a police woman?

There isn't enough space to list everything that's happened to Manda, or what she's learned from it. But by using the rich fabric of her personal life, psychology degree, varied work experiences, and amazing characters she's met, Manda is able to populate her books with believable in-depth characters and enjoys pitting them against situations which challenge them. Her books are full of suspense, twists and turns and the unexpected.

Manda lives in the beautiful countryside of Essex in the UK, the area's claim to fame being the Wilkin's Jam Factory at nearby Tiptree. She can usually find jars of jam which remind her of home wherever she goes. As well as writing books and reading, Manda loves walking her dogs and keeping fit. She lives with her husband of over 30 years, who, along with her son, is her greatest fan and supporter.

Manda is thankful that one of the more unusual, and at the time unpleasant, turns her life took, now enables her to spend her time writing. Confirming, in her view, every cloud has a silver lining.

Photo by Carmel Jane Photography